MORS OBLIVISCENS

Allyson McCollum

Ballast Books, LLC
www.ballastbooks.com

ISBN: 978-1-962202-90-9 (Paperback)
ISBN: 978-1-962202-91-6 (Ebook)

Printed inthe United States of America

Published byBallast Books
www.ballastbooks.com

For more information, bulk orders, appearances, or speaking requests, please email: info@ballastbooks.com

Dedicated to those without an identity, to those who had theirs stolen from them, and to those who have yet to discover the right one. You will not be lost forever; you will find your way home.

TABLE OF CONTENTS

CHAPTER ONE

Gray water laps over the smooth pebbles at my feet. I stand alone on the rust-colored bank of a lake, a thin yellow nightgown clinging to my skin as a frigid wind mercilessly whips through the fabric. The horizon steadily grows closer, as if I'm walking toward it. I am walking toward it, but my feet drag through the sand and pebbles, hauling some invisible weight along my path. Pine trees, thick and green and dark, pass by on either side. Water rises higher, up to my hips, my throat, filling my ears. Clouds part to reveal a violet sunset, or is it sunrise? I can't tell, not with those cruel, red eyes leering at me through the rays of light. Why will they not help me? Who does that hideous stare belong to? Gradually the gaze of my final witness consumes all the scenery around us until my vision goes black entirely. I compress down until I fold in on myself and disappear into the darkness.

The sudden blankness surrounding me is sharp and blinding, but it eventually dims, and I feel nothing. No pain or sorrow, but as if everything between my bones were hollowed out, as if I were floating even though my feet rest on presumably solid ground. I can't really see what I'm standing on or tell if I'm even right side up. Everything is the same shade of white except for my gold-brown skin and whatever keeps darting in and out of my peripheral vision. Spinning to chase the mysterious visitor gets dizzying after a while; there's nothing to hold on to so I can steady myself or orient my sight.

Gradually that changes as the emptiness fills with doors scattered on either side. No one comes in or out of them, and it may be the disorientation throwing my senses off, but no sound slips through the cracks between them and their frames either. None of the holes are big enough to peek through to test this theory. Maybe opening one will clear things up. The first one to my left could easily be mistaken for a palace entry; it's one of the more ornate, gilded and inlaid with blue tiles the size of my thumbnail. Its patterns are soothing to trace, even with a trembling hand. A spiral handle fits perfectly against my palm but will not turn no matter how hard it's bent.

My shy "companion" finally stops hiding after I trip myself circling around and searching through the barred doors for an exit. Floating alongside me are two tiny black orbs. They follow my every move, dancing ink fireflies in the white void. There are always two of them, right beside each other, always the same distance apart, constant as the silence. Hiding and attempting to outrun them proves pointless. They aren't attacking or chasing me, but they aren't terribly helpful without hands or a mouth either.

My own voice is gone, replaced by a deep burning that chokes any sound I attempt, so I can't ask the spots anything. I don't know that they would know anything, but it wouldn't hurt to try.

Another doorway appears beside the first, equally beautiful but more rustic than artistic. Carvings of animals and strange symbols climb the frame, perhaps telling a story my mind can't decipher. The dark wood is warm to the touch, and the black metal handle looks worn from much use, but it refuses to open just like its neighbor. I turn to the thing trailing me, hoping for a sign to keep going or help, anything other than this maddening quiet.

Two black rings appear around the dots, the innermost perfect circles, the outer ones more oval-like. The outer layers are thick and much darker than the others. A silver band rests between the rings, and it is then I realize that the orbs are in fact a pair of disembodied eyes. They seem curious, if the raise of the accompanying eyebrows is any indicator. Do they recognize me? Should I not be here? Again, with hope slowly replacing some of the confusion that's settled in, I try to ask these eyes what they see but only manage a pained sputter. Though their expression grows concerned, they can't offer any help.

In a sense, I let the eyes pick the next door. The next one I try rests behind them, and they hover behind me while I investigate. This door isn't quite a door at all, actually, at least not one made from wooden boards or a sheet of metal. It's soft and taut, like a sheet pulled tight over a mattress, but it's not cloth either. Leather maybe? More symbols are painted across its surface, though the hunting scene depicted is easier to read than the one before. Tethers of the same material are looped together along one side, but no amount of tugging will undo their knots. Talking may be out of the realm of possibility, but grumbling and muttering aren't. What good is a door that won't open? And a hall full of them with no signs saying which goes where or how to gain entrance?

Time here is immeasurable, with no day or night to go by; I don't know how many moments pass until the rest of the body forms. Each time I turn to look, another piece has fallen into place. A long, narrow nose soon appears, the skin on it so pale it almost blends in with the white around us, but it's just dark enough to be noticeable. As quiet as it is, its breathing should be audible, but I never hear a single sigh, even when it's two feet away. Sometimes the floating features venture close enough for me to touch, but if I reach out they back away.

Despite my mounting frustration with the uncooperative surroundings, my hands continue their odyssey to each closed escape route. These doors may not even lead anywhere, or may lead somewhere worse than this, but any change would be welcome at this point. This is the kind of place that could drive anyone up the currently nonexistent wall. I keep waiting for a mouth to materialize so maybe my "shadow" will finally speak and offer some guidance, but instead a hood envelops the shape of a head, casting shadows to form the other features. Black hair trickles out from within, long and thin like campfire smoke. The hood is black too, but it's easy to distinguish the hair from its dense, coarse material. Even easier to separate from the body are the massive raven wings that rest against its shoulders.

The sight of those stops me in my tracks; what in the world is this thing? It looks almost like a person, but no person I've ever met had extra limbs like that . . . did they? Try as I might, no such memory surfaces. Not of bird-people, not even of regular people. What do the people I know look like? What do *I* look like? Aside from my dark hair dangling down my back and the skin visible below me, I have no idea how to describe myself. Young or old? I feel small, but that could just be this space. The word *señorita* pops through my head, followed by "missy" and "her," so I draw the conclusion that I'm a girl, whatever that may mean. Not much at the moment. I need to get somewhere

where things like that matter so maybe the rest of what's going on will start to make sense. Ignorance is not, in fact, anything like bliss.

A bright red door bearing twin dragons fails to yield to my shaking. Its comrade to the right, marked by intricate knots along its edges and a tree in its center, does the same. So do the two covered in stars. Now the figure has formed a stick-thin torso, a floor-length robe with trumpet sleeves, and spindly white hands, but still no mouth. It is a man, judging by the way he carries himself, the set of his steely eyes, and his towering height. Now that the rest of his body has materialized, he looms over me, at least six and a half, if not seven, feet tall. Should that frighten me? Probably. But if he means me harm, he's had plenty of time to cause it and hasn't yet. He could be biding his time, waiting until I give up on the doors altogether and wander away before dragging me farther into the abyss. He could be what's keeping them all shut tight, or what's keeping anyone inside from coming out again. Until he says otherwise, I'll never know his role here.

No rustling of his cloak nor shuffling of his feet disturbs the silence, and he still doesn't speak while we wander around the emptiness together. This grates on my nerves endlessly, until it occurs to me that maybe he can't speak unless spoken to. My throat hurt too much the first few times I tried to talk to even consider a lengthy conversation, but it doesn't burn so badly this time. A choppy "hello" croaks out before it starts to ache again.

He gives no vocal response and only turns to stare at me expectantly.

After catching my breath, I try again, this time asking a question. "Wh-ere are . . . we?"

Nothing.

"Who are y-you?"

As if they'd been there the entire time, his gray lips open in reply. A voice comes out that's smooth as velvet and rough as sandpaper all at once. "I am Death. I have come to escort you onward."

"Oh."

The world falls from underneath me, or at least my legs do. The floor isn't cold like a grave should be, or maybe it is and I can't feel it. What do dead people feel? Anything? It suddenly feels like all the weight I've ever carried in my life has suddenly slammed down on me at once, but I don't even recognize any of it. How do I know it's my weight to bear? What do I mourn first?

"As for your other question, we stand in Purgatory. This is not a place; it is between places." Death stares down at me without menace, draws out his scythe, and for a moment I think he's going to cut me down like stalks of grain in a field. Running comes to mind, until I remember how relentlessly he followed me before. It would only delay the inevitable.

However, he proves there is no need to flee at all. He drives the tip of his scythe into the air and slices a gaping hole in it. Behind the white façade, golden light shimmers through the tear. Is that the source of light here, or did he open a gate to somewhere different? He slashes into the whiteness three more times, cutting out the shape of a rectangle and handing it to me. It feels downy and comforting in my hands, like a worn-down baby blanket. "Clothe yourself, child, and tell me who you are."

I didn't notice how exposed I was until he mentioned it; where did my pajamas go? Before the embarrassment can take hold, I cover myself with the sheet. Much to my amazement, the cloth fits itself to me, becoming a strapless white dress; my feet remain bare and my hair messily braided. Did I die sleep-walking? Is that how I got into the lake?

After thanking him, I shake my empty head. There are no solid memories inside of it to give him, only more questions he may not be able to answer. "I don't remember what happened before I died or . . . who I was. It's all gone." My name, my family, every memory ever logged into my brain have vanished like shreds of *papel picado* in a gust of wind. I'm shocked I can even speak a coherent sentence or remember how to count past one if I can't recall the other things that once made up my mind.

"Then you came to me before your proper time, somehow." His apologetic smile doesn't quite reach his ice-colored eyes. "In that case, you will reside with me until your place in the afterlife is prepared."

"Can you not open these doors?" I asked. Death goes on to explain that staying with him is my only option, which does not sit well with me. His gaze follows my gesture to the hall at our backs. I continue, "If this is part of the afterlife, shouldn't there be a door to Heaven or Hell here to send me through? Isn't that your job?"

"If I took you back to the living Earth, through this door here," He motions to a plain blue door I hadn't noticed before. "you would become a ghost, haunting the living until you allowed yourself to move through your grief. Wandering spirits are notorious for holding out for decades, if not centuries, and some even for millennia."

That's not what I want. If I can't revive myself by going back, there's no point in going back home, wherever that is. That would be like wandering here forever but tormented by the presence rather than an absence. All that was stolen from me—all I never experienced in life—would be right in front of me, just out of reach.

While there's also the possibility of learning more about myself if I choose that route, there must be an easier way than the one full of heartache. I recoil from the door and the idea itself. "No thanks."

"Hell would take you regardless of the circumstances, of course. They care little for rules except those of their own devising. But I do not cater to their whims and doubt you belong to that realm at any rate." Death indicates a cold black door in the distance. It's hard to tell from back here, but if I squint hard enough at the doorknob, I can faintly make out what look like claw marks along the edges. Definitely not my dream destination.

"Can you tell for sure? That I'm not . . ."

"Souls that belong there reek of their sins." He snarls at the door, which retorts by rattling as if it wants to swallow us and the rest of Purgatory whole. "You give off no such stench, regardless of what you may or may not know of yourself."

He goes on to add that if he took me to Heaven at the improper moment, the balance of the universe would tip off-kilter and no one would get any peace. He doesn't elaborate but is adamant nonetheless that neither outcome can happen. One little soul is all it takes to move the world one way or another. The Reaper turns to walk toward our next destination.

Skepticism creeps into my hazy thoughts, and I refuse to follow him at first. If he really is Death as I think I know him, then he is completely neutral and has absolutely no reason to deceive or harm me. But if he isn't Death, then who is he, and can he be trusted at all? And if he is Death but isn't the caring guide he claims to be, then what? With no one else here to speak for or against him, there is nothing to rely on but my own judgment. And how can I know someone else if I don't know myself?

He stops once he notices my absence and turns back to face me. "There is no need to be afraid, child. I cannot harm you, nor would I. I only want to help." He reaches out for me, even though my hands are tucked beneath my arms, which are crossed over my chest.

"It's just . . ." My fingers work frantically at the fabric of my gown. I don't want to offend what looks like my only way out of here, but something deep down is tugging me in the opposite direction. "Why don't I remember anything about myself? Is that normal?"

The Reaper shakes his head solemnly, lowering his hand. If he is growing impatient with me, he does a wonderful job of hiding it. "It is a side effect of your premature death. Your soul is not where it belongs, so some of its pieces have been disturbed. You will regain your memories when you pass over."

"Oh. Okay." As a lackluster way of apologizing and indicating that I will follow him, I inch closer and lower my head sheepishly.

His thin lips form what could nearly pass as a smile, and we begin walking farther into the white abyss. "If I could do so safely, I would take you where you likely belong, but as I said, I cannot disturb the balance of the universe for one soul."

"I will get to go, though, right?"

"Of course, someday. Perhaps soon." His bony hand lays gently on my shoulder, guiding me through the barrenness of Purgatory. "Death is the fate of every creature, and while one can delay it or run headlong toward it, fate cannot be changed." His eyes meet mine as his grimace slowly fades, and he bitterly speaks one last line, mostly to himself. "In the end, we all follow the plan laid out for us."

The blankness begins to diminish the farther we go; colors start to peek in here and there like the beginning of a watercolor painting. Nothing is completely solid or defined, but there is a noticeable difference between this place and the one I started in. I wonder how far we've traveled. How much time has passed since our first meeting and our exit?

Death falls silent again for a time, but unlike previous times, he breaks the quiet first. "I need something to call you, as we will be spending your remaining time together." He watches me as he speaks, considering all the options before him. Nothing in my mind can help in his search; without my real name or anything else about me, he's on his own. In watching him back, I notice his eyes aren't focused on my face—they keep hovering over my heart. "Humans' souls reside there, in the middle of their ribcages," he says. That's what he's using to rename me, the little broken pieces of the universe rooted inside.

"It flutters, like a hummingbird hovering over a flower," Death muses softly, his eyes tracking my heart's every move. "Never rests in one place for long, always jumping away the moment it seems to settle on one side or the other. And it occasionally leaps upward, rather than side-to-side." Most of them, according to previous observations he's made, have a steady pulse or a pattern to their flashing, but my light is erratic, flickering. Excitable, he calls it.

How would that have shown up in life, I wonder? Would such an unpredictable soul be a sign of happiness or anxiety? Unquenchable adventurousness or excessive caution? Or is it only a symptom of my odd circumstances? Neither of us knows.

Only one could even wager an educated guess, and they all come up short of sense.

He admits he can dimly make out my physical body too, though it takes more focus to see me that way. He describes the bare outline of me as fairy-like and delicate. It makes sense for him to compare me to something tiny, given that he's over two feet taller than me, and it's from this image that he finally decides. "The name Flit suits you, in my eyes. You move in such a manner . . . it is the first word that came to mind."

"Hmm, that's an unusual word. Not really a name, but it'll do," I reply. My agreement might seem shallow without other choices, but I really do think that's a nice name for now; it fits into the space where my real name goes, filling up the unnerving emptiness. Shrugging the pang of sadness off, I roll the word around in my mind and let it slide out into the air until it doesn't sound like a word at all.

Flit. Flit. Flit. Flit. Flit. Flit. Flit.

"There are much worse names to be called," The Reaper offers.

He tries to smile one more time, only to snatch the flicker of happiness away from himself again. "Come, I have finished my rounds for today and wish to retire." He shakes off the melancholy clouding his face, then takes his scythe and rips another hole in Purgatory. This time a doorway materializes, rather than a dress. Beyond the edge of the whiteness, a log cabin hides on the edge of a pine forest, its reflection shimmering in the lake at its front door. The Reaper glides soundlessly across the surface with me in tow, my feet brushing the tips of the small waves lapping at the shore. Mountains cut the skyline across the horizon, their peaks tearing the clouds open.

In this light my gown looks yellow, like the one I remember in my vision.

Is that tree the same one I saw before I woke up?

These rocks are darker than they were before.

Shouldn't there be people inside?

Just outside the portal, I stop short, hovering over the water like mist. I'm not see-through, which surprises me, but still as insubstantial as morning fog. "Are you sure this is okay? You said I couldn't go back to Earth or I'd become a ghost and get stuck."

Death stops at the shore's edge, beckoning me to follow him again. "We will be safe here, that I promise you."

The portal is gone.

"What is this place?" is all that tumbles out once I come ashore. The rest is a blur that fades into noise as I take in the scenery.

He opens the cabin door without a key, and dust swirls over the threshold. No one has been here for quite a while. "When I take my leave, I like to fill in the empty places of the world, the ones where living humans no longer tread and time does not pass. There is peace in those places that can be found nowhere else." His footsteps don't disturb the layer of gray on the floor, nor do mine. But books, pillows, and chairs move as easily as if we were regular people milling about our home.

"It's beautiful here." The bay window overlooking the lake looks especially comfortable, even if the cushion is a little worse for wear. The layout is open and inviting, as if it were meant purely for gatherings and sharing space with loved ones. Cruel irony has emptied this home of joy and filled it with lost, lonely ghosts.

Standing at the opposite window, he gazes out into the woods that surround the cabin. At last, he manages to tug the corners of his mouth up and keep them that way. "Indeed.

Nothing will disturb us here. I made sure of it when I first discovered this place." Despite his voice's confidence, his eyes scan the horizon as if he's searching for intruders and spies.

Outside of our cabin, there's no sign of life as far as I can see, not even any animals to speak of, and without us in it, this house would be lifeless too. Well, I suppose it's still lifeless with us in it. I'm a dead girl and he's Death incarnate. Perhaps the word I'm looking for is "uninhabited." A deep forest glowers back at us, waiting for one of us to step too far into its outstretched limbs. The trees sway in the wind, beckoning us closer, but now they have claws instead of buds, and we are unprotected against their grasp. I will not go toward them alone if I go at all.

Waves curl across the shallows, their soothing crashes slowly lulling the fear away. Some violently splash against the sandbar, trying to slither up the bank to wrap around our ankles and drag us out with the tides. All the rocks along the edge are free of moss; they are slick with water, treacherous to untrained feet. There is no end to the lake with no other shore within reach.

Few clouds dot the pale sky right above us, but just beyond the mountain peaks, a storm is creeping up. The water will rise with the coming rain, maybe enough to reach the back steps or even to climb them. Branches will snap and fall in the gales, blocking exits. Lightning will disperse every shadow, if only for a second, and thunder will shake the foundations.

The dangers here don't dim the beauty, and the beauty fails to hide the dangers.

Turning away from the outside, my eyes sweep across the shelves beside the bay window. This cabin can't have been abandoned too long ago if there are still books and knick-knacks waiting to be dusted and rearranged, and they don't look antique. Two ceramic teddy bears function as bookends, neatly holding the romance novels and crime thrillers together. A wooden trinket box stands beside an angel figurine with a broken wing. I search in vain for the missing piece and instead find a jar full of smooth rocks and more books.

There aren't any picture frames, not even empty ones, but photos aren't typically abandoned for lengthy periods. Irreplaceable things like pictures must be maintained or destroyed altogether, not left to rot. A vacant shelf is sandwiched in the middle of the occupied ones; I claim this one for any treasures found outside while following The Reaper.

It dawns on me that, while I have a name now, my companion has yet to tell me which of his titles he prefers. He said he was Death, but asking seems more polite than assuming that's what he goes by. "What should I call you, since you have so many different names?" The broken statuette is smooth in my hands as I carry it back to my window. If we have nowhere else to be today, I'll spend more time searching for its little wing and something to reattach it with. "Do you have a favorite one?"

He seems taken aback by my asking, and I worry I might've offended him somehow. His entire body stills, like the lake when the wind stops blowing. His gaze passes right through me as if I weren't standing there at all, not just my physical form but my jittery soul too. Panic from watching the forest and the sorrow I glimpsed in Purgatory mix in his pale eyes to form some miserable, unnamed look. Maybe it's his own name he tries to hide from out here where nothing lives. Without life to take for miles around, he doesn't have to be Death, so he grants himself some small reprieve by seeking this cabin's solitude at the end of the day.

Before I can apologize for my question, he glances down and catches sight of the tiny figure cradled in my hands, and he snaps out of his trance to reply, "I . . . no, I do not have a favorite. They all mean the same thing, after all." He shrugs, leaning his scythe against the frame of the back door. It's his turn to take me off guard when he removes his ink-colored cloak to reveal the dull gray armor underneath; the subtle tones of black in his wings stand out more now that there's less darkness to compete with. He is the same kind of beautiful as the view we share out these dusty windows, entrancing but undoubtedly deadly.

"Maybe one of the short ones then, since my name is short too?" I offer, following his steps to the sofa in the living room. Because of his wingspan—each one spreads out as long as I am tall—I have to curl up in the armchair to his left. "Death seems a little too formal, though, unless that's what you want."

He relaxes into the cushions, lean limbs taking up the entire space with no room to spare as he considers my question. If we follow the same rules as with my name, his would be a one-word summary of his being. Him boiled down to a syllable or two. But it would have to be polite as well as accurate; I can't exactly go around calling him "dreary" or "cryptic" can I?

The Reaper, what I've been calling him in my head up until now, is a little on the nose to say aloud. None of the others that filter into my thoughts make much sense either, not with the limited context that comes with them. Calling him The Pale Rider or The Horseman seems silly without a horse anywhere nearby. I'm beginning to wonder if those names even apply to him at all, since he has wings and a dimension-ripping blade. A horse would be kind of impractical for global transportation, supernatural or otherwise. The only other name that stands out to me is *Santa Muerte*, but his saintliness is still up for debate. As for that particular name belonging to a feminine depiction of Death, I suspect the human concept of gender might not matter in this case. He might even be able to shapeshift to become *Santa Muerte* or any of the other forms he's drawn in.

After some internal debate on both our parts, he chooses a moniker for himself. "Grim will do, I suppose. Not too archaic or religious." He shakes his head dismissively. "That would not do at all. I do not belong to any one order or sect; they all know me equally well."

"That's true." My eyes meet his for a moment as they study the midnight blue wings hiding all the other furniture. Are his feathers soft and downy or hard and sleek? Could I even feel them at all since I don't register temperature or texture like a living human? Would permission be granted to try, or does no one have that right but him? So many questions bounce around my mostly vacant head that they're starting to echo and give me a ghost of a headache. To quiet the constant stream of curiosity, I think of his new name over and over as I did my own until all the other thoughts become meaningless static.

Grim. Grim. Grim. Grim. Grim. Grim. Grim.

As I tilt my head to one side to watch the light play with the ends of his feathers, my fingers absently running over the remaining wing on the statue, one of the questions falls out. "If you don't mind my asking, what are they like? Other people like you?"

His eyes widen slightly in surprise. "I wondered when your curiosity would get the better of you. Normally, such questions immediately follow my introduction." We both agree that my situation is a bit odd as a whole, so asking about everyone else's wasn't high on my priority list at first. He shrugs and continues, "The demons of Hell's Court are precisely what you expect: nasty beasts, and most are far from bright. The exceptions to that rule are beyond cunning and especially cruel." He starts removing the bits and bobs from around his belt as he speaks, setting them all on the end table by the sofa: an empty brown satchel with a symbol carved into the fabric and a dagger in its sheath.

"Can you tell them apart?" Maybe the higher-ranking ones are all whip-smart, and their underlings are like cartoon villain henchmen. But if it's smart enough, wouldn't a demon know to disguise itself to be less threatening if it needed to? Going against one in any situation probably requires years of study and training to pick out weaknesses like that. Surely Grim of all people would know the answer to this.

"Never, under any circumstances, put any faith in an infernal creature. No matter your desperation." No room for negotiation exists in his tone. "They were made to commit atrocities against every other being in existence. None have been known to make exceptions." Not that I was planning to go out and befriend any of them, but one can't help but wonder how desperate you'd have to be to seek out help from down below . . .

"Deities are as unique as humans; the only true difference lies in their powers. They are born or made. They live as long as they are meant to, and then they perish just as humanity does. The major creator deities are still around, but not in the way they once were, not like when humans first recognized their existence." Grim asserts that no one variable is to blame for the faith famine going around these days—except for the demons, but they're the root cause of everything wrong with the world—it's the natural course of the world.

As he leans forward to brace his elbows on his knees, his eyes find the tiny angel in my hand again, and his silver eyes darken to an iron gray. The thin smirk forming at the corners of his mouth flattens back into a straight line. Any amusement brought to him by revealing the secrets of the world to me vanishes, replaced by disdain. "Angels are nothing like that statuette. They are soldiers, not garden cherubs or holiday ornaments." His wings expand even further, spreading to their full height as if he were a bird trying to ward off a rival. The tips brush the walls to either side, and the tops are running out of room between them and the ceiling. I'm glad his scythe is well out of reach; if it were still in his hand, the urge to back away would be much harder to fight. "Be wary should you ever cross one. They protect their righteousness before even thinking of their Father's beloved creations," he warns. I try not to remark on his nails digging into his legs like bone-white daggers. Less successful is my attempt to hide the steps I take out of his reach afterward. Note to self: angels are a touchy subject.

Part of me knows better than to ask the first thought that pops into my head after that reaction, but the part of me that couldn't resist is much louder and a bit of a bully. It's only logical that I wonder, given what little I know about these beings and the one sitting across the room from me. One of his names is the Angel of Death, but it may be another case of false advertising or a misunderstanding. "Aren't you one, though?"

"No, I am not. Reapers are our own kind." His low, frigid voice chokes off any follow-ups. Whatever he is or isn't clearly isn't knowledge I'm meant to attain by interrogating him. With our conversation now as dead as I am, I take my leave of the living room to explore the rest of the cabin. If we're gonna stay here for the foreseeable future, at least one of us should try to cozy it up a bit.

FLIT

The main and guest bathrooms are useless between the two of us not needing the showers or toilets, never mind the lack of running water, but the lace curtains and duck-themed décor upstairs are too cute to ignore altogether. Someone with a strong attachment to ducks must've stayed here before us because this room is jam-packed with knickknacks—knick-quacks, you could say—and artwork of duck ponds. I guess they were inspired by the spring and summertime view out the lakefront window beside the shower door. One of the ceramic ducklings migrates via my hands into the living room as I pass back through on my way to the kitchen.

Dust is worse in here—another obsolete room for Death and the dead—and nothing of more than fleeting interest can be found after rifling through the drawers and cabinets. Only one chair remains at the table, and neither of them sits evenly on the floor. Pockmarks remain in the linoleum from the missing seats, but they're nowhere to be found. Three bedrooms in the back reward me with a jar full of buttons and marbles, more novels, and a ragged quilt to tuck into my window seat.

The bedroom connected to the duck bathroom has two walls of empty shelving much like the reading nook, so I claim them for future treasures too. Something about this room feels off to me, though, quite unlike the rest of the house. The closet door doesn't sit on its hinges right; it creaks open no matter how hard or tight I shut it, like somebody yanked it open wrong and didn't bother to put it back. A single nightstand stands crooked beside the bed, drawers slightly ajar. And it's not fully against the wall or perpendicular to the mattress but in the middle of the floor, as if someone had been looking behind it and left it there in a rush. All the covers on the bed are thrown back and disheveled as if they were recently slept on, not neatly tucked in, or missing altogether. This room's bareness seems rushed and unnatural compared to the other rooms, like I narrowly missed whoever emptied it. I don't stay in this room long and lock it behind me.

The cellar door in the back corner of the living room refuses to budge, no matter how hard I yank on the handle. Grim kneels at my side and tries himself, unlike with the doors in Purgatory, but not even he can pull it free. "It must be stuck in its frame or tied to something below us. Perhaps there is an outdoor entrance—"Thunder booms overhead, making us both jolt and stagger backward. He recovers quickly, shaking his head and chuckling at our reaction. "We can look for that another time. Wading through thick, wet grass is far from pleasant."

"I'll look for a key in here while it's raining." A flash illuminates the house, and the latch to an attic appears in the hallway. "Guess I'll start up there, if you don't mind uh . . . pulling the ladder down." My arm's reach stops well below the string that dangles from the door, while he nearly brushes the ceiling. This door gives way much easier and drops much more dust to the floor waiting below. Trapped heat seeps into the air, followed by a stale, moldy scent and the patter of raindrops on the roof. Grim can't follow me up the rickety stairs without breaking the steps or hitting his head, so he peeks through the opening as best he can.

"Oh boy . . ." Exploring the attic proves to be a bigger project than it first appeared. Cardboard boxes and wooden trunks covered with sheets line the walls so that only a walking path remains. "Why would someone leave all this up here? Are they not coming back?"

Grim's voice rises into the attic. "I have been coming here for quite some time now, and no one has returned to claim it. At least one year has passed since any mortal person has entered this house, by my estimation."

Guess that explains why the place hasn't totally caved in yet. Unless there are leaks or other damages we haven't found hiding somewhere, there hasn't been time for half the floor to rot or for sections of the wall to go tumbling down. Maybe this is a vacation home and no one has had a chance to get away from it all in a while. Or it's an off-the-grid hideout and its owners got caught before they could escape and destroy evidence. Only one way to find out. "If I hand you something, can you go put it in the window seat?"

He nods quietly, but something in his eyes tells me that he's only half-listening and watching. What could he possibly be daydreaming about? Perhaps while I snoop, answers will find their way into my hands. Someone else's mementos could nudge some of my memories out of oblivion, or a returning thought may lead me to a clue about the previous tenants. There may be no connections to be found at all. Nothing so far has contained any names or important dates to go by. I also didn't fail to notice that there isn't a single clock or calendar in the entire house either. Not that it really matters much, since I don't know how long I've been dead.

CHAPTER TWO

FLIT

I spend most of my mornings combing the shore of the lake for trophies. Knowing Grim lurks just out of sight numbs some of the fear that leaks out of my mind into the landscape. So far my collection consists of driftwood and smooth stones, but anything's better than the empty state the cabin started in. I've come to dislike things that aren't filled up or colored in, full of life and teeming with detail. Blankness reminds me too much of the gaps in my memories, some of which came back while the waves chased me up and down the bank.

As of today, I know that I'm sixteen years old, or was right before I died. Grim assumed I might be younger after watching me traipse around plundering through everything in sight, but I distinctly remembered a sixteenth birthday cake with glittery number candles on it. Both were blue like the flowers around the cake's edge. The six didn't want to light at first, but somebody finally got it going before the wax from the one dripped onto the white icing. My name wasn't on the cake, so it remains a mystery, as do the voices of those singing "Felíz Cumpleaños" to me.

I also learned that a few of the words in my vocabulary were Spanish, but most were English, so I'm bilingual to some degree. Grim doesn't think I have a strong enough accent to determine a regional dialect with either language, though. I could be from anywhere on the map of America we dragged out of the attic. On rainy days, and in between conversations, I sit and stare at each state, willing my mind to find even a single thread of memory to pull on. So far this land beneath us is the only one I know.

I lived in a quiet neighborhood, wherever it was; the house was white with a green roof and the number 1120 on the mailbox. The street sign must be farther away than I can see in my memories, so that part of my address is still a mystery. Our house was always full of people and warmth, though all the finer details are muted for me now. No names remain, no faces. Curtains billow around the missing pieces in my visions of home, as if the wind blowing off the lake wishes to sweep away what little is left of those days as I'm searching for them. That wind already visited our cabin, leaving behind only a barely legible *carne asada* recipe and a bookmark covered in lilies. The recipe finds a new home pinned to the fridge, while the bookmark actually gets put to use. Hate to waste it when we have a private beach and the start of a library.

Another house that sat at the edge of a desert appeared alongside the first, where I could see the sun rise and set because nothing interrupted my view of the horizon. Coyote howls and cattle lowing filled my nights there, the pain and hunger of the world ringing through the stars like church bells. "Watch for rattlesnakes and scorpions," someone chides me as I race outside to play with several faceless children. None of them know my name either. This is only fair because

I don't know theirs. I find no toys in the cabin, except for a dried-up watercolor set and a frizzy paintbrush. Maybe all the children that existed here were grown by the time they left or remembered to take their toys along.

A fuller version of how I died still escapes us both; Grim says he can't read my fragmented soul like he would a whole one to find out what happened before my memories begin. He suspects that it could come back to my mind like the other bits and pieces have, but there's no guarantee that I'll regain those events or my name before my time comes. Without knowing those pieces of myself, I can't bring myself to invest in the few that I've gotten back or the memories I'm making now . . . if I even get to keep those in the end. Grim never said if I would remember him or any of this after I move on. I hope I do . . .

Before I can start digging through my head again—while digging for a large quartz rock in the shallows—Grim emerges from the back door and beckons to me. The sunlight catches fragments of color in his wings; little black-tinted rainbows flash across them as he stretches the feathered limbs in the breeze. His cloak isn't yet tied back together below his throat, so his armor catches sunbeams and turns them into white-gold sparks. In the morning light, there are blue undertones in his hair and even a little in his eyes if he stands at the right angle.

Scrambling to gather this round of sticks and stones up without dropping them, I jog up the bank to meet him. After wiping the wet sand from my hands onto my skirt, I set my trophies along the edge of the stairs to dry. "Something wrong, Grim?" Searching for an expression on his face has become a game of sorts since he always goes to such lengths to hide them. I try to match his gestures and face to the ones in my broken memories. What does his sadness sound like, a quiet sigh of wind or a dam bursting? Does anger make his hands shake or his jaw tighten? How long can he smile without it burning him out?

So far, he has three readable faces, though I hope that list will expand the longer I'm here. When he talks about ordinary things, like the moth-eaten clothes in the attic or how we could arrange the bottles we found under the porch, he's softer and more inviting, like a parent thumbing through a fairytale by the glow of a nightlight. The one I recall having was a lavender cloud, I think, with yellow stars. Maybe pink; that memory didn't linger long enough to study. But I did know what Grim's wings felt like after standing outside in the noon sun, and I even earned a handful of molted feathers for my shelf.

"What makes them come out like that?" I asked that day, turning the feather over in my hands like a knife. Its edges were solid and sharp but not enough to cut into skin. Several other feathers littered the floor and the back porch, dancing in the breeze.

"Old ones fall out on their own periodically, as these are." He picked another off his shoulder and placed it in the bundle I had started. "Stress is another factor, as well as external damage."

"Does it hurt when they come out?"

He shook his head, dislodging even more. "Only if they are removed forcibly, much like if I were to pull your hair rather than brush it out gently." We had actually found a hairbrush—minus the handle—under the sink in the duck bathroom that morning, so I had a chance to repair what was left of my braid. Grim had to help brush the ends after my arm got sore, an honor once reserved for my mother, whose face I could no longer picture.

When he answers my questions about his duties or himself, his voice stays even and flat like a teacher listing notes off a markerboard. My only recollection of school is a gym teacher in red shorts who wore her whistle on a stretchy cord around her wrist. She had short, silver-blonde hair and always carried a tape measure. Grim asked if any of the other subjects or material had come back to me yet, but my recitation of a few algebra equations didn't impress him all that much. Such inane things matter little compared to the grander sights he's seen, but he still makes time for them. He told me of reaping monks in snowy highlands, their steady souls floating alongside him as though they were old friends, and of crossing the last believers of ancient religions and the divine beings themselves to their afterlives. Most deities put up spectacular fights at their demise.

I would too if I thought I was immortal until the last minute. At least then I'd have more of a chance than what I had against my mortal demise, what with powers and all. Surely the divine have escaped his grip before? Somehow I doubt flirting with Death would work too well, though . . .

"Where do gods go when they die?" I asked two days later, at least I think it was two. Trees towered over us, hiding the sunset from sight. We spotted a bear foraging at the edge of the woods and decided to follow it for a while. There hadn't been any reapings for us to go to so far, so cabin fever quickly gained a foothold in me. Grim resisted at first, but my threat to go without him nipped his arguments in the bud.

"Depends on the god, really. If they have been kind and generous to their followers, they join them in the afterlife as a benevolent ruler of sorts." He shuffled behind me, eyes everywhere but on the bear twenty yards ahead of us. "If not, well . . . you can infer the rest. As I said, they are not so different from their followers." The bear finished its meal of berries and roots and lumbered farther into the woods than we cared to travel. Our cabin's roof was the only part visible from there, and neither of us were inclined to get lost. I was sure we could get back in no time, but Grim wasn't keen on testing that theory.

And when the wind isn't strong enough to stir dust, and the clouds turn red at twilight, he's fearful and hypervigilant. I've only ever seen that expression on a child tiptoeing through a dark hallway, seeking refuge with her parents after a nightmare. But he doesn't sleep, and it isn't the dark that frightens him. It's water still enough to see your reflection in. It's birds diving down to snatch unsuspecting mice from the clover. It's the back door swinging open without warning. He calls it nothing if I ask. I don't believe him, of course.

"Sounds like there's something in the woods. Hear it?" Most of my nights are spent in the window with one of the novels in my lap, but this night we were both kicking around the walls outside trying to find the cellar door. We scrubbed at sand and uprooted weeds until the screeching of broken branches interrupted our search.

Grim froze mid-pull, eyes wide with terror. "Do you see anything?"

"No. It's off in the trees over there." I pointed over my shoulder and kept digging until my hands scraped across wood rather than dirt. Finding the bottom corner of the trapdoor led to finding the rest of it, and unlike its counterpart inside, it wasn't locked tight. It opened with a thud that muffled the wingbeats emerging from the forest and Grim's footsteps behind me. I didn't even get to my feet again before he ushered me into the basement. "Hey, what's the big idea?"

"That's no bird, but it will carry you off like a mouse. Stay below until I come back."

The next thing I knew, the door shut and blackness consumed me. Beating on the exterior door and calling for Grim to let me out accomplished nothing but knocking dust loose from the boards. Time crept by agonizingly slowly, until desperation led me down the rotting stairs into the basement so I could find my way back into the house. My hands found cracks and holes along the walls and my feet uneven flooring, but the room itself was strangely empty, even of typical creepy basement things. Despite flailing my arms above my head and finding a string to tug, no light illuminated the musty corners. And, unfortunately, ghosts don't glow either. I couldn't see if there were any mason jars full of mystery goo or dusty relics that held the missing clues from upstairs. All the drop cloth–covered chests and cabinets were in the attic. This place must've been part of Purgatory, as bare as it was. Even the dirt floor was clear of disturbances. All of that combined made me want to leave even quicker than if it had been full to the brim.

When I found the opposite door—which was locked from this side—Grim was already waiting with his hand over the handle. The scrapes along his face made the irritation that swelled up at the sight of him disappear almost instantly. I was safe, not trapped.

We didn't go back to the cellar after that.

Now, as it usually is, his face is so neutral it's a bit unsettling. "No, nothing is the matter, but I cannot leave you here alone." His skeletal fingers work at the clasp of his cloak, shutting out the blinding rays shooting off his armor. "I do not have the means to protect the house once I leave, and I have souls to collect today."

"Protect the house? I thought you said nothing bothered you out here?" If there were any substance to my body

I wouldn't risk leaning on the collapsing moss-green rails, but being no stronger than a weak breeze in this form, I thought nothing of it. Grim probably thought about as much of my objection, having grown used to my inquisitiveness. Most other times—when I asked to hold his scythe, every time I dragged something out of the attic to tinker with, each memory I asked him to sift through—he nodded along without resistance, but not this time. A fourth expression appeared to match blows with my stubbornness: an impatient glare.

"I did say that. No one seeks out my company but those on a desperate fool's errand, but I am no longer alone." He made a point to seek out the physical plane so he could stare directly into my eyes and attempt to unnerve me. "There are those that would claim your soul and use it for less than noble purposes without me to deter them."

"You never mentioned I'm in danger."

"I am mentioning it now." His tone leaves little room for dispute, no matter how exasperated this information leaves me. Did I not deserve to know that something might be trying to spirit me away and throw off the "balance" Grim is so worried about upholding? What if these phantom pursuers were the cause of my death and held the answers I'm searching for? By no means would I take off and confront them myself, obviously, but not knowing they existed had to be even more dangerous than that. "As long as we stay together, you need not worry about creatures with ill intent. But if you are out of my sight, I cannot guarantee your safety. I am not omnipresent."

"Fine. I'm gonna be in the way, but if you insist." While the thought of watching him work admittedly sounds fascinating, it also holds its own dangers.

"Flit . . ."

"No, no, it's fine." My arms cross over my stomach, and I squint up at Grim while I wait for him to suggest an alternative. Could a lesser reaper not keep me safe here at the cabin while Grim goes about his day? He said there were other, smaller reapers out there working too. Did he not have any "magic" or whatever it's called that could serve as a barrier? He isn't known for creating things—unless you count grief and sorrow, but they aren't really his fault—but surely he could manage a gate! He made a dress from the fabric of reality and cut open a door in the air to get us here, so it stands to reason that a fence isn't an outrageous request. When he offered for me to stay here to escape Purgatory, I was under the impression that the cabin would be my only view until my hour struck. Nobody said anything about traversing the world while he mows down the wicked and the virtuous. I didn't sign up to be a tag-along. All I asked for, all I have come to expect, is sanctuary from wandering the lonely world. I gesture impatiently at the empty air beside us where a portal would fit. "Let's go."

Anger, cold and sharp as a razor's edge, threatens to slice through his fragile mask of calm the more I needle him. It bleaches his irises white and darkens the skin around his eyes to the color of deep bruises. "Very well. Stay close. Do as I ask, and you will make it back here in one piece." His mouth wants to curl into a snarl, but as with his fear, he smothers it until it straightens back into a flat grimace. "Behave otherwise, and I may not be able to save you a second time."

The scythe's curved blade carves a line from the peak of the mountains down to the rotting boards beneath our feet, and I step through behind him.

GRIM

Predawn black replaces late morning blue above our heads once we finally emerge from the doorway; the moon leers down between the oak branches at the edge of a large backyard. One of my underlings waits by a tire swing, their scythe propped against the tree. At times, I wish they all had individual names so I would have something to greet them with, but remembering them would only be another burden to bear for us all. Their faces all look alike at any rate: dead-pale skin stretched too tight over skulls that are barely human, with dark hoods drawn over their brows. Some of them have scars or tears in their cloaks from run-ins with other beings, but I cannot claim to have seen them enough to remember what injury belongs to which reaper. Anonymity keeps our job much simpler and neater. Fewer personal details to get in the way, you see. If Flit finds the newcomer fascinating, she does not let on and marches past us to examine the house and grounds.

"Good evening, sir."

"Clear and cool, is it not?"

"Yessir." Ordinarily I do not see my subordinates at reapings unless they occur on a large scale, such as a battlefield or natural disaster, but this one called me here. I only personally reap a select few souls, ones from lineages of great import known as Lines, but occasionally a soul meant for me finds its way to the list of a lesser reaper. They rifle through their cloak pocket to retrieve the cloth satchel issued to each reaper at their creation. Inside the satchel are enough coins for each soul to be reaped that day, engraved with the proper details of their respective afterlives. Religions are indicated by symbols pressed into the center of the coin: crucifixes, runes, blank spaces, and the like.

Destinations—up, down, or start over, if you will—are scrawled across the top in the traveler's native language, and their full names cover the bottom. Birth dates take the left side and death dates the right. The little reaper's bony fingers sift through the pool of coins until the errant one surfaces and they hand it to me. "It's one of the Lines I've got for you. Recognized the surname, Levitt. Don't know how I got it."

A six-pointed star rests in the center, with גַּן עֵדֶן above and *Felix Oliver Levitt* below. The date reads May 24, 2010. That is quite the jump from the time our cabin resides in. "It happens. The universe is far from perfect."

They agree and begin to leave without further comment until they catch sight of the ghost at my heels. Flit took up residence in the swing while we conversed and occupied herself by staring absently at the manor. It appears that her being cross with me is the only thing that will put a stopper in her curiosity about the afterlife. She has not uttered a word since we left the cabin, and we walked half a mile up the driveway to get here. "One get lost, sir? I've never seen you leading a soul around." The other reaper's head tilts so that we are both in their line of sight.

Flit briefly glances away from the lamp-yellowed windows to acknowledge she had been mentioned, but when we make eye contact, she turns around so fast her braid swings with the momentum. I believe her aim would have been to hit me with it had I taken a step or two closer.

"Yes, I found her in Purgatory, luckily before anything else did."

"Purgatory?" The little reaper's eyes dart between the two of us as if pure fear had struck them dumb; Purgatory serves only as a path between the realms we serve, not as a dwelling place. Angels use it to deliver messages to their earthly charges without being seen by others. Demons use it to spread their chaos more effectively without drawing unwanted attention from their heavenly counterparts. We use it to travel long distances across time and space in seconds. And humans only take a handful of steps through it when they pass on, rarely registering they spent any time there.

Lesser reapers would not have interfered with a wandering soul without orders to do so; they likely would not have seen her at all in the area where I found her, so far out from our usual routes. The celestial and infernal creatures, however, have little other purpose than seeking out helpless souls to serve their own ends. Flit would make a fine beacon for their greedy eyes to follow and an even better flame for one side or the other to snuff out.

"She died before her time and was not sent to an afterlife realm." My tone should have been sufficient in deterring further questions, but this particular reaper has an inquisitive streak not unlike their query. They again glance from the human to me and back, confusion and curiosity mingling dangerously below the surface.

"Must be from a Line. Normal souls don—"

"She does not remember, and I cannot discern it."

Flit's ears no doubt perk up when I raise my voice to silence the underling—some reaper business is not meant for mortal minds—but again she whips around as soon as I glance in her direction. Suits me all the same if she overhears or if her eavesdropping fails. Let her ruminate on stolen bits of knowledge and not ask me for clarification, see where it gets her. I shall not reveal secrets to her of my own accord if she wants to be petty about her safety.

The smaller reaper gets flustered after being reprimanded, coiling in on themselves. "Yes, yes, of course, sir. W-well good luck getting her home, and with this soul, sir. Good night, sir." And they vanish with a nod.

Meanwhile, my wayward charge wanders closer to the house, and in its shadow, she truly looks the part of a ghost. The moon's cold light washes the copper from her hair, the gold from her eyes, and the bronze from her skin. The night drains Flit down to a grayscale facsimile of herself, all but her voice. She always speaks eerily softly, like most humans do when they enter unfamiliar houses of worship. No reverent fear colors her words, though. At last, she aims a sidelong glance toward me. "So are we going in or do we wait out here all night?"

"We go in. Souls typically stay with their body until they are claimed."

"Except me."

"Yes, except you."

She did not request an explanation, so I follow her steps onto the creaky porch, silent as a shadow. Two rocking chairs, side by side, sway under her hand and the breeze that preceded us. A swing clacks against the wall at the far end, a lonely sight with no humans to occupy it. Even without our influence, the place already seems haunted.

We pass through the unlocked front door and into a foyer already lined with wilting flower arrangements. On a table beside a flickering menorah, greeting cards lay scattered, some read and others unopened. Both well-wishers and premature mourners offer condolences in equal measure, but judging by the other pile of envelopes nearby, that was all they contributed. At the end of the hall, our destination is lit by a single Tiffany lamp and blinking lights on a plethora of medical devices.

Despite this man's valiant efforts to delay this meeting, Death has arrived.

"You would come at a time like this." His dark eyes snap open upon our entrance, and he makes sure to get the first word in. "I don't suppose you and your little friend could be troubled to wait a few minutes? I'm expecting someone."

I detest sneaking up on people and stealing them away, but giving them a warning is not always the wisest route to travel. The ones that fight back make my already taxing job more difficult. He did not have the air of an easy negotiator, though he truly had little room to argue. To humor him, I glanced at the grandfather clock wedged into a corner and then at the numbers etched into his coin. To my ill-concealed surprise, Flit and I had in fact arrived ahead of schedule despite our chatting on the lawn. We could indeed stall for a moment to give him the closure he sought. "Time waits for no man . . . but we are a bit early. You will not miss them, Mr. Levitt."

"I didn't realize you could see me too." Flit's demeanor softens as soon as he recognizes her presence, and she tiptoes over to offer him some comfort in return. I sense a fragment of her soul briefly connecting to an image of a grandfatherly figure seated in a kitchen preparing a meal; the features she could make out resembled Mr. Levitt's in some ways, and this fleeting link drew her closer. Mr. Levitt gladly takes her tiny hand in his bony one as she perches on the edge of the mattress, rather than seeking consolation from me. Unlike her, most humans are quite put off upon meeting reapers in person and would prefer any other company to ours.

She scarcely makes a dent in the comforter lovingly tucked around him, even when she leans closer to speak. "Who are you waiting for?"

He is the first being to interact with her directly since we met, and even without tracking the days, it is clear such lengthy isolation did not agree with her. Though she vehemently resisted leaving the cabin, she could not deny her longing for her own kind nor how poor a substitute I have been.

"My daughter, Melody." He reaches over to a nightstand with his free hand and brings a framed picture closer for Flit to inspect. The photo's edges curl under the glass pane, worn soft from being carried for many years; humans tend to inadvertently destroy things by loving them. It is not their nature to let go, even when they should. "I-I have to tell her goodbye. Her mother couldn't . . . I-I can't leave her like that."

Flit's ire returns long enough for her to shoot daggers at me across the room as if she believes I directly choose which humans die and when, but she quickly turns it off again to speak to the dying man. "I'll wait here with you." Her eyes glaze over with tears that are blinked away as she holds the aged photo in her lap. In it, Mr. Levitt sits on an antiquated couch with his family surrounding him: a young woman with the same creases around her mouth leans in from the left, a man around the same age stands behind them with his hands on their shoulders, and a tiny boy with thick curls is sandwiched in the middle. "Where is she?"

"Getting ready for bed." He points to the staircase outside the door that leads up to the pitch-dark second floor. The only illumination I can detect seeps from under a closed door to the left of the landing. The sound of faint sobbing carries down the steps, but not far enough that the other two could hear. "She'll come down to say goodnight. Then I can go."

After some deliberation and a minor attitude adjustment, my companion decides she can address me once again. "Will she be able to see us? No offense, Grim, but uh, you might freak her out. Just a little." Her own appearance did not concern her as much as mine did, for obvious reasons.

"More than a little in my experience," I correct her. "But unless she is coming along to Heaven with him or is clairvoyant in some way, we will remain invisible to her." With time drawing nearer, I bestow the coin upon its owner so that he might pass in peace. An angel will gather his soul from the portal as it closes on our end, and they will put the coin away to be counted with the rest collected today. Mr. Levitt does not recoil from my touch as the coin exchanges hands. In cases of such fear, I usually set it down and allow them to pick it up on their own, and in the cases of the extremely unwilling, I give it to their escorts.

Mr. Levitt chuckles at his destination while inspecting his ticket to the afterlife. "Oh, so all those nights in Vegas didn't count against me after all?" Flit wonders aloud what he meant by that, but he determines she is far too young for the details necessary to explain. She is too busy marveling at his age to pursue it further. Or perhaps biting back her jealousy . . . she has no wild tales, nor a family to regale them with.

"Not as much as you might have feared the morning after," I reassure him to keep the joviality intact. "You more than repaid that debt, judging by your soul's luminance."

Unlike Flit's, this soul is whole and intact, so his life can "flash before" my eyes as well as his own, if he so desires. Some wish to skip that part of the process, some linger until time runs out. Mr. Levitt served as a doctor for many years in this rural Colorado setting, bringing the gift of life and easing the burden of death for those who otherwise would have been alone. He utilized both the technology of the times and ancient practices passed down through his Line; if one did not work, he turned to the other before seeing a lost cause. Sometimes he did not see it then either, and often this worked in favor of the patient. His wife, Lana, departed for a decade now, acted as his nurse even before they married and became a saint to the ill in her own right. He is certain she loathed to leave so suddenly—unexpected heart trouble—but also that she left at peace with her legacy. Their daughter learned her mother's traditions before a reaper took Lana onward, and she still had her father to guide her until his time came. Now, the universe believes she can hold her own, so he must come with me.

He regards my statement skeptically, tucking his coin into the pocket of his pajama shirt. He could not see the steady glow that all but enveloped his side of the room as I could. "Judge, jury, and executioner, eh?"

"Only a modest harvester really." I indicate my scythe leaning against the wall, more a tool than a weapon, but capable of being both. "I collect the 'crops' when they are ready and take them to their proper destinations."

"Seen your fair share of nuts then, I'll bet," he teases, his breaths beginning to thin out and grow farther apart. Flit cannot help but giggle, which turns his waning attention back to her. "And you're hardly a seedling, haven't even broken the soil yet . . . robbing the cradle ought to be a crime, you know." I nod in assent, and Mr. Levitt pats Flit's hand again.

Taking the young and innocent is the worst aspect of this job without question. I would transport every last caterwauling, writhing soul of the damned singlehandedly before I would willingly take hold of a whimpering child's any day. The pain of hellfire is only wrought upon those who deserve that fate, and I take immense joy in throwing evil into the flames, but the gates of Heaven are open to its people whether they are aged or youthful.

Above us, the light clicks off and the bathroom door creaks open, softly signaling the end drawing nearer. The grieving daughter will bid her ailing father goodnight, and he will follow us to his eternal rest as agreed. He turns again to me before she descends. "Will Lana be waiting for me?"

"Your wife will be as you remember her, in the prime of life." Scenes from events stored inside his mind, some he may not remember and some he may treasure dearly, materialize in the air between us so we may recount his vices and virtues. Many of Mr. Levitt's thoughts center around Melody or his practice, and of course Lana is present in them all. "You were both healers in life, and in death you will be restored as were those under your care."

"Fah!" He feebly dismisses me just as his daughter slips into the room. "I hope they do a better job than that!"

Melody is none the wiser to the otherworldly beings in the room, but Flit still jumps out of her way as if her mere touch would scald her to the bone. She hovers in the shadow of my wings, waiting patiently to escort her new friend out. Melody takes her place on the edge of the mattress after wiping tear tracks from her face. "Guess the line went dead back home. Asa said goodnight and he loves you." She sniffles a few more times while her puffy eyes search the room. "Who were you talking to, Dad?"

After a short coughing fit, he shakes his head at her. "I was telling that ol' bone farmer he can't have me just yet. His sickle isn't sharp enough."

"I must give you points for originality, Mr. Levitt," I retort, speaking over Flit's renewed giggling. "I have earned many names, but that has never been among them until now."

His daughter fails to find the humor that my young charge has and struggles to keep unspent tears from spilling out as she scolds him. "Oh, don't talk like that! I'd rather not dream about skeletons tonight."

"I know, honey." He apologizes to her but aims a wry smirk over her shoulder at me. He will have the last word in this exchange one way or the other. "I'm muttering to myself to pass the time. Old habits y'know."

She huffs not with impatience but with affection and annoyance in equal measure. "If you say so. Need anything before I turn in?" Although she indicates the kitchen with a toss of her dark hair, she does not move herself from his side by even an inch. She may be unable to see who waits in the corner of the room, but she knows I am near. It is futile to fight against my coming; the only solution is to arrive before me and make the most of that limited time.

"Not a thing," her father rasps quieter than the second hand of the clock ticking by. The stroke of the hour is his time, and he can sense it closing in the longer she lingers. He does not want her to bear witness to his end and hopes to shoo her away before it is too late. I do so hate how the living carry on after a brush with a reaper, as if the whole business is not unpleasant enough without the guilt they summon with their cries. At last, Melody sweetly kisses her father's forehead and returns to her own quarters knowing what she will wake to in the morning. I am both unseen and too obvious to ignore.

As soon as the door swings shut behind her, we assume positions on either side of the bed, and Mr. Levitt takes both our hands in a confident grip without prompting. Leaving his corporeal body behind, we lift his soul up and guide it to stand at the footboard. He glances back at himself beneath the quilts and tangled wires—humans and their morbid curiosity—but not for long. He is ready to move on.

"This way, Mr. Levitt."

"You don't have to tell me twice. Being old and sick is no cakewalk, friend." He struts past me and down the hall before the last syllable of his name leaves my mouth. Contrary to the drained image he left behind, this version of Felix Levitt has substantially more vitality. Equal levels of snark exist on both planes, however. "You know about half of that, being older than dirt, don't you?"

"Dirt is only half as old as you think," I reply as soon as we catch up to him. If I were human, I would be out of breath from running after him. Fortunately for my stoic public image, I am not. He stands expectantly by the tire swing while Flit trots up behind us with her much shorter legs, and I prepare a portal for him to cross into. The portals reapers use are vastly different than the ones souls pass through; those that lead to various afterlives pull at mortal souls as a magnet does a scrap of metal, tugging individuals toward their fate no matter how they may rail against it. Reaper portals leave the direction up to the traveler. Their one similarity is that both must be opened by someone wielding a supernatural blade.

"Bit of a wisecrack, hm? Keep him in line if you can." While his eyes follow the scythe's tip through the night air, Mr. Levitt's elbow nudges Flit and then angles toward the stars. "I hope you find your way up there, kid. Maybe our clouds will bump into each other."

"I'll be sure to look you up," she promises, her own eyes trained on the portal with pitiful longing. She knows what waits for her innocent soul on the other side and that she cannot behold that splendor yet. Waiting with that knowledge undoubtedly reminds her of the pain she left behind with her living body; incorporeal beings do not always experience physical agony. To her credit, she hides it well enough to not alert Mr. Levitt as he departs. Her wave goodbye is cheerful and congratulatory until the streak of light vanishes. Only then does her smile wilt away like a dying flower.

"If only they were all that pleasant when they go." I offer her a comforting hand on her slumped shoulder, which she takes without protest. She leans into my side with a dejected sigh, her footsteps aligning with mine. Heartbreaking as the peaceful crossings are, I hate to sink her mood further with a warning about the worse ones, but it must be done for her sake. "Of course, some of them have reason to behave otherwise."

Fright glimmers in her eyes as the next portal is torn. It is jagged and dark around the edges and reeks of thick, choking smoke.

CHAPTER THREE

GRIM

Flit's unease increases tenfold when we emerge in the confines of a women's prison deep in the Appalachian mountains; being a spirit, the negative energy radiating through the cells and corridors hits her as a brick wall would a speeding car. All the other ghosts lingering behind bars form such a wall, with their anger and regret forming a cloud that suffocates those with clearer consciences. This place is not unlike Purgatory with its liminal state of existence. Everyone confined here is on their way to another place, be it the freedom of a second chance on the outside or execution and damnation. We are obviously not here for the former; rarely does the universe allow a soul to escape its fate. Especially not one so vile as the woman we are here to collect.

Before we enter the execution chamber, I pull Flit aside and kneel before her. Even on my knees, the top of her head scarcely reaches my shoulders. The way she gazes up at me—with trepidation and awe and the beginning of trust—makes her seem even smaller, more fragile than she really is. You would be surprised how difficult humans are to break irreparably.

"I must warn you now," I say as she edges closer so that my wings touch behind her back. "Heaven is not the only destination I send the dead to. You may witness terrible things, but you must not be afraid. Any being that could do you harm would have to cross me, and few are so foolish."

She nods, glancing anxiously at the door to our right after every other word. "I'll stay close. I'm not interested in a fate worse than . . . well . . . you." Her smile is hardly convincing, but it will have to do. She cannot be left alone, not here, not with the creatures lurking just out of her perception.

"I am sorry for the things you may hear or see on these journeys. If I could leave you in peace at the cabin I would but . . ." Down the hallway, ghosts' screams and wails mesh together into a cacophony only they can hear. If the living on the other side of the door notice them, they elect not to investigate.

"I didn't do it, I was framed. They're still out there!"

"It was an accident, a horrible accident . . ."

"I was protecting myself. I never meant to go that far."

Further unnerved, Flit puts her back to me to face the spirits rather than risk one sneaking up on her. "You're not early to every death, are you? I don't want to be here longer than we have to."

Wrapping her in my right wing, I guide her through the wall into the waiting area of the execution chamber. The reporters and guards are filing out the door opposite our entrance, so there's less of a chance that a gifted one might see us. "No, we are right on time to this one."

We round the corner and find a small group of people still standing in front of a one-way mirror. The spirit of an older woman with long gray braids and amber skin watches without a hint of emotion on her face as the appointed people remove tubes and wires from the deceased. To her left is a younger woman, presumably a still-living relative judging by the similar complexion and dark features of their solemn faces. One striking difference, however, is in the younger one's eyes; the left is so dark it nearly matches the shade of my cloak, but the right is so blue it's almost white.

I freeze, but not before covering Flit entirely.

Call it an old superstition if you must, but in many cultures and my own experience, beings with this type of heterochromia are far more likely to possess some form of psychic ability than those without it. That is a chance I cannot take. Never mind the other ghost standing mere feet away. Flit doesn't see it that way and of course objects to being swathed in feathers without warning.

"Grim?! What are you do—?"

"Quiet." I allow her to peek for a few seconds to keep escape attempts to a minimum. "If they see you, we may have trouble." If the living woman does have abilities, then odds are she has powerful connections in the supernatural world, and in no situation does that work in my favor. If she sees me alone, it will likely be enough to encourage her toward the nearest exit, but Flit will bring unwanted attention from every plane. Demons are reckless and angels are meddling. Humans are often both. The sooner the living vacate the premises, the sooner we can go on our way as well.

Tense seconds pass as if everything in the room were slowing to a halt; her mismatched eyes find me and pause fleetingly, but her spiritual companion draws her attention before it can linger and find something amiss.

"They call this justice," the old woman mutters as she shuffles toward the exit, "but justice would be her trading places with the ones she stole from us."

"She isn't going to the same place as you or them, *Elisi*." the younger one replies, turning away to follow her grandmother. "Not after all she's done. All that greed ate her up and left us with that." She gestures to the corpse they are leaving behind before turning back to me. She doesn't ask outright, but her expression suggests that she wants to know the fate of the soul I've come for. Judging by my brief read of hers, any answer I give will bring great pain.

Her father, Yona, his twin sister, Inola, and their father, Biyen, were all murdered over the contents of a safe that was burglarized by the condemned: family heirlooms, proof of their lineage that reached almost back to the beginning of the Line, money for hard times, weapons for protection. Most of these material things got sold or pawned for money that failed to keep the authorities from pursuing the guilty party. Her accomplice turned her in to save herself from meeting me in the same fashion. Dikanodi—the one staring me down—was the one to discover her family's demise and the theft of her inheritance. Her one solace is that her grandmother, Tallulah, was not at home at the time and that she did not see the fresh crime scene; her heart could not have borne the sight that haunts the last of the Walker Line.

As if this crime were not horrific enough on its own, the condemned is her own mother.

And she is right, a trade would be unequal in this case. Souls bound for Heaven or its sister realms are far purer than those going to Hell, so she would not even be worth half what she took. Not even a fraction. I hope my words do not frighten her into hysterics—this has happened more than I care to admit—but I must say something to ease her listless soul. "There will be justice in the end."

Her grandmother regards me cynically, dusting off the skirt of her tear dress. "We will see when the end comes, won't we?"

"Seriously?!" her granddaughter hisses, stepping between us, though whom she means to protect from whom is unclear. "You want to bicker with the Grim Reaper, but I can't watch *Buffy* because it attracts bad spirits?" I develop the suspicion that the frown lines beginning to grow on her face came from several previous discussions on the topic with the incorrigible matriarch.

"I'm already dead, what's he gonna do?"

Dikanodi casts a fearful glance over her shoulder for answers and comes away surprised by my response. "The end has come for your tormentor, Mrs. Allred, not you." Despite my reassurances, the elderly woman stands defiant and unmoved. "Punishments befitting her crimes will be hers within the hour, while peace and reunion will be yours when your journey ends."

Tallulah crosses her arms and nods to the smudged window on the right-hand wall, the one that opens into the death chamber itself. "Do you yourself pass out these punishments? What do you know of her fate, *Ganatsaysdi*?" Past the glass divider lies a woman strapped to a gurney with a vacant expression on her face and many needle marks in the bend of her arm. We watch silently as Marcy Allred's body is zipped in a black bag and removed, leaving her soul seated on the table, numbly observing us.

"She will know eternal torment at the hands of someone far crueler than I. My only participation in her afterlife is handing her over to them."

"I wish to see this fearsome creature." Dikanodi balks at her grandmother's bold assertion. "Unless he is the lowest of the low, he is not low enough for her."

"*Elisi*, please." She begs to leave this place before true evil arrives. Though I am uncertain of the extent of her abilities, it is clear she can sense the approach of a powerful darkness even before it is summoned. "If he says she's going to Hell, then I'll gladly take his word for it. He looks like he knows what he's talking about."

"Go if you like. I will follow when I am through here." She firmly roots herself across the glass from her former daughter-in-law, and the tension skyrockets. Either of them could easily cross through it and confront the other directly, but neither takes that step.

Flit, unable to hold her peace any longer against the building suspense, emerges from her hiding place. "We won't be long. Your grandma is safe with us." The older woman gives her an approving nod, but the younger is quite startled by her sudden appearance from seemingly thin air. "It's not her time to leave, like he said, so you don't have to worry so much."

Unlike her aged family member, she is not inclined to argue with either of us, and with one last pleading look that falls on a stubborn soul, she shakes her head and trudges back to her vehicle alone. Once the door clicks closed behind her, the remaining three of us turn to face the murderess at our backs.

"Flit, wait out here. If she makes any attempts on me, I want you well out of reach."

Her new companion scoffs, her eyes never wavering from the other woman's face. "Snakes don't know how to do anything but bite. Expect nothing less from her."

Marcy's face never so much as hints at regret as she stares back. "So you're him, huh? The Devil come to collect his due?" She regards Flit and her ex-mother-in-law with little more than contempt and disinterest. "Aw, and you got a little angel on your shoulder?"

"I'm not an angel," Flit retorts, her usual bite lessened by the anxiety seeping into her voice. "Grim, please, hurry up." Her expression indicates that she wants to bolt into the nearest portal that will take us away from here, but some patience is required in reapings like this one. Without said patience, I would be unable to tolerate the cocky ones, the ones that think if they are clever enough, I will be lenient with their punishment.

They fail to realize none of that is my personal decision; if I personally oversaw punishing wretches like her, I would make the wickedest of the Court shudder in terror. There are ancient realms far worse than Hell that could stand one more resident; luckily for the world's worst, there is a balance I must honor, and taking them anywhere other than their prescribed location wouldn't bode well for either of us.

"If the Devil had it his way, he would come to claim you himself, but for the time being that responsibility falls to me." As a member of a Line, one of the Court must claim her in person lest she go to the wrong realm and count toward the power of one of their siblings instead. One of them being minutely stronger than the other would not do at all.

Were it not for Tallulah keeping Flit company, I suspect she would keep inching toward the exit, and if she started moving about on her own, I would fear for her wandering out of sight and getting into trouble I cannot spare the time to deal with presently. For now, they stand together facing me and the murderess, the dawn framing them through the window like a painting. Both try to ignore the cries of the trapped ghosts down the hall, until something out of my sight catches Flit's attention.

FLIT

Flashes of garnet and navy peek through the window to the corridor we came through; there is no solid form, just streaks of color darting in and out of cells and doorways. In a way, it reminds me of meeting Grim, only less accidental. Where he just kind of stumbled onto me somewhere I wasn't supposed to be, this . . . whatever it is . . . seems to be on the hunt. Its movements are more deliberate than his were. No uncertain hovering or lingering in empty spaces for this being, no way. Its presence makes the ghosts' wailing grow louder, more desperate; however, the creature itself is inaudible. Grim condemning the lady behind me could also be drowning this thing out, so I won't know unless it gets closer. But until he gets a look at it and determines if it's friend or foe, it can stay right where it is. Better yet, it can hang out there until we leave altogether.

"This is your last chance to repent and perhaps save your wretched soul," Grim snarls as if he doesn't want to offer her a path to forgiveness. Something tells me that isn't entirely his decision, but he has strong opinions about certain cases. "Do you have any remorse for the actions that led you here?"

"Even the blind could see she doesn't." Mrs. Allred mutters, crossing her arms and scowling even harder. "She's only sorry she got caught."

"Is she why you haven't passed on?" I ask. Grim mentioned ghosts lingering on this plane because of unfinished business but never clarified if that was the only reason spirits didn't cross over or how to tell if that was the case at all. In hindsight, the question seemed a little too blunt, but so did Mrs. Allred. Maybe she wouldn't mind.

"It is part of our people's tradition to stay for a time after our body has died. I would be here in spirit with or without her actions." she replies, "I get the feeling that your traditions are not the same. If not for him, you would be elsewhere." Her tone suggests a deeper meaning to her statement, but it's lost on me.

If Grim hadn't found me in Purgatory, I would still be wandering through it instead of wandering around Earth at his side, so she's right about that. And if he'd been able to leave me at the cabin, I wouldn't be surrounded by the horrible ghouls down the hall or anywhere near the woman he's collecting, so that's part of that truth too.

I shrug it off with an attempt at a joke. "Probably not. At least I hope I wouldn't be in prison if I were still alive." She raises her gray eyebrows at me, asking without speaking. "It's hard to say with no solid memories."

She hums thoughtfully. "So your traditions are lost, I see. And the ancestors you could call on for help too." This saddens her, taking some of the edge off her voice. She pats the folding chair next to hers, and I sit to collect the sudden influx of thoughts.

"Oh . . ." I hadn't thought of it like that before. Missing a whole lifetime of culture and traditions kind of took a backseat to trying to figure out the more everyday things about myself. "We don't even know who my parents are, or where to start looking for that matter."

"I do." She places one barely wrinkled hand over her heart. "The mind may forget, or try to hide or deny, but the soul remembers the knowledge of our ancestors. Everything is passed down that way, even unspoken things. Look hard enough and something will come of it." She nods to herself resolutely, as if that were the whole truth and nothing but.

Skepticism has taken root in me, however, and uncertainty blooms at one end of it. "How will I know if what I find is right or not? Everything we do know is jumbled and out of order."

"Your intuition will never lie to you. It will lean toward the truth as a tree leans with the wind." She gestures across the room to the other woman, who has gotten off the gurney and is puffing up at Grim like a schoolyard bully. "Take her, for example. I knew from the moment she met her little co-conspirator that we had lost her to evil. But the others wanted to give her second, third, and fourth chances, against their intuitions. And this is where that left us."

On the opposite side of the glass, Grim's target huffs, leaning forward with her hands on her narrow hips. Even with her arrogant sneer and stance, the fear swirling just below the surface is pouring out of her wild eyes. She isn't fooling anyone here. "Oh, so you're gonna preach to me too, huh? Like I slaughtered a bunch of saints? Those leeches—"

Grim stiffens. "Yes or no will do."

"Nah, then. I ain't sorry. Nobody wanted to give me what belonged to me so—"

Mrs. Allred hums again. "What does he do if they repent, I wonder?"

I do too. Neither of us ever brought that up in our discussions before. What would a second chance look like for someone like her? Is that even possible? Forgiveness feels way out of the question in this case, but maybe humans don't get to decide that in the end.

In the midst of our contemplation, another shape appears across the corridor, this one dark and menacing. It's smaller than the first one, but it brings a wave of cold that fills the space between us. A growl echoes through the hall, not as an audible sound but as a rumbling that shakes the floor like the start of an earthquake. Mrs. Allred checks her seat to make sure it isn't causing the wobbling, while I leap out of mine back toward the door to get a better look at the confrontation. The first presence moves toward the second, but it doesn't budge.

"If you do not repent, then you will face an eternity of suffering for your sins." Grim swells to his full size, wings splayed and spine straight until he fills most of the room and cuts her off from any escape. His face isn't visible to me now, and judging by his booming, frigid voice, I'd rather keep it that way. "You have committed several homicides of the most heinous nature and betrayed those who called you family. Therefore, you will spend eternity in the bottommost layer of Hell, Judeccan, the unclaimed realm of traitors. For the last time, Marcy Eileen Walker, do you repent?"

His words echo so that even the things outside are paying attention; all that's visible of them are streaks of red and black between the cell bars all the way at the end of the row, but they've clearly stopped moving. They're listening. At least one of them has noticed me trying to watch Grim and them at the same time, but their attention is equally terrifying, so I'm unsure which it is.

Even after his final offer of redemption, Marcy remains shakily defiant, "I-I'd do it all again. Th-they owed me."

"What she was owed, she was given, and still she took more." Mrs. Allred sighs, a single tear escaping with the quiet exhale. "She took everything."

For a fraction of a second, all the sounds around me die as suddenly as a candle being blown out. Nothing moves except the light playing across the sharp edge of the scythe. I beg myself to turn away, to seek the things beyond the bars or stare at a rivet in the door or the corner of the ceiling, anywhere but at the blade.

Don't look. Don't look. Don't look.

Of course, I can't help but stare.

The cold air filling the prison vanishes, the growl becomes a whimper, and the black mass disappears into tendrils of smoke. Whatever Grim's about to do is apparently more than even that dark beast could handle.

Grim, rather than cutting her down with his scythe, pulls his curved dagger from his belt; he takes her arm roughly and carves the Roman numeral IX into it. No blood pours out, unlike if she were still living. "The only thing you are ever owed in this world is your life, and you have stolen more than you could ever repay."

He takes the scythe from the wall after returning the dagger to its sheath, opening a rift that glows a cold blue. She doesn't have to walk to it; from the realm beyond, what I justifiably assume is a demon emerges. He's about as tall as Grim and just as uncannily almost human. Two horns, both broken off just above his matted blonde hair, jut out from the back of his head. Two antennae stand at attention by his temples. The whites of his eyes are black as tar, the irises are corpse gray. Most disturbing are the thickly encrusted stitches sewn through both of his lips so tightly the shape of his mouth is distorted.

Mrs. Allred, far more shaken than expected but still not willing to flee, shuffles from her seat to stand between me and the newly arrived demon. My back is unguarded in either direction, no matter how I turn, but she is appreciated nonetheless. Her steely attitude might give him cause to hesitate if he considers coming in this direction. "Wonder if she'll get the same mouth treatment as that down there?" If I don't laugh, I'll scream and run all the way home alone. So I chuckle and shrug.

The creature gestures to the damned with the tip of the jagged spear in his left hand while holding his right out to Grim expectantly. With disdain for both apparent in the half of his expression I can see, Grim speaks to the demon. "This soul belongs to the lowest realm, and for her passage there I give you this coin. Do what you will with her." Unlike the single Star of David on Mr. Levitt's coin, there are two symbols on hers—a cross and a faded bird's head. I don't catch either of the full dates, only the year listed on the right side. For some reason it startles me a bit seeing 2003 printed there. How long have I been dead now? Is this before my time or somewhere in the future I never made it to?

The murderess changes her tune a beat too late; it's out of Grim's hands now. "Wait, wait, I changed my mind! I'm sorry! I didn't mean to kill Yona, he walked in on me cracking the safe and—" She stumbles through a half-hearted explanation that falls on several pairs of unsympathetic ears.

The demon impales her on his spear before she can finish her excuses, then yanks her like a doll being dragged by its pull-string through the portal. Our last view of her is marked by her nearly limp arms clawing at the edge of the rift and a sickening, bloody gurgle. Our last view of him is a cold stare that lands squarely on me and only disappears when the portal seals itself.

Grim deflates a bit once the demon is gone and turns to where I am cowering alone in the lobby. Mrs. Allred was smart enough to leave after Marcy was gone and before Hell's messenger got a good look at her. "Flit? It is done. Are you alright?"

"*Hell of a thing to ask me after what I just saw . . .*" I mutter to myself, suddenly paranoid that he'll change his mind and call that thing back to take me off his hands. I know he said I'm not destined to spend my afterlife breathing fire and brimstone, but I would prefer not to push him to make an exception this one time. As I start to answer him, the blue and red being catches my eye again. This time it's much closer but still not totally clear on the other side of the door.

The nearer it gets, the more I worry that our demonic visitor didn't come alone; like his presence, this one makes my incorporeal body shiver with nerves I have never felt in life. Maybe it's because I'm not a physical thing anymore that these entities are affecting me so drastically. I mean, Grim did say that only the dying and other supernatural creatures can see him—and me now—so it would make sense that the only way to acknowledge demons and whatever else is lurking around is to be on the same plane as they are, or to be specially attuned to it like the living woman who saw Grim earlier. In this case, however, the fear comes from not seeing it rather than coming face-to-face.

"Someone . . . something's outside." I snap out of my frantic search long enough to inch closer to him. "I don't know what, but we need to go. Please, let's go, Grim."

Grim takes my place across from the entryway, his silver eyes drinking in every detail of the hall beyond the door, though he comes away unconvinced. "I do not see anything—" He starts to object until a wave of tension seeps through the wall and hits us full force. Whoever is in the hallway locks stares with him, and neither of them are happy about the encounter. It starts moving toward us, rather than pacing the corridor parallel to the chamber, and Grim staggers back into me.

He makes no attempt to mask his fear or explain; he only rips a crooked portal into the air and practically shoves me through. "Come, our time has passed here."

⁂

A PRISONER OF JUDECCAN

Snow used to be so beautiful to me.

How could someone not love watching its tiny crystalline forms drift slowly downward, carried by the slightest breeze? Who would not enjoy the barren winter world being lined with the finest lace made by nature itself? Or the hush that falls over the land as everything stops in awe?

Now I pray to never see it again.

Too long I've lived in a frozen wasteland, surrounded by ice so thick and deep that the bottom appears black. There is no reprieve in the open from the wind that stirs the frigid air, nor shelter deep enough to truly escape it. The sun has never shone here and never will. My winter is unending and devoid of any warmth.

I used to love other people too.

My family made up my entire world for eons. They were all I knew and all I wanted, from nurturing my younger siblings to learning from the eldest, I couldn't have asked for anything more. Even our more distant kin were precious to me, no matter our differences. I would've given anything for any one of them.

Now the presence of others fills me with dread through to my bones.

The only people around me now are my sick tormentors and the others suffering at their hands, and the latter are all but ice sculptures at this point. I haven't seen a new arrival in this cursed tundra in years. Judeccan may be small compared to the levels above it, but it's not so small that everyone congregates in one particular area. There is no safety or solace in numbers anywhere in Hell, especially not here. Everyone here is out for themselves, from the highest of the Court to the lowest of the damned. If they're down here, they know better than to trust anyone else they see. This is the realm for traitors, after all. Not one of us is worthy of those we left behind in the living worlds. We had our chances, some more than others, and squandered them all on our own wants. On foolish notions. On pride.

One would hope that the possibility of such eternal torment would convince more people to lead kinder lives. They don't have to follow the whole system, or any of its many variations, just the few rules on how to treat other living beings. Most of them are fair and straightforward. Children understand the concepts and typically have little trouble; it's the adults who struggle with no cheating, no stealing, and no lying.

Take me, for example. I had one rule to follow, one thing not to do. I also had doubts that could not be silenced. Would it really be so bad to break this one rule? Why, if this action had such catastrophic consequences, was it even an option at all? It became one of the oldest known cases of "what could possibly go wrong?" The Court and their lackeys were my answer.

Speaking of, Prince Mammon seems to have found his way into my domicile today. His realm is five levels away, but none of the rest of the royal demons can be bothered to enter this one, so they bully the smallest of their number into collecting the souls bound here. I've never heard him complain, but that could be the crooked stitches across his mouth at work.

He's dragging what's left of a woman behind him on the tip of his spear, leaving a bloody trail through the already sludgy snow. He pays me no mind—what a relief—as he searches for the perfect place to deposit his prize. Should he toss her into a cave or roll her down an embankment? There are plenty of empty stalagmites to impale her on nearby. He could call a pack of hellhounds to take care of the new guest, or any of the other underlings. My only wish is that he does not linger to torment her himself. The longer he stays in my vicinity, the more likely he'll be to pay me a visit before he goes. And unlike most residents of Judeccan, my mobility is not limited by breakable ice but an inescapable cage. I'm a special case, you see.

The sixth-born demon finally decides to send the soul careening down a hill to his left and into the chasm below. Then he reconsiders, taking a step back to examine her more closely. As many non-human beings can, Mammon can peer into a human soul to seek any information he may need to determine their fate. A reaper likely performed this same ritual before she was sent here, but it didn't satisfy the demon.

If he's seeing the same things I am, he knows she slaughtered a good portion of her immediate family in the midst of a robbery. Two men, one much older and the other her same age, and another woman. She had an accomplice in someone she considered a friend. They weren't a very good one, however, given that they sold her out to reduce their own sentence. From betrayer to betrayed, how hilariously ironic.

The pair stole several artifacts from a safe concealed in a closet, as well as a stash of money. None of the items, except perhaps some of the knives or rings, had any real monetary value. However, one item immediately caught my eye as it passed from the lockbox to their greedy hands: an old handmade doll that was quickly discarded in favor of the riches beneath it. Well, not so much the doll itself but the pattern on its dress. I'd seen that pattern centuries ago while being tortured by one of Mammon's vile relations, Prince Asmodeis. He'd manipulated some humans into stealing it from their brother after they'd sold him off like livestock and then proceeded to try and convince me my own siblings had left me to a similar fate. But I knew better.

I also knew that pattern could only belong to a member of a Line.

"So that's who you are." She obviously doesn't hear me, nor does he, over the biting gales and distant screams, but now my new neighbor makes more sense. The Court doesn't just go and fetch any old soul, they only personally ascend to a reaper's call when it concerns members of certain families. And this woman lolling about on the ground, not unlike the toy she once disregarded, belongs to one of them. My, how far some of them have fallen.

Mammon seems inclined to agree that she has sunk far below her rightful place, so much so that he viciously snaps off her arm bearing the number for this level and tosses it off the cliff. The sound that wrenches itself out of her mouth is guttural and inhuman. Pain like that is indescribable until you feel it yourself. He ignores her cries, grabbing her by the matted tangle of black hair on her head and dragging her toward the nearest exit. No doubt he means to add her to the ranks of his dominion rather than let her soul go to waste down here in the unclaimed pit. Though he is the Prince of Greed, and theft is not beneath him, the surrounding circumstances lead me to a different conclusion than simple petty thievery.

The end, at last, is approaching . . .

CHAPTER FOUR

GRIM

I cannot risk another encounter like the one we had at the prison. There is too much at stake for another slipup like that; regardless of my previous intentions, this will be the last reaping today. I doubt Flit will disagree, and I hope she will not ask too many questions. An apology is in order, as the warnings I gave beforehand did little to prepare the poor child to witness such violence so close. "Perhaps that was a bit much for—"

"Oh no!"

In the middle of the gravel crossroads lies a tabby cat and a Beagle puppy, both struck by a car while chasing one another, both belonging to the household of a Line. Contrary to what some believe for whatever odd reason, animals do indeed have souls to be collected, and if a Line considers them part of their family, they come to me at their death. The cat's soul is yowling indignantly. The dog is confused but happy to see Flit. She, on the other hand, is devastated.

"This is just as bad as that awful woman! Poor things . . ." She stoops down with such a forlorn expression to pet and kiss the dog. "*Lo siento, perrito*. I'm sorry people are so mean."

I have always been partial to felines and their languid indifference to circumstances that inconvenience them; this one seems only mildly perturbed that she is dead. Lolly—the name on her tag reads—is more incensed at Oscar the puppy for chasing her out of their yard. "This was not all human error in this case." Cradling the cat, I turn to Flit so she can pet her as well. "This cat knew this area well but still ran to the road. The dog knew little of this place and failed to pay attention."

In that vein of thought, Flit's distress from moving from one scene of carnage to another clouds her mind, so our own pursuer does not even register with her. The scent of sulfur must not be strong enough for her to pick up on, and she must have avoided the lingering cold patches in the sunbeams, otherwise the fear of another demon's presence would send her into a panic. As weak as it appears, it likely is not a member of Hell's Court, but their lackeys are far from a better alternative. The Knights are just as cruel as their masters, and those below that rank are unruly at best, indiscriminate destroyers at worst. Even the smallest imp could steal an unguarded soul, and animal familiars are speedy messengers, so we must act quickly to escort these two onward before we become targets ourselves.

A snarl from deep in the forest informs me that my thoughts come too late.

The hellhound prowls through the underbrush, not brazen enough to come into plain view but cunning enough to wait for my back to turn. Judging by its size, it is a Prince of Hell's personal guard dog and not one of the smaller mongrels spawned from them. Attacking it would alarm Flit and alert its master, wherever they may be skulking, so my only choice is to remain in this standoff until we leave or it attacks us first.

She is far from convinced that people are not at fault for the loss of the other two creatures and continues to sulk. I, however, suspect the hellhound to be the culprit behind the fatal chase, not the puppy. "And the human didn't stop fast enough. Or bother to look for their owner. Or move them out of the road at least." Her fingers disappear into Lolly's thick striped fur and behind Oscar's floppy ears, and her voice fades into a dejected sigh. "I hope I didn't die in some stupid accident. Or worse . . ." Her mind clearly swung back to our previous errand with the murderess, and undoubtedly to the age-old question of what fate was worse, being intentionally or unintentionally killed.

I have no answer for her in either case. All I have is a half-hearted apology. "Without your memories, I cannot tell . . . I am sorry Flit."

"Oh, it's not your fault. I was just wondering. Hoping, I guess." She watches the dog bounce around us and the cat purr in my arms. I hand her Lolly in order to open the portal to the Garden of Eden. Animal souls are the only ones permitted to reside there now, after the incident with the fruit tree. The cat wriggles away and trots into the opening without so much as a backward glance, but the dog remains at Flit's side, eagerly wagging his tail.

"Go on, it's alright. Follow the kitty," she urges. Oscar whines as if asking Flit to walk with him; he has been trained to follow, not to lead. "Go to the light. I can't go just yet, but I have a friend over there who I'm sure would love you until then. Mr. Levitt seemed like a dog person, didn't he, Grim?"

"I hardly think he would hold anything against the cat either." She smiles back and nods in agreement, and since it appears that she has accepted her wandering fate for now, perhaps my suggestion will not be too dangerous. "Perhaps if you walk toward the portal, he will follow you. Walk to the side of it until he passes through."

In her eyes, for a brief moment, simmers curiosity about what would happen if she walked into the light herself. I could not stop her if she were to bolt at the last second. Someone on the other side would be swift to remove her, however, and she would be at their mercy.

Perhaps I should have kept my mouth shut and shepherded the dog myself, but who would keep the wolf at bay?

"Here, boy! Come with me, this way." Flit gives a sharp whistle and pats her leg to get Oscar's attention. He immediately trots to her side, his tail wagging so hard the entire back half of his body swishes along with it. She leads him into the opening, her own form only inches away from touching it. Inches away from disappearing into the afterlife before her proper time. It takes every ounce of my composure not to snatch her back and slam the portal shut behind the dog.

I can see it in the way the glow dances across her eyes, painting gold rings in her irises and threading the color of her hair with holy fire; she wants to go, the call of Heaven pulling her in the farther she gets out of my reach. She admires it far too long. Her hand aches to reach out, the pieces of her soul long to be whole again.

"*Not yet.*" I will her to stop and turn away from paradise. "*Not yet. Not yet.*" Those tense minutes stretched to their limits finally end when she turns to me and steps back from the closing doorway. I hate that I am relieved by her compliance with my unspoken plea, but she cannot know this.

She will not be led away from me.

She cannot leave.

She must not be taken.

As the portal fades into the pastoral scene behind her, the birdsong is interrupted by an unearthly howl few have survived to describe. As loud as a foghorn and bone-shaking as an explosion, the bay of a hellhound can only mean that its patience has worn bare. Flit leaps away from the forest just in time to miss the massive beast crashing through the underbrush and onto the road.

"Get back!" Brandishing both scythe and dagger, I command the dog to return to its place of origin, but my ghostly ward is the only one that complies. She darts behind me and into the yard belonging to the deceased pets, hoping the picket fence will offer some protection should the beast charge us. I do not have the heart to tell her this mutt could raze the house itself to the ground if it so chose.

"Grim!" Flit cries out in terror at the same moment its jaws snap at my throat.

The sweeping blade dissuades it from jumping up again, but only until it dips underneath and strikes at my feet.

Kicking it away only gives the creature more room to get a running start at me, but it moves too quickly to land a solid cut from this distance. I will have to let it get closer to even have a chance of striking the right blow. And if I fail . . .

"Grim! A portal!" Tears rolling down her face glisten in the morning light. "Make a portal and close it!"

I sidestep the cur, and it collides with a tree, shaking leaves from every branch. "Flit, I cannot portal it away. Its owner will find us and send more." The only thing worse than one of these mongrels is a whole pack at the beck and call of a demonic Knight or Prince they guard. If the dog fails to destroy me, its master will make a more successful attempt and kidnap her to add insult to injury. And as long as this monster breathes, I cannot portal her away either, lest it slip past and discover our hideaway.

There is only one ending to this battle.

I just need an opening, one missed step on its part, a distraction.

Behind the hedges, a garage door whirs open, startling all three of us. Perhaps the owners of the pets have come searching for their lost loved ones at last. This only adds another human for me to protect, and he cannot even see or hear any of us. I am sure once he rounds the fence and sees all the dust flying and hears the ungodly snarls, he will not think twice about fleeing, but that would give the hellhound an invitation to chase and maul an innocent man.

Flit came to the same conclusion, without the concern of her invisibility, and scrambled to her feet to stop the unsuspecting bystander somehow. Ghosts have been known to influence the living, but those instances typically speak of much older spirits. She has no experience manipulating anything but inanimate objects, an innate ability of the wandering dead, but far be it from Flit to let that stop her. "Stop, stop!" She places her tiny hands on the man's chest and shoves him backward. "Grim, get the dog! He won't stop for long!"

He did in fact stagger a bit, but not enough to halt altogether. She pushes again, harder, and he catches himself on the fence. "What the hell?" He whips around in search of an attacker or offending object that would have tripped him, only to find an empty driveway.

"Get back inside, please!" Rather than pushing, Flit decides pulling will work better and grabs hold of the hand closest to her. "Come back with me, come inside," she begs him as I fight, each plea keeping time with the blows against the hellhound.

He resists at first, but after the third time she speaks, he looks directly into her eyes as though her voice had finally cut through the veil. Her target, though immensely confused, eventually follows the tugging on his arm back the way he came out. Over the pounding in my own head from blood loss and the scrape of the scythe handle through the gravel, I hear the door slam shut.

She is safe. For now.

Now that I do not have to split my focus between the hound and the humans, our melee can truly begin without fear of unnecessary injuries. I finally managed to land a few hits while Flit was making her rescue, but so did the mutt. Dark spittle drips from the dog's jowls, pooling on the dusty road. Feathers, torn from the flesh beneath, flutter in the spring breeze like dandelion tufts. My scythe blade is coated with grit and streaked red from tip to hilt.

"Back to . . . your master . . . you foul cretin."

It grumbles in retaliation, limping around to circle me.

"Your miserable life . . . does not have to . . . end this way."

Another snarl, an unwavering glare.

"Take another step toward that house and there will be nothing left to send back to Hell."

It pauses, its dead-black eyes flickering between me and the front door. It sniffs the air, searching for its intended victim. Right now, I have no way of knowing if Flit is the soul the creature seeks, or if it was sent for one of the homeowners. Unless its controller travels with it, hellhounds seldom announce their agendas to the opposition.

It huffs in a mimicry of exasperation, facing away from the house and down the path a car took only moments before we stepped fully through our portal. Regarding me with one last glower, the hellhound concedes the fight and flees after its prey.

Not Flit. She is safe.

Moments later, my companion comes bounding out the front door armed with a metal bat, only narrowly missing the truck barreling around the corner. "Is it gone? Did you—?" She searches the crossroads for a body that is long gone. Once her eyes find my wounds, the hound is all but forgotten. "*¡Ay, Dios mío!* Grim, are you okay?" She reaches out to comfort me but recoils for fear of adding to the harm.

I do not know how to respond without frightening her; these slashes are not fatal, but they are signs of worse to come. The Court is growing restless, desperate even.

We are not safe. We never were.

"I will be fine. We just . . ." She steps forward and takes my hand gingerly in hers. "We need to go home and rest. Today has been a bit—"

"Much? Yeah, just a bit. Let's go."

I shakily open a rift to our quiet lakeside haven so that we may retire from all the excitement. My shredded cloak practically falls off my shoulders upon entering, so Flit drapes it over the sofa. It is little more than a ceremonial relic really, but it alarms fewer people than the armor underneath. She does not mind either way but often gets distracted and trips over the train. "Very good. . . Perhaps I ought to keep you on as an apprentice."

Flit considers the offer as she steps in behind me. "Maybe I could reap the animals and the nice people. I'd never want to deal with people like that horrid woman or anything else from Hell."

How I wish that were an option. "Unfortunately, pure souls are not the only ones that require transportation from the mortal plane to the afterlife, and humans are not the only beings that travel. Imagine if that thing had found you alone."

Flit slumps into her window seat, rolling the wingless angel in the palm of her hand as if it held the deeper answer she sought. "What did it want? It didn't even come after me really." Her finger slides over the jagged edge where the missing piece should rest. If she were alive, I would be concerned that she would slice her finger open, but instead I worry about her finding a real one and—

No.

We are safe here.

We are protected and hidden.

"That I do not know. I suspect it was after the animals and we interrupted its hunt."

She is shaken and disturbed, her innocence disrupted. Before these traumatic incidents, I suppose she was the closest a human has ever come to being as Adam and Eve were before their Fall. She has no knowledge of the massive cruelty of the universe, no bias in her heart until given evidence, and complete faith in the one guiding her. How easily that naivety is ruined.

I open the back door and all the windows for the breeze to sweep out the suppressing, stale air inside the cabin. It reeks of abandonment and the regrets of the forsaken; if these walls could speak their piece on what they have seen, they would only chant, "*How dare you? How could you?*"

Flit wanders under my wings onto the porch while I linger in the doorway. She leaves her angel on the windowsill, its sculpted face peering through the bottom pane, and collects her stones and driftwood from the staircase. Though she passed as a young woman, her childhood lay not far behind. This much was evident in her care for the trinkets she gathered from the shore; only children care so much for small things without worldly value. She had not abandoned these values for an adult's care for material wealth and never would. In fact, there were many things she would never have the chance to do if she stayed. She would never relive the pain of her last moments or know the injustice of all that came before.

I envy her deeply.

FLIT

It hadn't taken long to discover every secret the cabin had to offer; there were stretches of time that Grim and I stayed here the entire day or only had one reaping to attend, so I had a chance to explore as far as I felt like going. We watched sunrises the mornings after thunderstorms because the clouds were more vibrant. We found unused animal dens and spent the dark hours following their trails to their new homes. Sometimes I would find bones hidden under rocks or bushes and would bring them home to match the décor to the inhabitants. Grim's favorite was the bird skull we found in the hollow of a dead tree. I made wildflower crowns for both of us as the afternoon dissolved into twilight; we wore them until they dried, and then we sent our fragrant little boats adrift in the lake.

I also found an empty journal tucked in a drawer that didn't pull open all the way and, miraculously, a working pen. Grim was a bit apprehensive about me keeping a diary lest some poor living soul find their way here and stumble across it, but I managed to reason with him that, for one, nobody had even come near us the whole time we'd been here, and, for another, most people wouldn't make it past the skulls in the living room. With that line of thinking, I decided it would be best to hide it under the bear skull on the middle shelf. Nobody would find it there.

"Are you writing to jog your memory? Or about your time here?" He asks now, inspecting his new scars in the window. The gashes from the hellhound mostly healed as time wore on, but some were too deep to close all the way. He claims he could erase them all just like wiping away dirt, but he sees no need to expend his power on something so superficial. I think he looks cooler with them anyway.

"Both, kinda. If I remember something, I jot it down if we're here, but the little pieces don't usually make any sense by themselves." Like this morning, the color of my *Quinceñera* dress flashed through my head while I was trying to remember what kind of fruits I liked. I also remembered I hated cold weather but always wished for snow when winter came. As for keeping track of our day to day, it's the only way I can think of to keep up with the passage of time, or try to at least. It doesn't seem to pass normally here, and it's hard to figure out if it's passing elsewhere when we don't stay out for long. There could be decades or more between each reaping. We could be going into the future or the past for all I know. Grim continually avoids answering when I ask.

"How old are you anyway? In human years?"

"I have not been keeping track, if I am to be totally honest." He chuckles, "Younger than the first humans, that much is certain. I did not awaken until after they were cursed to mortality."

"Maybe you should write stuff down too, then. Guess you'd need more than one journal, though. Maybe one per century, you think?"

His smile drops, and he shakes his head. "What I know in the wrong hands would be catastrophic. Even telling you these things is dangerous." Ever since the hellhound attack and the prison, he's more visibly paranoid about being discovered. Whatever or whoever sent that thing to harass us that day had him peeking out the windows every time a breeze swept the tree branches the wrong way or an unexpected thunderstorm growled over the mountains. He missed entire conversations watching the horizon and nearly tripped over passing shadows at reapings. But no matter how many times I beg, demand, or interrogate him about if something is wrong, he waves me off like he doesn't pace holes in the floor daily. I guess I won't know until it's too late at the rate we're going.

Just like I'll probably never find that missing angel wing in this house.

I have searched every corner of the bottom floor from ceiling to ground, wall to wall, and still haven't found even a piece of a piece! So, refusing to accept defeat, I pull down the attic door and begin my upstairs search anew. I turn out every chair cushion, clear every drawer, and even look under everything that had space for something to hide, and still nothing turns up.

Grim, while supportive of my hobby, can't fit into the spaces I can and chooses to perch on the staircase and observe instead. "Still nothing?"

I can't help but groan, "Unless it's hidden under a floorboard or buried outside, I don't think it's even here. Maybe somebody threw it away by accident." Thinking of the poor little figurine sitting in the window with its limb missing only made me more acutely aware of how much of me was gone. Of course, the thought then crossed my mind that someone had thrown me away too. No one came looking for me when I died.

In the silence between our voices, I try to scrape together more memories, aside from the eerily familiar lake, from the hours leading up to my death.

I can picture the nightgown down to the pink embroidered flowers around the collar and hem. There are 108 steps between the start of my death march and its end at the shoreline. My hair had been braided but was coming undone because my scrunchie had come off as I tossed and turned. No lights were on behind me. I was alone outside. I didn't fight the force tugging me toward the water hard enough.

Now, as I turn to trudge back toward the stairs, the jarring sensation of being lifted off the floor suddenly hits me, and I latch on to a dresser to ground myself. A vision washes over me, but whether it is memory or dream remains unclear.

Dead-cold hands yank me upward, sending beads of water rolling off my lifeless body. Two voices murmur over my head, one deep and scratchy, the other so soft it's almost impossible to catch. The grip on my shoulders and beneath my knees tightens. Someone grabs for my leg and misses. The voices grow louder but remain unintelligible. Feathers float by on the wind, but I can't see what color they are. The lake slowly fades like paint washing down a drain. Purgatory swallows me then, and the revelation vanishes, along with my mysterious captor. Or savior?

Does that mean I was *deliberately* taken too soon? Did the one who pulled me from the depths lure me there in the first place? Grim said angels and demons used human souls to supplement their power, and it stands to reason that if one came after me the other would follow and at least try to stop them. I don't remember any other enemies from my life so far, and certainly none serious enough to warrant murder and soul-napping.

Grim turns from glancing down the hall, giving me little chance to right myself before he sees how the fear rattled me. He doesn't hear the near-collapse or sharp gasp that stops me from coming down, or he would've torn the room apart seeking the invisible force that triggered the panic. His response to my earlier musing doesn't help much, despite his gentle tone. "Perhaps they did discard it. I doubt the former inhabitants expected anyone to pity a broken figurine this much."

A mask of irritated humor falls over my frantic expression. "You can't open a portal to the missing wing and bring it back, can you?"

"I am afraid not. I can only ferry souls, not knickknacks."

"Some help you are. Do angels even really have wings? Maybe the statue having wings is inaccurate." Or maybe I'm afraid to match the image in my head with the doll in my hand. If an angel took me, were they saving me from someone else, or was Grim right about them being irrepressibly self-righteous? Who was trying to use my soul, and why?

He nods. "Most angels do, yes. Some look like humans with wings . . . and some can look like whatever they need to look like at the time, or nothing at all." Grim doesn't go into great detail describing the qualities of the various choirs of the Heavenly Host, just enough to differentiate between them. The seven Archangels and Archeia look the most human of them all; only Gabriel has the white wings and fair hair people usually associate with angels.

He goes on to describe Hell's occupants, disgusting as he may find them. "Most demons are flightless, thankfully. Some of the Court can fly, but most of the lesser ones cannot."

Flight isn't as necessary for them as one might think. Unlike Heaven, which is all connected and on one level, Hell is split into nine sections with one for each member of its Court of High Demons, and the members tend to stay in their own areas unless provoked otherwise. However, Purgatory and the bottommost pit are unguarded. Purgatory is kind of like a bus stop for other religions; virtuous people who aren't part of Heaven's system wait here for their deities to collect them for their afterlife.

"Go there much?" Most of the wobbliness is gone from my legs, so dismounting the stairs with his eyes trained on me isn't such a chore.

"No, unless one of my charges is routed there. And even then, it is only a brief visit at most, as Purgatory only allows one to linger there as long as they are meant to."

"Would you reap any of the Court or Host if they died? Where do they go?"

He hesitates as if he doesn't want to go on at first. "No angel has perished since the war against the Rebellion, and I did not attend their deaths. Demons return to the flames when they perish; humans kill them every day in exorcisms. Their fates afterward are in the hands of their creators."

Grim helps me climb down from the attic, then follows me back into the living room. My little angel, still half-wingless, does not turn from watching the lake to greet us. I leave it be and pull my journal out for the evening. "Maybe angels go back to Heaven then, into the clouds or whatever else is up there."

"Perhaps." Grim stretches across the sofa, contemplating his otherworldly knowledge. "We will know for certain if a member of the Heavenly Host passes before you do. The death of a celestial being tends to turn into a spectacle."

"Oh yeah?" My pen stands at the ready to scribble down any details he passes along. Maybe he won't notice or ask, considering his opinion on keeping records of the supernatural. This won't be the only occasion of note-taking on my part, and he doesn't need to know that either.

"I forget you have never met another celestial directly. The lot of them are melodramatic to say the least. Prone to tantrums, for lack of a better term." He sneers, "Especially if they fancy themselves a leader. They take anyone or anything they can catch hold of down with them."

The way he describes the deaths he's seen is beautiful in a melancholy kind of way. Some of them dissolve into embers and blow out with the wind, while others melt like candles and seep into the ground. Some explode into infernos that swallow mountain ranges whole. Or implode and leave no trace at all but the last memories of their deeds. No two are the same, not even identical twins. Grim can count on one hand how many have taken their demise gracefully; most of them were the other incarnations of death passing the mantle along before slipping into peaceful eternity. He left them in their chosen resting places to decay out of mortal sight. "Some of them may still be there, even all this time later. Centuries have passed since the last one perished."

"So, do they die when no one follows their religion anymore?"

"That is not always the case, no. That only weakens divine creatures." His fingers work at the straps of his armor, readjusting the greaves and plates absentmindedly. He never takes it off entirely. "Other such beings may kill them, just as humans kill each other. Not all immortals are truly immortal, so there are some who grow old or become incurably ill."

I glance up from my diary and observe him for a moment; he may be one of them, and I may have little experience when it comes to non-human personalities, but he hardly behaves like what most would picture when they think of a supernatural entity. They're all people technically, but the way he talks about the others sets him apart from them, like he's closer to a human than to something primordial. At the same time, he moves and speaks like no one in the living world. Maybe he's somewhere in between us and them. That makes me wonder . . .

An awkward silence falls long enough for me to continue my thought aloud, "When we reaped that woman in prison . . . we both saw something in the hall. I know you saw it because we left so quickly after you looked out that window. Was it something that could kill you?"

His face goes as blank as Purgatory's landscape, and he doesn't even pretend to breathe. What little color he had to his skin drains away like fresh paint under a faucet, and he recoils into himself, wings contracted and gaze distant. Without uttering a word, he answers my question.

GRIM

Panic is an ugly emotion. The feeling that the air is tightening until not even time can move, that growing dread that can swallow any living thing, makes even the mightiest cringe with fear.

If Flit has that much figured out, what else can she deduce on her own? Does she know more than she lets on, is she testing to see if I will lie? If I lie and she finds out, what will she do? She cannot harm me, of course, unless she possesses a weapon I am unaware of, but human teens are known for their brashness. What is to stop her from fleeing from here and being snatched away by a demon? Or being found by an angel and "cleansed" from walking the Earth as a ghost? The risk of her finding other people, mortal or otherwise, is catastrophic at best.

One wrong encounter and the truth will find her before she is ready.

Luckily for me, before she can press any harder on the matter, one of my subordinates appears on the porch and taps nervously on the open door. "Sir, I came as fast as I could. I—" If I am not mistaken, this is the same reaper from Mr. Levitt's death; they seem to recognize Flit, and the sight of her trips the words tumbling out of their mouth. "I found one of your coins in my satchel again. This one is the end of two Lines."

"Come again?"

"The Lines of Elijah and Lazarus, sir." They shy away as though my tone frightens them. "And not by natural means. Demons are afoot, I suspect."

In the corner of my vision, Flit visibly recoils at the mention of the infernal race. Two brief encounters with lower-rung beings must have been enough to squelch any budding reckless curiosity about those creatures for her. "Like . . . hellhounds or something bigger?" She addresses the smaller reaper.

"Much bigger." Their brow is drawn into a concerned grimace, their eyes studying my ghostly charge for longer than necessary to reply to her. "I fear it may be one who holds their leashes. Not the Court directly, but not far below them either."

Regardless of their rank, demons are under no circumstances to terminate the end of a Line unless they face them as vessels in battle with the Host. To do so invites the wrath of things much more fearsome than a simple death for the offender; gods do not take kindly to interference with their great and delicate machinations. Ending a Line removes key players from the equation, and when plans fail to balance out, chaos spreads like errant weeds. Of course, knowing demons as I do, that is likely their goal.

Rising from my fleeting comfort, I draw my cloak around my shoulders and pass through the back door. Opening a portal inside the cabin would prove foolish if a demon waits on the other side, especially one with this sort of mischief in mind. "Have you any more deaths to attend today?"

The reaper shakes their head. "This was meant to be my last for the evening. Why do you ask?" Flit now stands beside them, hesitant to follow me into a reaping akin to the last two she witnessed. "Do you mean for me to stay behind with her while you collect the soul?"

"I mean for you both to come along and for you to aid me should it become necessary. Hell is growing bolder by the second, and I will not stand for their meddling in my affairs." The portal shimmers a cold, dense black at its edges. Both figures behind me remain motionless except to huddle closer to one another, fearing the possibilities that await us across the tear in time and space. "If you stand about here instead, there will come no warning if I fail, and you will fall into their grasp yourselves. Come."

She takes the first step forward but remains shielded behind the smaller reaper's back. They inch forward before she collides with them, but neither looks any more convinced than they were a few moments ago. "And if you fail, what are we supposed to do? I can't fight or outrun these things," Flit points out.

"Not alone, you could not. But you will not be alone this time."

We emerge from the other side of the doorway onto a quiet forest path in the dawning hours of the day. Nothing stirs save for a chilling breeze jostling the wintered branches above our heads. No wolves howl at our disturbance. No birdsong rings in the growing sunlight. No one stands on this side to greet us.

"Are you sure this is the right place, Grim?" Flit wrings her hands and twines her hair around her fingers. "There's nobody out here. Unless it was a bear attack or something and they're off in the bushes."

Instead of replying to her, I turn to the other reaper for answers. "This is the location, correct? The human is nearby?" We stand at a fork in the path; the right side leads into the darker depths of the wood and the left into bright meadows.

They nod, guiding us down the left road. "Yes sir, this is close to my initial portal site. I had to walk a bit, but only around this next bend I believe. That's . . . well, that's where I thought I smelled brimstone."

"Did you see anyone?"

"I didn't stay to search for them. I took one look at the coin and came straight to you. If the Court was here and had come after this person, I knew I stood no chance against them." they admitted, their head hung low and eyes averted. Flit cast the reaper a pitying glance, but her sympathy was quickly replaced by panic. Branches in the near distance snapped as loud as gunshots in the silence, followed by an indistinct voice calling out ahead of us. Its words were carried away on a strong gust of wind, far out of our ears' reach. However, where we could not hear our mysterious companion, we could certainly smell them on the same breeze, and the reek of sulfur is a hard scent to confuse for another.

"*Dios mio* . . ." Flit did her best not to gag, but her hands could only block out so much of that odor. "Yep, something is definitely dead out here."

"That is hellfire you sense, not decay." Flit withdraws into herself, and the other reaper's eyes pale with fear as well. "If the demon has claimed the soul for itself, we will have battle on our hands. Where is the coin?"

The reaper fumbles through their pockets before placing the small metal disk into my hand; every detail reads as expected except for one. Her name still means "blessed, bringer of joy." Her birthday still occurred the day before that year's winter solstice. She is still bound for Heaven's golden streets. But her death date, though I have fought and prayed for it to be, has not been altered. Surrendering to fate is not an option, so I press on despite my looming failure. The others cannot know.

"I pray it doesn't come to that, sir." They shudder. "Those nasty creatures—"

I conceal the coin in my palm and march toward my waiting foe. "Will be sent howling on their way shortly. Wait here unless I call for you."

"And if you don't come back?"

"Then you guard her until her final hour has rung. Or yours. Whichever keeps another soul from the reach of those who seek them so greedily."

FLIT

Without a word of goodbye or a promise to return, Grim stalks off into the forest without looking back. His stride never falters over roots or stones in the path. He may be walking into all our certain dooms, but he doesn't trip himself once. Not even when the foul-smelling wind kicks up again, reminding us just who he's up against.

"Do you think he'll be alright by himself?" I ask the smaller reaper pacing back and forth across the road. "I don't know how powerful he is, not really. Or how powerful anyone else we may meet doing this is." The thought occurs to me that I should mention the incident at the prison, but the thought following that suggests that Grim may not want his subordinates learning there's something out there that he fears enough to flee immediately rather than engage. There's also no guarantee whatever is out there is the same as a hellhound or what came after us in the prison. It could be a huge misunderstanding. It could be something worse than any of that. Without knowing for sure, frightening my only remaining guardian falls under the "stupid move" category.

"Well," they mutter, "if it's a lesser demon . . . a Knight or lower, he'd likely make short work and send the imperiled soul onward without much fuss."

"Sounds like there's a 'but' in there."

They nod gravely. "But Knights of Hell seldom travel alone, and the Princes won't be far away if this is under one of their direct orders." They tap their spindly fingers against the side of their mouth. "This is all highly irregular to say the least. First, coins turn up in the wrong place, and now a rogue demon chasing souls? This absolutely smacks of Hell hoping to start problems."

"Isn't that all they do?"

"Fair point. But this . . . their motives are rarely so complex or unclear. They aren't complicated beings, nor are they powerful enough to interfere with these coins." Several of them jingle in the pouch at their hip. "That's the bit I don't understand. Souls, of course they want souls. But these?"

"So they can't do anything with the coins? Like make them into weapons or hide them from reapers?"

"Only a god can destroy or create a coin. Not even our scythes can damage them." To demonstrate, the reaper sets a random coin on the ground between us and lets me read it:

Heaven

August 17, 1981–July 23, 2008

Rory Aisha Monroe

I wonder who this person is in the grand scheme unfolding around me; did they die peacefully or get dragged into the unholy mess slowly rearing its ugly head at us?

The tip of their scythe hovers over the cross at the coin's center like a needle above a record, then the entire blade is swung downward. Golden sparks fly as the metals meet, and the coin jumps off the ground from the impact but lands unscathed at my feet. Not so much as a scratch can be seen. "Our blades can cut through most everything else with ease. These coins are protected by their creators, or they're supposed to be at any rate."

"And hiding them?"

"Pointless. They gain no power from them and draw our attention to boot. The last thing they want is to be discovered."

"Could somebody be interfering with them directly? Not with coins, but with the gods?" I hand them back the crash test dummy coin after a thorough inspection. "Or whoever sends you guys the coins?"

Fear is an inadequate word to describe the emotion swelling across their face. Utter horror, maybe. Despair is close too.

Nothing lands close enough to what I see. "Keep this between the two of us, hmm?" The reaper stows the coin away and huddles around their scythe. "May I have your word you will not speak of this to any other?"

"You want me to lie to him?" I gesture down the lane in the direction our third companion had stalked off. The thought of this deception alone is enough to make me hesitant to go on.

They shake their head, dislodging some of the hair from beneath their hood; unlike Grim's, it's mousy gray and curled at the ends. "He will not know of this if you say nothing to him. He is not completely omniscient." Their eyes dart about the forest, wary of eavesdroppers other than Grim as well. "Please, my brethren do not understand my worry. I have doubts where they do not, and you clearly do too."

Stars wink out like dying candles.

A reaper pleads for a lost soul to understand.

At last, I give in to the burning desire to know and be known.

"Fine. I promise not to tell. On one condition . . ."

GRIM

As dawn crests the horizon of the lake, I break through the undergrowth, and the full-blown stench of the demon hits me like a physical strike to the face. If I had taken but a few more steps forward, we would have collided. My feet snarl themselves in the grass waving along the hillside, ending my stride far enough away to discern exactly whose presence I stand in.

His helmet scrapes against the plates on his shoulders as he turns to glance my way, the bull's horns on either side glistening like daggers in the growing sunlight. "You're late." The Knight of Sacrifice huffs and snaps his fingers mockingly. "I thought your lot always came when called."

"A simple view for a simple mind." As high as this creature stands in the Court, one would hope he knew better than to whittle our duties and abilities down to their basest form, to assume a mortal death summons a reaper as a bell does a handmaid. "Do you not have someone else to torment elsewhere?"

"Oh, believe me, I'm done here, and I have no intention to hang around until somebody else finds out about this little rendezvous." His boots squelch with each step away from the lake, dispelling water into the already dewy weeds. "Angels may not usually pick fights, but they'll surely finish them."

"I suppose the old adage about stopped clocks is right after all, in your case."

With an unamused scowl, he gestures to the water where the body of his victim drifts beneath the choppy waves. "You gonna go fish the soul outta there or what? If not, I can throw it to the first hellhound I find and go on about my day."

If he were truly considering that route, he would have done it well before now and thought nothing of it. He fears the consequences of Heaven discovering his deed and raining their fury down upon his impudent head. Ending one Line entirely is no frivolous decision, much less two. This act against humanity makes a declaration; Hell means to start their game of war anew, whether Heaven is prepared or not.

"How generous of you to not snatch the soul and run like a common burglar. I would hate to have to chase you until your last breath." That will likely be his and his brethren's fate in the end regardless, stubborn as demons are, but that day has not yet come.

He raises a skeptical eyebrow. "That's not a very convincing tone I'm hearin' sir."

"Astute observation." Water parts beneath my feet, revealing the stony lakebed and all its hidden treasures: sun-bleached animal bones, trees long since rotted to their cores, and man-made debris. The soul and its body have drifted farther out than the ripples they left behind, farther down than they could have traveled in life. I find her lying with her back to me across a flat boulder, as though she were a sleeping mermaid. Her braid lies limp and soaked across her shoulders, her pale yellow bedclothes plastered against her ashen skin. She seems even smaller now that she is completely silent and still.

Strangely, the soul has not risen from its mortal shell to address me. Did the wretch behind me spirit her away and return for some sort of infantile prank? "Moloch, what have you done to her? Why is she not waking?"

He tilts his head—rattling his few braincells together to conjure a response, I suppose—before the thought returns to him. "Wh— oh! Guess I forgot to undo that. Didn't want anyone interferin' so I . . . persuaded her out the door." With a curl of his claws, the soul releases itself from the corpse and drifts up into my waiting arms. She still does not speak but is slowly rousing herself. Time escapes from me with each blink and tentative stretch.

"Is that how you say 'possessed' in your Circle?"

"Nah, didn't have to go that far. She was half asleep and didn't want to get up."

As we return to the shore, the waves crash together, resealing the glassy surface of the lake. The body remains where it lies, waiting for its own rescue. It was not mine to interfere with once the soul was removed. Her assailant, however, is another matter. "One would imagine not. Few are so eager to leave behind a life they had scarcely lived, especially when a demon is coercing them to do it."

"I didn't scare her or anything. Not until we got out here anyway . . ." Moloch frowns like a scolded toddler at first but quickly twists his face into a hateful grin. "You should've seen her fighting it. I've never had one hold eye contact like that before, all the way to the last bubble." His pupils grow darker the longer he gazes down at the poor child, and he reconsiders letting her slip away so easily. Souls of Lines are terribly powerful, those at the end of them especially. It certainly would benefit his masters to have even just one on their side of the battle, ill-gotten or not.

"Pain and suffering do nothing to satisfy me, fiend. We are nothing alike." One swing of the scythe would wipe that fool's errand from his mind, but that would require setting the soul down out of his reach and not being ambushed myself. Demons typically travel in packs like the beasts they are, so I cannot be assured Moloch is in fact alone. Out of sight does not mean absent.

"You can't lie to me like that. I know the things every last being on this planet would sacrifice to save themselves." His laugh is a mean and vulgar sound, making my skin crawl with loathing. He lunges for the soul but finds empty air instead; each step back I take, he follows, always reaching. "What you've thrown onto the pyre is written all over your face, Reaper. Might be able to fool your little cronies and those ignorant humans, but not me."

Before he could clamp his hand around her ankle and snatch her away, a peal of thunder loud enough to rattle the nearby trees jolts him out of the pursuit. Where the sky had previously been lightening to winter's blue, it suddenly darkened again with black-violet clouds that swallowed the sun whole. White bolts pierced the water and struck the earth all around us. But no rain fell. No wind stirred the dust. And our voices were all but drowned by the roar that followed the storm.

"Unless you want to be torn asunder like old rags, I would slither back to the hole you crept from!" Moloch would receive only one warning from me and no help whatsoever. He got himself into this bind; he can weasel his way back out again. The demon hastily retreated toward the cover of the forest; all the armor in the underworld would not save him here if he lingered much longer.

Sparing no time for fear or more guilt to take root, I cut a portal into the veil and seal away my sin before it can be discovered by those who followed me here or those seeking vengeance on her behalf. Neither could ever hope to understand my motives, and neither would be inclined to try. Heaven thinks themselves the law above all else, and poor Flit could not bear the pain of knowing I brought about her wandering fate. The Knight may have stolen her final breath, but it was my actions that buried her beneath the waves.

FLIT

"What condition is that?" the little reaper whispers, afraid that the pine needles or sleeping moths will overhear. "Be swift about it, I fear we don't have much time."

"Can I give you a name?" They tilt their head like a puppy hearing a strange noise. It's definitely a strange request. "So if we see each other again, I'll know it's you and that we can talk," I explain.

"Oh, I see. Of course, if I can have yours as well." They wave away their confusion and replace it with a worried smile. "None of us have spoken names of our own, like humans do. We have these sigils to tell each other apart, but we're the only ones who can read them." They point to the medallion holding their cloak together, where a series of sharp lines form a strange symbol.

"Figured as much. That's why I asked." It doesn't take long for me to think of something to call this reaper; it was one of the first names that came to mind when I first met their boss. "Grim calls me Flit. Does Muerte sound alright for you?"

They consider the name just long enough for another rancid breeze to whip past us. Still, their smile brightens for a sliver of a moment. "I quite like that, actually. It still means 'death' but isn't the same word aloud."

It's also one of the few Spanish words and phrases that remain in my brain from before this afterlife. "Now, what do you want to tell me?"

Muerte's smile vanishes altogether. "Even before Death came across you outside Purgatory, things in the supernatural world have been steadily tilting off-kilter. Coins out of place. Lines rapidly dying out with little cause. Divine and demon activity in equal measure, barely canceling each other out. World-ending catastrophes kept piling one on top of the other without ending the world somehow. Someone has taken it upon themselves to cause an uproar left, right, and down the middle, but no one knows how or why."

"Who would do something like that?"

"I-I don't know, and my suspicions are entirely circumstantial." Their hands flutter, so shaky they can't hold on to their scythe anymore. "Demons would've taken credit if it were them, and the angels likewise. Gods seldom deviate from the plans already laid out—"

"Seldom? Or never?" Finality like that doesn't usually apply to humans, so why would these higher people be any different? We're supposed to be made in our Creator's image, so we had to get it from somewhere.

Their eyes darken to the flat gray of wet concrete, their gaze hardening to match. "The ones that do don't often live to see the results. Full-scale wars have been waged over less."

Then who would be stupid enough to press their luck like this? I'm sure they weren't the first or only case, but were the angels who were cast from Heaven for rebelling not enough of a warning? The punishment for interfering with the universe at such a scale as this will be Hell at the minimum, though I can't imagine much worse than that. Well, maybe Purgatory, if they were dropped out where not even the reapers venture. Whoever is behind this would have to know the consequences better than us and still think their scheme is worth the trouble.

"Who does that leave?" The question answers itself before the last word passes my lips, but hearing someone else say it provides solidarity. That's what both of us have been looking for after all, someone to tell us we aren't alone in wondering.

"Reapers" was rendered inaudible by what I thought was the rumble of an earthquake that instead turned out to be the loudest thunder I've ever heard. But there's no other word Muerte could've uttered. It was set in their jaw, the way their eyes fearfully darted around, and the unsteady step they took toward me just before the boom. Lightning erupted around us, white-hot bolts striking down trees that tore at the clouds' bellies. Perhaps I spoke too soon about the world not ending like it should. Grim still had not returned.

"Quick, in here!" My new ally ushers me into a hollow redwood stump and then covers its entrance with brush. "This does not bode well, not at all."

My anxiety doesn't truly rocket into the stratosphere, however, until another even more deafening sound echoes through the woods. If a hundred trains were derailing all at once, or a hundred tornadoes were bearing down on one house, it still wouldn't match the volume or sense of impending doom. Wave after wave of *they're coming, they're after me* sweeps over the meadow as I cower in the tree's corpse, the little reaper standing guard outside.

Their scythe will do nothing against the unseen source of this maelstrom.

We're sitting ducks.

Worse than dead, caught.

Silence returns, leaving my ears ringing. I want to scream for Grim to save us, but what if something else hears instead? Never mind the demon he went after, now there's the sky-dwelling enemy to contend with too. Besides, he might not even be there anymore; we have no idea if he prevailed over the monster he came here for before the new one showed up. For all we know, it could've claimed the departing soul and took Grim out for trying to stop them, and we're its next targets.

Another blaring horn muffles the noise, but someone is coming back up the path he left on. They're too far away to see clearly through these leaves and twigs, but they're large and dark even against the swelling storm. And all I know right now is I'm not going anywhere with anybody without putting up a fight.

My hands find a dead tree limb at my feet and prepare to swing it like a baseball bat.

Before a third blast sounds, my name fills the quiet in a familiar voice, and the stick is almost abandoned. But Muerte blocks my way just as I'm about to sprint out of the hiding place. "Wait! That could be the demon meaning to deceive you," they whisper hoarsely. "Stay here. I'll verify who we're dealing with."

"But—"

"Please, stay." They turn their back to me to face the being across from us, scythe clutched in both skeletal hands and wings unfolded. I didn't think the smaller ones had wings, but my view is now obscured by rows of vulture feathers. They make Muerte seem much bigger than before, less meek. Unlike the gentle and reserved tones they've always spoken in around me, the voice that comes out now commands even the grass stand still and listen. "How do I know you are the High Reaper?"

What I hope is Grim stops in the middle of the road, his own scythe acting as a walking stick rather than prepared to do battle. He looks incredibly surprised that his underling is puffing up at him where previously they always shrank back. Guess they took that "guard her with your life" bit to heart. He also does not fail to notice the fallen branch clutched in my hands, waiting for a target to approach. "Believe me, were I the Knight that once stood in the next clearing, I would not stop to chat. Nor will those causing this racket." Our eyes meet over Muerte's shoulder. "We have to return home before we are caught in the crossfire. Moloch has likely found himself in rather unpleasant company, if Heaven has sent someone to intercept him."

"Moloch?" The other reaper shudders as they help me out of the stump. "I'm loath to imagine what he did to that poor soul . . . did he take them?"

Grim shakes his head, smirking. "We arrived in enough time to remind him how foolish crossing a reaper is. Had we taken a moment longer, he would have at least attempted to escape." He rips a portal between the three of us and we all pile through, all too eager to escape the stench of Hell and the blows from Heaven. The doorway takes a lot longer than I would like to close behind us.

"So now what do we do? That's two demons at least that have gotten too close for comfort, Grim." He doesn't turn to me in response, instead busying himself by the lakeside window of the cabin. After discarding his scythe across the couch, he unsheathes his dagger and sets to work carving strange symbols over the doorframe and windowpanes. They glow a silvery-white before fading into the wood as if they were never there at all. "What're those for?"

"None may enter this house except those currently inside it," Muerte replies in his place. "Those are Enochian marks of protection. They'll keep angels and demons out unless they're invited in."

"And in the state they will all be in, that will not be happening." Grim finally speaks again, gliding into the next room to continue his carving with the two of us in tow. "That idiot Knight went and kicked the biggest hornet nest he could find and left everyone else to bear the consequences."

"Meaning?"

He stops mid-line, his expression sharp and cold as the blade in his hand, "I paid no heed to the year on the coin, but all other signs point to Moloch trying to restart the apocalypse."

"*Restart?*"

CHAPTER FIVE

FLIT

Every morning for the past week Grim has scoured the perimeter he set up around the cabin for anything out of place. At this point I wouldn't be shocked to learn that he knows which way each pine needle is supposed to be laying on the ground and if the wind shifted one. Not only did he carve the Enochian runes into the frame of the house, but he also drove his knife into every tree trunk that could withstand it. Inanimate objects were much sturdier for that sort of magic, apparently; if a living thing is marked and it dies or the mark is disfigured by an injury, then the effects of the mark disappear. Marks on things, however, work themselves into the fibers and foundations and are much harder to mutilate. You'd have to destroy the whole object to destroy its mark.

"Would marking a ghost do anything?" I ask when he comes back inside. "Since I'm not alive, would it affect me at all?"

"It would most likely drive you mad." He cuts any budding suggestions for experiments off at the knee. "Unless you can commune with the supernatural world on your own, humans are not meant to wield Enochian. The last time one was marked, it was a curse, not a blessing." Considering neither of us knows if I had any unusual abilities premortem, I'd rather not find out the hard way.

"What about speaking it?" Pen scratches fill the space between our voices; ink fills the spaces on the journal page. "It's a language, right? Can you speak it?"

He shrugs. "Doubtful. I only know a few pieces here and there, not enough to hold a conversation." His eyes skate over the carvings in the room. "Enochian is mostly ceremonial at any rate. Angels and demons can converse however they like."

"Reapers too?"

"Reapers too. Of course, we are far from the most talkative group of celestials." He actually manages a little smile, the first I've seen on him in ages. "That title would belong to Hell's inhabitants. They enjoy long-winded speeches, especially about themselves."

The longer I think about it, the sadder that statement becomes; reapers don't have anyone to talk to except who they're reaping . . . and that doesn't always go over well. They don't socialize with each other unless something is wrong, and even in that case, only one reaper has come to see us so far. Otherwise, they're entirely alone for most of forever.

Most humans couldn't stand that kind of eternal life. I know I couldn't do this without him here. We're pack animals at our core. A sense of belonging lives somewhere in everyone, even those who don't want to belong with others. Everybody wants to feel like they have a home to return to in the end, a family of some kind. Why else would most versions of Heaven include reuniting with those who have gone before us?

My journal falls closed in my lap; no words can describe the sorrow that steadily blooms in my heart like the herb garden

Mama used to keep in our backyard. Every breeze through the window brings back the scent of the leaves drying in the kitchen, or the smell of them cooking into a dish. The sudden jolt of memory drives the pain deeper, spreading it thick. Worse still is realizing Grim doesn't have anything like that to miss now, but the minute I'm gone, he'll know the human kind of mourning.

"Grim?" He hums in response, distracted by his own thoughts, but I go on anyway. "Can you visit me when I cross over?"

The question snaps his stoic expression into a million pieces. While we had spoken of me staying on as an apprentice of sorts, he had to know that may not be an option. Even if I didn't want to be with my family again, which is not the case at all, that didn't mean we could stay together. At the same time, leaving him all alone after what we've been through won't be an easy task either. He's my only friend for now, and I'm beginning to think I'm the only one he's ever had.

He doesn't get the chance to collect himself and respond, however. "I know you all must tire of my barging in like this, but it's happened again." Muerte comes dragging their feet up the porch steps, their face a mix of disdain and weariness. The coins already rest in their outstretched hand, two this time. "At least this event was on time. No demons mucking about."

"That you are aware of." Grim pulls a mask up over the devastated face he wore moments ago. He's all business now, and probably will be the rest of the day, especially with more coins being out of place. "Which Lines have died off this time?" He answers himself with a single glance down into his palm. The names concern him so greatly that, in his haste to collect these souls, he nearly leaves me behind.

"Oh dear, he's right." The smaller of the reapers holds the portal just wide enough for me to squeeze through. "Things are getting quite out of hand now. Other reapers have started noticing with so much going amiss. Be safe out there!"

Hopefully Muerte hears me request that they follow that advice as well.

GRIM

Beyond the portal's entrance, all that is visible is the dark of a stormy night sky and the knowledge that everything could soon be turned on its head. At least, that is what my racing mind chants to me with each unsteady footfall. All the time spent maneuvering and manipulating the few wheels of the world my grasp could reach, wasted.

Fate, unavoidable as ever, despite exhausting efforts.

I tried. All I can say is that I tried. Tried to protect her from a role beyond her comprehension, beyond what she should have to endure. That will not be her perspective on it, most likely, not when all the years of grief and pain she does not even know she carries around with her finally breach the surface.

Flit calls for me to wait, her voice paired with the thump of her diary dropping onto the floor and falling open. She sounds as though a wall of water stands between us. The raging tempest in the empty desert drowns out her voice further, even when she crosses over. She glances around to get her bearings, the distant lights of the Las Vegas Strip catching her attention briefly, then finds her way back to me. "Grim, is something wrong? Why did you take off without me?"

"It was not my intention," I snap without meaning to; my mind is occupied entirely with examining the coins in my hand rather than satisfying her curiosity. Each detail is in order, each etching a crack in my careful façade. "Do you see anyone out here?" She glowers back, incensed, but shakes her head no. Our queries must have wandered off in the driving rain.

We emerged along the shoulder of a highway, so perhaps if we follow the road, we will find those we seek. I can make out a dim silhouette of smoke not far ahead, which seems promising. I would confirm with the smaller reaper, but they left separately. Oh well.

We eventually reach the remains of a vehicle that has come to rest at the bottom of an embankment; clearly the car swerved off the paved road to avoid hitting something, and it flipped several times before slamming into a Joshua tree. Little remains of the metal body, or of the two humans inside. Flit gasps and jumps away from the wreckage as if it reached out to grab her on the way by. She does not make any attempts to peek inside, which is the best course of action on all accounts. There is nothing that she could make sense of in those ashes.

A soft whimper breaks the cacophony of thunder and sludgy water rushing underfoot; a woman's voice is calling for help, and Flit sees her first. "Grim, over there! By those big tumbleweeds." I do not have time to warn her that it could be a demon in disguise before she bounds off into the dark, her white dress the only speck of light this side of the horizon. Just beyond her stand the two spirits we have come for, a middle-aged couple named Joseph and Liliana Torres. As Flit reaches Liliana, my breath hitches in my throat and refuses to release.

I take my time approaching them. No need to rush the inevitable.

"Hello, I'm Flit," she greets them uncertainly, not being used to leading these interactions. "We're here to help you cross over. What are your names?"

Liliana pauses her wandering to reply but stops short and tugs on her husband's sleeve; ironically, she looks as if she's seen a ghost. "What did you say your name was, *mija*?" She stares in disbelief at the sight before her, only turned away by a crack of lightning that strikes the ground nearby. "I'm sorry, it's just that you remind me of someone."

At last I reach the trio, startling all three. "She is not your daughter, Mrs. Torres. You will find your child and other family waiting for you once you cross." These words of comfort feel hollow yet heavy, like a casket of lead. None of them seem to believe me.

Flit whips around, confusion and hopefulness waging war in her eyes. "But Grim, I could be who she's talking about. You said that—"

"You are not their child. I may not be able to see your memories, but I can see theirs clearly. Their daughter has already crossed over." I try not to leave any time for questions or answers between the three of them—we have already lingered too long while searching and chatting. "Take these coins and present them to your guide. They will take you where you're meant to go."

Thinking Flit would stop at my behest was a fool's dream, having known her long enough to predict her temperament. "I'm sorry about your daughter." She cuts in between them and the doorway to Heaven. "What happened to her?"

Mrs. Torres gives me a nervous glance, but Joseph barely hesitates to speak over the gale. "We don't really know. We went on vacation for her birthday, and she just vanished one night." He gestures a puff of smoke with his hands while studying her face more closely. With her soul being fractured as it is, they can stare all they like, and she will come in no clearer than a grainy photograph taken from too far away.

His wife gathers the courage to speak up. "They never found our poor Bea. She was just gone, like she was never there at all . . ."

"How old was she?"

"Fifteen," I interject, ushering Flit away from the portal so the couple may walk through. "I am sorry to bear the news of her death in this way, but she died before her sixteenth birthday actually occurred. She can better explain the circumstances to you once you are reunited." The Torreses are no more satisfied with me than their fellow restless spirit, but with the portal flickering, they have no time to argue. And I have less chance to worry about Flit darting for it herself; she is too tongue-tied with unanswered questions and growing frustration to make a run for the door before it disappears.

Flit recedes into herself, her thin arms crossed tightly over her chest and her head hung down, eyes cast to the earth. Corporeal beings would need to worry about the floodwaters rising all around them, but no such disaster could claim us two. No, something much more powerful looms ahead for her and me. "In the end, we all follow the plan laid out for us, whether we know it or not." I break the quiet, and the dark, by opening a portal back home. "I was only saving you from breaking your own heart, Flit. They were not your missing pieces, no matter how much you wanted them to be. You will be whole again when the time comes. Understand?"

She says nothing and sweeps past me into the cabin, one last peal of thunder shadowing her steps.

Grim cutting us all off and rushing them away last night doesn't sit right with me. He's a private person on a good day, but that seemed totally unnecessary. He wouldn't let us talk like he did before with other people. It's like he didn't want me there at all; he almost left me behind! He said we have no reasons to distrust each other, so I don't get—

The ink is barely dry when Grim steps in, and I slam the diary shut. He wants to keep secrets for no reason, fine. I can do that too. My inner thoughts hardly compare to the "inner workings of fate" or whatever he used as an excuse yesterday, but I still got my point through to him. He scowls at the *pop* the paper and leather make when they come together, then sighs, "I hope you do not plan to hold a grudge for long, Flit. You have seen what prolonged negativity does to the dead on this side of the veil."

"Only as long as it takes you to be honest with me. Totally honest," I snap back, shoving the diary back into its usual spot. "You can't tell me that you trust me and then hide things from me like you don't. I don't remember much about life, but it doesn't work that way."

"You would be surprised how life works at times, my dear. Rarely ever does it go the way of human ideals."

"Wouldn't be here if it did." Grim flinches a bit at that remark. He cares in his own way about us insignificant mortals, but his non-human mentality always seems to have its fingers wrapped around his moral compass like snakes around a kill; the other side of him is afraid to reach for it and take hold. Both sides fear making a fatal mistake on behalf of the universe, and I'm starting to wonder if it's too late to worry. The *I-shouldn't-be-here* and *something-is-horribly-wrong* hadn't really sunk in until now, but it's like everything in the house has been shifted a few centimeters from where it's supposed to be. The change is invisible but still a palpable, smothering tension. And then it ruptures like a burst dam.

"Flit, listen—"

"No, Grim. I don't like being lied to. I don't care if you think you're protecting me, I deserve to know the truth!" The tightness in the room pulls us closer and closer together until only the doorframe separates us. "The little reapers may follow you blindly, but I am not one of them. Either tell me the truth or—"

"Or what? You will flee into the wilderness and get captured by something far worse than me? Yes, that will teach me a lesson and get you exorcised or something equally unpleasant."

"And if that happens it'll be on your head! All you have to do is answer one simple question."

"If it were as simple as you believe, do you not think I would tell you without fanfare?" He starts out hissing with anger, but it doesn't hold on long before fading to pain. Can he weep? "If I tell you what you seek to learn, all of this we have built here will . . . none of this will ever be the same."

If this argument goes much longer, I won't be able to keep myself from crying. The rage that swelled into my lungs until my ribs nearly burst open lodges in my throat, trying to escape; now I'm choking on a sob full of betrayal and hurt. "It won't anyway. Now that I know you're keeping secrets from me, how can I go back to trusting you?"

Grim slumps, defeated. He knows we're both right, and he loathes it. Whatever he's hiding is enough to potentially tear us apart, but continuing to lie to me is a definite means of driving a wedge between us. He's backed up to the edge of a cliff with the blade of his own scythe at his throat; there's no painless way out of this. He takes a deep, ragged breath that sounds like pure regret even though it's wordless. When he speaks, it is decisive but remorseful. "You will not know peace if you choose to know. But you will not rest until you do . . . nor will I."

I shake my head, though I'm not sure what I'm disagreeing with. "I've never thought badly of you, Grim. But this is making me wonder if I was right in doing that. Please, just tell me what was going on last night."

"Very well. You shall have what you so desperately seek . . . and if you hate me for it, then I will have earned it." He props his scythe against the back of the sofa where his robe is already draped.

Satisfied to finally get answers but wary of them nonetheless, I retake my seat in the windowsill to prepare for however long of a story he has. "Hate you? Why would I hate you?"

He remains in the doorway, facing toward the lake as if he can't bring himself to look at me anymore. "You may not. I hope this is the case, but there are those who would paint this as an action of my own volition rather than an unavoidable happening." He pauses, steeling himself. "Those Lines that ended last night, they are not of any minor set. Their deaths herald the End of Days, as they are the only two current Lines to combine and produce an heir."

Mathematically, at least in my skill range, that doesn't seem possible. How is it that, with the number of descendants each

Line must have by whenever now is, there has never been a child from two or even more of those families? "Why does that matter? I'm sure this isn't the first time that's happened, is it?"

He shakes his head. "You are correct, there have been many of these children over the centuries. Some are born into powerful dynasties and influence the progression of the world. Some are born into persecution and poverty and fail to thrive at all. Those who design the ways of the universe do their best, or so they say, to prevent such an unbalanced dynamic, but one always manages to slip through their divine fingers." He withers even further, the weight of the words sitting heavy on his shoulders. "And then it all falls down like so many poorly stacked cards. Lines dying off narrows the field for either side to pick vessels for battle. In this case, with the parents being gone, neither of them can take the place of the child in such a fight, so whatever side has found them will start off with an advantage."

"And we don't know what side that is, because no one has made a move . . ."

"Correct again."

Silence engulfs the cabin for several minutes as the situation's gravity settles around us. End times are coming, presumably soon. Grim, through his work, is an unwilling harbinger and not only has to carry on his usual duties but also whatever being on Apocalypse Detail requires. And he has to worry about me now too. Will I be witness to the horrible battles that will tear the Earth to pieces? Is it even safe for me to leave the cabin anymore, with angels and demons on high alert for loose souls? Am I a target at all, or is that his paranoia running wild?

What does this mean for me crossing over? Is that an option anymore? What's the alternative if not?

"And you are absolutely certain," —my next words come hesitantly— "without a shadow of doubt, that I am not their child?"

Grim, on the other hand, is quick to reply. "Yes, Flit. While you may bear some resemblance to their daughter, you are not her. Do you not think your own mother would recognize you immediately, rather than being so uncertain?"

Well, considering my soul is fragmented—which he told me himself—and my memories are scattered, something tells me that doesn't just affect my perception of myself. Ghosts don't have flesh and bone bodies like the living do. Yes, we still appear as we did in life to those who can see us, but what about other dead people? All the ghosts I've seen so far have had an aura around them, something that conveyed their personality wordlessly. But all of them were intact and knew who they were and how they got to that point in time. I don't have that knowledge, so do I look odd to other spirits? *Would* my mother recognize me right away?

"I guess you're right." None of this sits right with my gut feeling, but my only other source of reaperly information isn't here right now, and calling them out in the open would only make Grim suspicious of my wandering thoughts. Slipping out of his sight for a quick Q&A with Muerte will be tricky, but it's also necessary to quiet my doubts.

"It happens every once in a while." He wraps his cloak across his slumped shoulders and takes the scythe up again, embodying a reluctant harvester more than ever. Before he cuts a portal to our next reaping, however, he reaches for his belt and unfastens the dagger's sheath from it. Then, he cuts a length of the black fabric trailing behind him, runs it through the belt loop, and offers the blade to me. "I do wish it happened less often. Take this, in case I am right and cannot protect you from it."

GRIM

We emerge inside a hospital ward devoid of the usual bustling about. No nurses wander the halls, no patients mutter about the subpar food or flimsy blankets. A plague has been visited upon this place, and its victims lie silent in their suffering. Their listless caretakers do not fare much better; weariness clings to every soul we see like a fog hovering over a moor. Hope seems a foreign concept on this floor, labeled ICU on the sign we pass.

"How is it possible that this place is worse than the prison?" Flit grumbles, wrapping her arms around herself as though she were cold. "Hospitals are creepy on a good day, but this one takes the cake."

"The spirits that remain here are far older than those were. That prison is much newer than this place, therefore its spectral inhabitants have not had time to grow as strong as they are miserable."

Her face scrunches up and is reflected in a viewing window. "Can you reapers not do anything about all these loose ghosts? Seems like you'd stay on top of things like that."

I see her petulance has not entirely disappeared. Wonderful. "If we were not awaiting our impending demise, I would expect the others to better maintain their assigned regions." Her expression does not soften to allow leniency for us, but she does not press harder. "We will be busy enough ferrying souls to and fro when that time comes, I assure you. None will be left to their own devices."

She only scoffs as we round one last corner before reaching our destination. Her stubborn irascibility is only shaken by the sight that meets us through the creaky door; a girl nearly her own age lies prone and intubated in the hospital bed. The room is pitch dark, save for the lights on the machines keeping her alive and what little seeps in from the shuttered windows. It is empty, save for a hard leather recliner and two tables on either side of the patient.

"Grim . . ." Flit whispers, horrified. "Do we really have to take her? Are you sure it's her time?" She steps closer to brush a stray hair from the girl's face and pats her hand gently. Our third companion does not respond to either the touch or to our voices.

"We are a bit early again." Her coin lies heavy in my palm, and not just from its physical weight. Reapings like hers and Flit's grieve us much more than we would ever let on. Life is such a precious and truly rare thing, and to see it cut so short is painful no matter how you bear witness to it. "You may sit with her until she goes, if you like, or wait by the door. She may react poorly to our news, so it is up to—" As I reach out to place the coin in her hand, a detail of its surface catches my attention. Or, rather, the lack of detail. It should read:

Eniyah Cadence Monroe

November 1, 2001

Heaven

. . . and today's date, which I am unsure of. However, both the symbol that belongs in the center and the death date are missing from the coin entirely. Missing religious symbols could mean any number of things: lack of faith, indecisiveness, uncertainty. The center being blank is far less concerning than the death date not being etched along the edge. That has only one meaning, one that proves correct my theory about Moloch's actions. This girl is a vessel, a human meant to bear the weight of an angel or demon upon her soul during the final fight for dominion over Earth.

"What's wrong?" Flit turns to investigate what interrupted our conversation and sees the empty bottom half of the metal disk. "Did someone switch it out for a dummy coin? Or did it come out that way?"

"Neither of those are possible. No one had the chance to interfere between here and the cabin. No one else is here or in our path that should not be." This cannot be happening. It cannot be real. It cannot have all been for nothing!

"What do we do then?" Irritation grows in her tone like dandelions in the sidewalk. "I'm assuming we can't send her onward now?"

"Ever the observant one . . ." I snap back. "Things are much worse than I feared after the last reaping. Travel to the afterlife is being halted altogether—"

"Halted?!" The room suddenly goes from humid and stuffy to painfully cold. Every machine that had been steadily beeping goes haywire, their shrill notes echoing the way bullets ricochet. "They can't just stop letting people cross over, can they? What about all the people that die every day? Or the ones already stuck here? What about me?" she wails, and the louder she gets, the more the machines try to drown her out. A few of them have stopped completely, their energy drained despite being plugged in.

Miss Monroe jolts awake as more of the devices die around her. Fortunately, the ventilator is not among them, but she is no less alarmed by her unexpected guests and circumstances. I fear Eniyah may have an episode of her own if the already-dead fail to find a bit of rest soon.

"Flit. Flit, please. I will fix this, I swear to you." The lights around us flicker with every panicked move she makes, so I attempt to back her into a corner away from the electronics. This only serves to fan the flames of her panic, and the lightbulbs overhead suffer the consequences. "Flit, calm down! Please, if this goes on much longer, someone might find us—"

"¿*Cómo*? How are you gonna fix this?! You don't even know what's wrong!" she screams, trying unsuccessfully to push me away. "You promised I could go home. You said you would take me as soon as you could. You promised!"

"And I still hold that promise. But I cannot fulfill it if you are taken from me." I check the door over our shoulders, which surprisingly has not let in a doctor or nurse to see what all the commotion is. Although if the few we saw on the way in are any indication, the staff may be too battle-worn to be concerned with flickering lightbulbs and drafty rooms. "You must control your energy. That dagger is a last resort, not a match with which to light a beacon."

"I wasn't trying to do all that. I didn't even know I could." Her voice levels out a bit, and so does the room; the temperature rises gradually, and the machines sputter back to life, but tension remains in the air. "Besides, what good is a soul if they can't take me anywhere?"

"That is not—" I start to correct her until an exterior light shatters unexpectedly, cloaking the whole corridor in darkness.

FLIT

Grim goes stock still, and his grip on my shoulders becomes painful. Watching his head turn toward the hallway reminds me of a slow-motion shot in a slasher movie; he can't get any paler than he already is, but the horror in his eyes grows with every passing second. Pale green smoke wafts under the door, filling the darkness with the choking scent of rot. Nausea hits me before the cloud gets past the divider curtain and sweeps full strength over the girl lying in the bed. She gags and gasps, unable to escape the fumes. Both of us are utterly helpless, despite our different positions. I am shoved so far into the corner I nearly pass through the wall and onto the roof.

"What is that?" I try to peek over his shoulder, but he suddenly rises to his feet and blocks my view even more. "Is that a—?"

"Quiet."

This isn't a gentle suggestion. This is a threat, a command. Who or whatever followed the smoke is a matter of safety or suffering. It has to be an angel or demon for him to be so shaken, but getting answers about which of the two we're facing is futile for now. Without letting go of me fully, he cuts a portal into the wall beside us and leans down to whisper harshly. "Listen well. If anything comes through that door, you go home. Do not wait for me. Do not turn back."

"But—"

His pupils narrow so much that I can't even see them anymore, and his irises are unmistakably glowing white. "Do not argue with me! Now is not the time for petty debate."

"I'm not being petty! I don't want to abandon you if there's something I can do to help." If not for fear of snatching my arm out of its socket—is that even possible as a ghost?—I would've jerked out of his grip to face him more directly, but I settled for hissing back. "You are all I have, Grim. You and me, that's it."

"And why do you think I am so desperate to protect you? Who else do I have?" His voice falters as he releases my shoulders to frame my face with his trembling hands. Such affection is strange and jarring coming from him; it deflates my mounting anger, if only for a moment. "You are the only one of your kind, Flit. If I lose you, I—"

BANG

The door rattles violently on its hinges and thicker smog billows in. I shriek and climb into Grim's arms like a child afraid of a thunderstorm.

BANG

Drywall splinters off the wall and crumbles to the floor. He tries to usher me through the portal but can't pry my fingers free from his cloak.

BANG

The machines' alarms go wild as the door comes free of its frame. I beg Grim not to leave me, to not let me go.

CRASH

A figure appears in the fog, silhouetted by an unnatural light, and time slows to an agonizing crawl. Grim doesn't want to separate us, but he can't protect me and fight at the same time, not against this foe. When my grip is finally wrenched loose enough, he tosses me onto the lakeshore on the other side. "Forgive me for this, Beatriz. I had no other choice."

We both realize his mistake a moment too late.

CHAPTER SIX

FLIT

"**G**rim?! Grim!" My feet move too slowly to scramble off the ground before the portal closes the rest of the way, and I am left alone in silence. Well, the thunder overhead is pretty loud, but all my ears register is that name he called with his goodbye. He didn't say Flit. He said Beatriz. That's not my name . . .

Is it?

My head spins through every interaction we've ever had. Every piece of my soul revealed to me. Every single time I asked for help and he answered.

Did he find out who I was and not tell me?

If I were still alive, I'd puke from the nerves, but nausea's ghost isn't strong enough to pierce the veil. When did it happen? What clicked for him that didn't for me? Thank God I can't hyperventilate and pass out either.

What if I never see him again and never get to ask?

Desperation hits like a second wind during a marathon and pulls me from the water into the dark, empty cabin. "I . . . I have to find help. I need to call, I—" The fragments of my mortal memories fill in the blank with 9-1-1, but my present thoughts leap to the only other creature it deems trustworthy.

Even in the fog of panic, my hands find my hidden journal and nearly tear it in two searching for the page I need. We prepared for this situation not long after the hellhound incident; Grim's paranoia and my sneaky notes are finally coming in handy it seems.

"What should I do if we get separated? Like, if one of us gets lost or somebody tries to take me?" I had asked him that night while he repaired his cloak on the back porch. Until that fight, the thought had never seriously crossed my mind, but losing sight of Grim for even those few moments was terrifying. "Is there a way to call you to me somehow?"

He smoothed the last wrinkle from his sleeves before turning to me and nodding. "In hindsight, I should have told you so from the beginning. Perhaps it would have somewhat eased both our minds today, but better late than never, I suppose." He beckoned me closer and held up the button on his cloak as Muerte later would. "All you have to do is carve this into a surface and call out to me verbally or in your mind."

"Does this work for all reapers?" My fingers traced the silver clasp, memorizing the lines to sketch into my journal. Maybe I should have started drawing this on my hand before we went out so I wouldn't forget it in the heat of a moment, or somewhere on my dress so it wouldn't rub off.

"It does, so be careful to carve the lines correctly, lest you summon someone you do not know," he warned. "There is no reason to distrust the other reapers, of course, but they may not be terribly helpful either."

I know Muerte will help me, if they can. Or they can go help Grim. Or find someone else who can help us.

Their symbol is drawn beside Grim's with their names in between; Grim's reminds me of a Christmas present with a bow on top, while Muerte's looks more like several letters combined into one image.

⌘ Grim   ⌖ Muerte

With the page in hand, I race back out the door to find something suitable for carving into. The cabin is already covered in sigils I'd hate to interfere with, so it'll have to be a part of the outdoors that bears this rune. A dead log at the edge of the forest catches my eye, and my blade sinks into its bark with little resistance. Their name echoes across my mind like storm sirens, pleading for hope and shelter.

Muerte. Muerte. Muerte.

No response. No appearance.

I carve deeper. I scream aloud.

"Muerte! Muerte! Muerte, please!"

Still nothing. Still no one.

I carve deeper still. I cry out again.

At last, a portal bursts into view beyond the trees, and Muerte comes stumbling through. Any relief that had appeared alongside them quickly vanished. I didn't realize reapers even needed to breathe until Muerte gasped desperately for the air to speak. "Oh, thank the Creators . . . you're alright." They righted themselves against a tree and gave me a once-over. "The High Reaper called several of us to his aid but ordered me here to defend you about the same time you called."

Horror washed over me; Grim had to call for backup for just one member of the Court or Host? It had to be one of them. He didn't fear their underlings like that. It had to be a high-ranking demon or angel to send him into such a panic.

What happens if they call in reinforcements too?

What happens if the other side wins?

Or we lose Grim?

Judging by Muerte's expression, all those worst-case scenarios are distinct possibilities, "What do we do now? I don't even know who he's fighting or if we can even help or—"

"Flit, dear, all we can do is wait this out." Muerte places their hands on my shoulders to catch my attention; their body trembles with every storm-swept gust blowing across the lake. "We are safer here than there, with you being within reach of a Princess. Our mutual friend would be quite distracted playing keep-away." There are girl demons like the one from the prison? I don't think Grim ever mentioned him having sisters. He always said "Princes."

"Should we call someone else to help them?" But who would we even go to for that? Angels are, with Grim involved at least, out of the question. Deities probably couldn't be bothered about it, and that list is far too long for me to narrow down with next to zero information on them. "How many other reapers came?"

"All reapers not actively collecting souls were summoned . . ." We slowly make our way into the cabin, both stumbling into holes in the sand. "I was the first to arrive, and it was only seconds before his attacker entered the room."

"So, you don't know how bad things got? If the others got there in time . . ." They remove their hood completely and drag their fingers through their disheveled curls, shaking their head all the while. The front door locks all slide into place under my hands, clicks echoing in the empty rooms. The little reaper stands in the middle of the circle of seats, unsure of which to take. Now that I think about it, Muerte hasn't been in here longer than a few moments before today. And we're alone, with Grim far out of reach. Just us and our secret from our previous meeting in the last place that doubt needs to take root.

And yet here I stand with another seed to plant alongside it.

"You weren't there yet when he sent me away either." As my unease shifts from gut-wrenching fear to gnawing suspicion, the thought crosses my mind that Grim calling me Beatriz truly was a mistake. He simply misspoke in the heat of the moment. It may have even been the name on the girl's coin, since I didn't get a good look at it. The following thought, however, recalls the lost daughter the couple we reaped spoke of. Why would he be thinking of her while trying to save me? Did he try to save her soul from a demon and couldn't live with that failure? He did say we resembled one another somewhat; is he using me to make up to himself for losing her? Could I be the key to finding her and he won't tell me? What piece am I lacking to glue it all down with?

I know who might have those answers . . .

"We barely missed each other, I believe, just as I missed the cavalry coming in behind me." Muerte's form stills except for their head tilting to the right. "Why do you ask?"

Of course Grim wouldn't tell them that he slipped up. He'd never admit to confusion or lying or fumbling. But that doesn't mean the other reapers wouldn't notice loose threads and holes in his stories—just that none would mention it to his face.

"Before he threw me through the portal, before it closed, Grim called me Beatriz." Muerte tilts their head further, still confused. "I told you, he calls me Flit. He said he doesn't know my real name, and I don't either. No memories have come back to me with my name in them."

"And you've met no one who knows you crossing over?"

"Well . . ."

As if invisible strings meant to hold the reaper up were cut in half, Muerte finally sinks into the loveseat across from my window in shock. "Someone knew you? After all this time?" They want to sound congratulatory, but the tension around us smothers that as quickly as a wet blanket kills a fire. Every ember of hope is doused the more I explain about what they've missed between visits. All the close encounters of the hellish kind. What Grim told me about Lines ending after we sent the couple onward. It all adds up to an answer that still eludes me, but maybe their outside perspective can connect dots thus far unseen.

"He's hiding something, that much I know." They nod, worry with hints of anger swirling in their silver eyes. "But what do you think it is? Has he always been this—?"

"Cryptic? Unyielding?"

Well, if I didn't even need to finish that sentence aloud, that answers that.

The storm outside fills the brief silence inside. Thunder rumbles through the treetops. Rain swells the waves until the stony beach disappears. Lightning carves sharper outlines along the growing shadows.

"You and I alone cannot solve this mystery, I fear. Our knowledge falls short of our goal, so I must seek out others to fill those blanks." Muerte leaves the sofa and approaches me, kneeling as a knight would before the one they swear their undying loyalty to. If my heart still beat, it would've fluttered until it hurt. "But I must do this alone, and you must not claim any knowledge of my mission if asked. Any repercussions will be mine alone."

"You think Grim would hurt us if he finds out?" I've never given Grim any reason not to trust me, nor has the reaper he called specifically to protect me and our home, so why would he suspect us of anything together? Is he that paranoid, and I just don't see it? Should fear replace my dwindling trust that lingers for the High Reaper? "If this will get you in trouble, then—"

"Don't you dare tell me not to help you," they snap, wings unfurling to pin me against the windowpane so there is no choice left but to look them in the face. "I will listen to all matter of convoluted theories and questions I've answered millions of times, but not one word of that nonsense. If there has been an injustice, it will be righted. If it is a misunderstanding, it will be corrected. Understood?"

When we first met, Muerte's features and Grim's seemed so similar, but this close up, Muerte's closeness to humanity is far more obvious. Grim wouldn't rebel against all he knew for the sake of one mortal and their unending curiosity. He wouldn't abandon the balance he upholds to put anyone at ease, not even for a second. And yet someone he taught to mirror his image has demanded, not asked, to do that for me. A deep pit forms in my gut the longer our gazes hold, threatening to pull my already sinking heart into its abyss. What if this is a fruitless journey and Muerte suffers for nothing in my name? I would never forgive myself. "On one condition."

"Name it."

"Be safe." Without thought or hesitation, my arms slip around Muerte's shoulders, pulling them closer. "Come back when you can."

They return the embrace first with their arms, then their wings, cocooning us together and sealing our promises. "That's two conditions, you know."

Grim returns with little fanfare just as the clouds break open to reveal the sunrise and the remnants of the storm's path. Last night's weather did no damage to the house, which is more than I can say for the poor reaper; whoever he met in the hospital did him no favors. I couldn't imagine his pallor getting any worse, but he looks even more sickly than when he left. He literally looks green at one point.

"What did that to you?" Muerte and I both search for a quilt to wrap around his shoulders and offer some comfort since warm food isn't exactly an option for us. None we discover are quite Grim-sized, but he doesn't seem to mind. If not for the frightening circumstances, him being crumpled up on the couch like he had a bad cold would've been an oddly humorous sight. Now it sends a palpable chill through the whole house. It's nothing short of a bad omen.

"Not what, who," he rasps, barely audible. "Pestilence herself nearly killed us all over that poor girl in the hospital bed."

Muerte scowled, though I couldn't tell if it was from suspicion or concern. "Merihem was out hunting for a vessel?" That would line up with what Grim said about Hell trying to start Armageddon on their own terms. They need souls for power, and the souls from Lines are more powerful than regular souls, and since Grim was meant to retrieve this girl before the demon interfered, that means her soul falls into that category. And judging by his pitiful state and the morose tone, I'd say Merihem or Pestilence or whatever her name is got exactly what she came for. Maybe she didn't get away with anything unscathed, but Death did not come out victorious.

"Considering the lengths she went to in order to claim her victim, I would wager that is her ultimate goal." Grim shifts uncomfortably, wrapping the blankets tighter around himself with every movement. "She has never been so covetous as to steal from me. Her want is so desperate that she risked dying for it."

"Did she kill for it?" Muerte now stands at my window, their back to us, and even from here I can see the tension coiling below the surface of their reflection. Were reapers lost to this battle? Could they have done more beside their brethren than riding out the storm with me? They don't outright ask these things, but the unspoken still follows what's said.

"Not this time, but the others may not be as merciful should we cross paths."

The smaller reaper casts a glance at me that his commander misses in his nest of faded quilts and tattered sheets. We both doubt it was mercy that spared them, and I can't help but wonder if it was a bargain . . . the helpless soul that lies between them for the safe return of the reapers to their duties. One small sacrifice to uphold the order of the universe.

After all, what's one mortal worth against many servants of Death, really?

"Fortune will not always be ours, true." Muerte takes up their scythe and readjusts their cloak. "So I will warn any of our kin I meet during my duties that Hell walks the Earth, as I'm sure Heaven does as well."

Grim's eyes narrow, but he does not object to this plan or make any accusations of conspiracies. Instead, he nods once before nodding off altogether. Whatever Merihem did to him must've finally taken its toll and drained the last of his strength away.

"He'll be alright in a few hours. Doesn't look like she touched him or like any of the poison she carries got directly into his system," the only conscious reaper reassures me.

"Breathing in that smog of hers isn't good for anyone, but at least it can be recovered from."

Together, we walk to the shoreline where they appeared yesterday, stopping by the crooked sigil in the log. With a wary glance back toward the cabin, I cover it in moss and peeled bark, in case Grim goes wandering without me and happens upon it. "If anything else happens, I'll call you back here."

"And if my search turns up any clues, I will find a way to send for you." Sunlight glances off the nearby water, casting the wisps of their hair in gold and deepening the shadows across their face. Even with such sharp features, Muerte's presence is nothing but soft and comforting. "Whether he knows about it or not. You will get your closure if it's my last act in this world."

"Don't let it be . . . somebody still has to escort me to the other side, okay?"

A portal springs open beside us, images of their destination swirling like paint mixing together, unfocused but still vibrant. Now more than ever, the temptation of fleeing to the unknown beckons me toward that warm, inviting light. Muerte even stops themselves from pulling me along behind them as they leave. "It will be my pleasure, no matter where your path leads."

GRIM

When next I wake, Flit has taken up her usual post in the bay window, journal in her lap and expression full of serene concentration as she scribbles. The smaller reaper is gone, leaving her to watch over me in my thankfully brief coma; she appears unbothered by our guardian–ward role reversal. One would think that, after being so near one of her greatest foes with no warning and then us being forced apart for several hours, I would have woken to hysterical relief. Instead, she lounges about in the afternoon warmth as aloof as a pampered housecat.

If I did not know better, she would appear content and untroubled, and we could carry on with our day as if our world was not turning up on its head with each passing second. But, after many millennia handling restless souls, her true mindset is easily discerned from the spiritual energy radiating out of her form. What begins as drops of impatience and irritation sprinkled into her otherwise sunny personality soon forms a pool of dissent and doubt out of which she cannot climb. That pool grows with every unsatisfactory answer and hiccup in her journey until it becomes a fearsome sea of unassuaged anger that threatens to drown us both if action is not taken.

Oh, how to choose between running the boat aground with hopes to salvage it or letting the waves claim the wreckage and praying you make it to shore . . .

"How long have I been sleeping?"

"Just a few hours," she replies coolly in contrast to the heat of her wrath rolling through the room. "I'm guessing we won't be going out later today, with the Apocalypse coming and all."

According to my empty coin pouch and the unwilling pact I witnessed only hours ago, she is correct. All normal operations in the living plane ceased the moment the first vessel was taken. Mortals may not take notice until the theatrics begin—those varying by which religion is putting on a show—but more subtle signs exist for those watching. "No, we will not, unless it becomes absolutely necessary."

"Guess I won't be crossing over any time soon either, right?"

"Flit—" She starts to interject, but I cut it off quickly. "Your time is approaching, I swear it on all that I am, but we cannot rush these things. If you pursue fate too ardently it will return the favor in most unpleasant ways."

"Oh." A sardonic grin catches the edges of her mouth, and she finally looks up from the book; her face is that of a cemetery statue, hard-set in its fury. "Is that what happened to Beatriz?"

She heard me.

"Who is she, Grim?"

"No one."

"Liar." She stares back, silent and cold as the grave.

"You truly desire to know of her?"

And thus, the ship is swallowed by the tide into which it dove so confidently, the captain's hand steering it headlong into the maelstrom. As tradition calls for, I will go down to the depths with it. "Very well. I will ruin our peace, as you request. I will show you how I let Beatriz grow, let her family love her beyond measure, and then had her taken away."

Gears in Flit's mind whir and click until a familiar scene aligns with my description. "You called that demon to steal her from her family? No, no, you . . . why?"

There were many reasons, but words fail me here, so I elect to show her through my long-silenced memories:

A lake appears before us, the rippling surface splashing against a familiar shore. Our cabin sits dark in the distance, in far less disrepair than its current state. Above the water, a hooded figure darker than the whole of the night sky hovers. The water parts, and they cradle a limp soul against them. As the head lolls to one side, Flit recognizes the face, although the wet, dark hair obscures most of the features.

"I did." I wring my hands, bending each finger until it pops. "I thought myself indifferent to humans, until your parents came along." Hesitating to console her shock will only lead to losing momentum, and I fear doing so will only lead to greater strife, so I press on. The two Hispanic families that make up her heritage had a history of cheating fate beyond what was reasonable, and by the time her parents came along, I had had enough of their dodging. "Liliana and Joseph seemed ordinary the first time our paths crossed. Your father was four and your mother was seven . . ."

Her father appears before me as a little boy lying bedridden with a deadly fever and no medicine nearby; a cut on his leg got infected and quickly spread until he was delirious with the heat in his head. His mother and her sisters tried every folk remedy they knew and asked around their hometown for more. His fever finally broke and he quickly recovered.

Then, her mother was helping her grandfather on their ranch; her horse threw her onto a rock, and she hit her head. She was unconscious for several days, but luckily there was no lasting damage. However, had the rock impacted an inch to the left, she would have never woken up.

"Miraculous recoveries are no strange thing to me, so I let the first time go without a second thought. They were young, and you know how I loathe taking innocents . . ."

"But . . . ?"

"But this was not the last time they both evaded me."

Her father was nine when he nearly suffocated in a house fire. One of the lanterns in the barn fell off its hook during a storm, and the wind carried embers onto the porch of the house. The whole family almost perished, but their dog finally caught a whiff of the smoke and woke up her grandparents. Joseph had to rescue one of the younger children but almost got trapped by falling timbers and smoke.

A bull attacked her mother when she was twelve; she and her father were trying to corral it into a trailer to be sold, and the beast fought back.

She missed being trampled to death by rolling under the water trough and crawling under the fence.

"Again and again, they slipped through my fingers. At the last possible moment, their lifeforce would return to them, and they would survive whatever misfortune befell them."

At fifteen, her father got hit by a car and was left on the street to bleed out. If an off-duty EMT had not driven by and seen him scrambling to stand against a fence, he would have taken his last breath in a ditch miles away from home.

After an argument with her mother, Flit's mother ran out into the front yard and was bitten by a rattlesnake hiding in a tire swing. If not for the antivenom at the local hospital, she would not exist.

"What has that got to do with me?" Flit crosses her arms to make her impatience plainer, as if it were not already obvious. "I wasn't even born yet! I didn't do that to you!"

"No, you did not. You were not my original intended victim. But it was as if, as you humans say, they had a guardian angel bent on thwarting me at every turn. Once I learned what they were meant to bring about, I had to prevent them from bringing a new generation into the world . . . but my effort came too late."

I followed them relentlessly for years. Claimed relative after relative, took the whole family with disease and war and tragedy, but still her parents evaded me. I was there when Liliana discovered she was pregnant with her first and only child. I am there when Flit learns her name again from a memory snippet so old she cannot believe it is hers. We hear it in so many different voices they all blur into one hum, so many different times it is as if the word is filling all the empty spaces still left in her mind.

Beatriz. Beatriz. Beatriz. Beatriz. Beatriz. Beatriz. Beatriz.

All the rage and hurt locked away with her forgotten memories comes spilling out in tears. "What did you do, Grim? What did you do to me?"

After Moloch leads the child to a watery grave, a vision of me appears in the background of her parents' lives, watching them run themselves ragged and spend all their savings searching for her. Together we watch them abandon the cabin in their grief and give up on bringing any part of her home.

As the last image fades, she remembers everything that came before it.

"I made this deal thinking your parents would soon follow . . . I thought if I ended those Lines entirely I could—"

By her logic, I did not let her finish living, so I do not get to finish speaking. "How long have I been here?" She leaps to her feet, stalking closer. With every footstep taken, more cracks begin to form in my final illusion. The cabin is showing its true age. Wallpaper peels off in sheets, and boards buckle and bow under her weightless feet. Windows break. Hinges rust. The blankets so carefully draped over me rot and fall to moldy pieces. Her vision is chained to her prey and she does not notice. There may be pain in my heart, but nothing I feel will ever come close to the depth my betrayal cuts her. "How many years have I been dead and rotting in the mud out there?"

I stop to count, not wanting to deceive her further. "Over two decades in Earth's time. Your parents passed on a year after you; their suffering was brief." The urge to reach out to comfort her aches like a festering wound, but that bridge is ashes now. "Now you can fully hate me . . . I took away the lie you have known as long as you can remember. I took your memories to prevent this anguish, but now you have them back."

All the poor girl can manage is a choked-off sob. "A child . . . I was a child. And you made me into a corpse."

I am dead to her now. Unforgivable. Any trust she may have stored for my use has been scattered to the wind by my own hand. It was foolish to reveal this to her, but if she were to find out without me admitting my crimes, it would have been worse. There is no absolution for what I have done, of course, but a confession is better than hearsay. Better I damn myself than let someone else—like the other reaper—do it for me.

Some desperate part of me wants to try and justify my actions further, to explain the farthest origins of this feud, but she will have shut me out completely by now. Anything beyond our recent history will fall like seeds onto fallow ground. Still, I cannot stop myself. "There is more to this than my resentment, but I cannot expect you to understand—"

"Oh, I understand you just fine," she hisses, just loud enough to be heard over the walls rattling. No divine force is causing the quake this time, only her unspent ghostly energy. She has gone twenty years without truly utilizing the abilities granted her in death, and this surge of rage has awakened them whether they can be controlled or not. "You couldn't take it, you couldn't handle them dodging you again and again. They took your stupid reputation and smashed it, so you took me."

"Flit, please—" Light fixtures swing and crack against the ceiling, and rocks and books tumble off her shelf, left to join the rest of the debris. Her one-winged angel remains standing against all odds, though its face soon becomes marred by the rapid passage of time.

"That isn't my name, and you know it! You can't even say my real name, can you?!"

How wrong she is. I can see it etched into the top of her coin—first, middle, and last. Her full name scarcely fits into its assigned space, but it is far from the longest on record. Her birth and death dates are separated by 5,839 days; she passed the day before her sixteenth birthday. The center bears a crucifix, and the bottom reads *El Paraíso*, which is Spanish for Heaven. Anything she wants to know about herself or anything else is only a question away, but none of those answers would mend what has been broken.

"Beatriz, I am sorry. You did not deserve to be caught in the machinations of this world. Few belonging to the Lines deserve what they are dealt." If she only knew the history of even one of those families, if she only knew what destiny awaits her, then maybe she would sympathize with my point. "You may believe that I robbed you of a long, happy life by taking you so young, but you have no idea what the world would have faced had I not intervened."

"Oh, so you're gonna throw some what-if apocalypse off on me like it's all my fault too? Because I was totally in charge of the entire planet right before I died!" she barks, trying in vain to stop the tears that keep falling. "I was in high school! I hadn't kissed a boy or gotten my driver's license or anything teenagers get to do! No balance in the universe is worth stealing my life before I got to live it, Reaper." She could not have spat the last word out with any more vitriol. Enough hatred burns from the deepest recess of her soul that she could reduce everything around us to ash if she knew how to channel herself. She has the power, only lacking the skilled knowledge needed to manipulate the environment in that way. Of course, that could be more dangerous than if her skills were honed. Loose cannons are more deadly than the anchored ones.

"If there were some way to go back and change this—"

"You wouldn't. You don't care about me or any of the other humans you reap. You care about doing your job and nothing else. That's all we are to you."

"That is false, and you know it."

"Do I? How do I know this isn't a lie too? How can I believe anything you say ever again?" Her fingers curl and uncurl into fists; she wants to hit something, but she cannot decide what deserves it more, me or the house she has been haunting. Much like myself, it once represented a safe harbor where she could rest without fear, and now it is tainted by my deceit. If she leaves, she will never return to either of us willingly. All the trinkets and keepsakes in the world could not tether her here.

I should not let her leave, but if it is meant to pass, nothing can stop her. I should have stopped myself when I had the chance, but that moment has come and gone. All I can do now is warn her and pray she listens. "I was not lying when I spoke of the angels and demons that will hunt souls such as yourself. If you think me untrustworthy, wait until one of them finds you. Their only thoughts are to use souls to wage war against each other. Many Lines have fallen in their wake."

"I'd take dealing with the devil himself over you! At least I'd know not to trust him."

"If you refuse to listen to reason, perhaps I should show you some memories of mine to prove my point about him and his ilk. Shall I begin with one of the Princes tormenting their subjects or the wrath of an Archangel against the unrighteous?"

She stands barely a foot away now; her anger straightens her spine so that it lifts her from the floor like a helium balloon. If she explodes, there will be nothing left behind but splinters and dust. "You enjoy our pain just like them. You'd never admit it, but you do. And you all think you're the only one that's right, regardless of the damage you cause." She snarls as she abruptly turns and pulls my scythe to her before I even consider reaching in that direction, closing her fingers around the handle as if she means to snap it in half.

It appears I should be more cautious of her than originally assumed.

Although she is not a reaper, the blade of the scythe is powerful enough to cause concern for anything it comes into contact with; no one is immune to its touch. Granted, she would have to strike a hard and precise blow to kill an immortal being, but I would prefer not to test her strength or accuracy with all that hangs over my head. If she kills me—she certainly has the motivation to do so—she will undo all that I have done to protect this world and then some.

I slowly raise my hands in surrender. "Beatriz, put that down. I do not want you to hurt yourself trying to get back at me."

"Don't act like you care. You're just afraid," she spits back. "And you should be . . . I'm going to find an angel and other reapers and tell them exactly what you did to me." She swings the scythe horizontally between us until it catches on a loose thread and rips a hole in the empty space. I try to reach out and stay her hand, but a final swipe leaves a gash from my shoulder to my waist; I recoil to save my neck in case she decides to aim higher. She tosses it away, shattering the bay window, and with one last heartbroken glance, she flees into the rift.

CHAPTER SEVEN

BEATRIZ

I want to forget everything after Purgatory, but there is no power in any dimension that could take my experience away from me. I transcended the mortal life I had been meant to lead, became a companion to the High Reaper himself, and followed him across realms mortal eyes were never intended to see.

And now I am free.

In the days we spent together, the cabin never felt like a prison, but now that I no longer live in his shadow, the reality of our arrangement becomes brutally clearer. For all his insistence otherwise, he did not genuinely love me as a friend. If he had, he would've let me pass on into the next world like I was supposed to. Like I *deserved* to. His pride wouldn't have shackled me to the non-place we inhabited together; he would've told me the truth right from the beginning without me having to beg for it.

In hindsight, I should've just walked out of the cabin or called Muerte back rather than jumping through a tear in time and space alone with no plan, but it's too late for that now. What I lacked in experience with using the scythe to travel I made up for with pure dumb luck. While I had originally meant for it to take me to my parents in the afterlife, I quickly realized that a reaper was necessary for that trip, and I had no intentions of taking that one with me anywhere ever again. Instead, the cemetery where they were buried, where I should've been buried beside them, would have to do.

No.

I shouldn't be buried at all.

I shouldn't be a memorial marker above an empty plot of earth, surrounded by wilted marigolds and melted candles. All that remains of me should not be a photo from my *quinceñera* and scraps of notes whose ink washed away decades ago. I should be a grown woman with a mildly irritating but still fulfilling job, a spouse who always forgets to take the trash out but always remembers how I like my coffee, three kids, and a few cats. Or a globetrotting businesswoman who doesn't stay in one place long enough to fully unpack her bags. Or a professional ballerina who lives with four of her closest friends in an apartment meant for one. I could've been anything, but the chance to decide was stolen from me and is now unattainable.

"Twenty years is a long time to live a lie, but soon I'll have eternity to regain my truth." I don't know if these words are to reassure myself or verbally defy him because he's not here to fight back. "I just have to find a way to my parents without catching the wrong kind of attention."

Muerte has already put themself in danger on my behalf, so I would hate to ask anything more, but that may be the only way to get my coin away from Grim. Surely he has the sense to realize the jig is up and he can't hold me back forever without consequences. Odds are he has mine hidden somewhere unreachable. Maybe there's some merciful god watching that can make a new one if we can't get the original, but there's no going back to him for me. I don't care if I do have to wander the world until it ends, I'll never go crawling back of my own free will. There will be another way if it has to be made from the ground up.

"No Grim Reaper or Pearly Gates can keep us apart now." With a mission in mind and a half-baked plan brewing, the cemetery disappears behind me, and I trudge to my future with wounded determination.

My old house wasn't far from the Happy Homestead Cemetery, as it turns out. I remember passing by it every day on the way to and from school, counting the tallest headstones between the gate rails and searching for funeral home tents among the hills and trees.

The moonlight turns the winding streets different shades of gray, so even my skin looks like old parchment when it isn't covered by the shadows. Everything looks so different than it used to, but that's to be expected after twenty years in a time bubble. The cars are much sleeker, less boxy than I remember. The houses are bigger, and they have different toys in the yard if they have any. I can't feel the warmth or chill of the wind, but the flowers and trees are in full blossom, so it's probably late spring or sometime in summer. Other kids are taking a break from school for granted, while I'm grieving the trips I never got to plan.

Home finally comes into view around the last corner, but no amount of preparation could've steeled me for the sight that waits at the end of my driveway. A rusty dumpster sits in the front corner. Shards from the stained-glass window around the front door litter the steps, spread in a halo on the dead grass and cracked concrete. What windows aren't missing their panes entirely are covered by sheets of plywood. The door itself hangs ajar, and the doorknob is nowhere to be seen. A dusty mailbox rests atop a brick pillar, missing half its numbers and letters. The flowerbeds have long since surrendered to weeds, and the paint to the unforgiving weather. Like me, this house is only a ghost.

Still, it's a place to haunt.

The inside doesn't look any better than the yard. Dust thicker than what covered the cabin floor coats everything left behind, which isn't much. Cords and screws are all that's left of the furniture; the red couch that Mama found at a yard sale when I was three, Papí's blue recliner in the corner, the boxy television set with the snow globes on top—all of that is gone. No pictures remain on the wall, no knick-knacks on the shelves, just like the cabin when we first arrived. Every trace of my old life was removed like a canvas torn from its frame; I can still clearly imagine where everything used to be, but it's only an afterimage.

Mice and empty bottles populate the kitchen that once was the heart of this house. Every holiday, birthday, whatever occasion, you name it, this room was full of people dipping around each other with dishes and ingredients; we didn't subscribe to the phrase "too many cooks in the kitchen." As a ghost I no longer feel physical hunger, but the longing for one of those feasts hits me like a ton of bricks each time a draft opens an empty cabinet. What I wouldn't give for a last meal, even if the taste were missing.

Hoping to starve my heartbreak but knowing deep down it will only worsen, I drift up the stairs past Mama and Papí's door. The quilt Mama's *abuela* gave her should've been tucked neatly over their bed, with its warm and vibrant patchwork. And the dresser's mirror should've caught my reflection as I passed.

Mama's rose perfume should've been clinging to the curtains and mingling with Papí's sage cologne. All that stands in their place is the ripped wallpaper and the empty space where my shadow belongs.

My room waits at the top of the broken staircase, and I have no clue how to handle that. Knowing what the rest of the house looks like, there is little hope for the state of what used to be my safe haven. Where are all my posters and drawings? Who has my clothes and jewelry now, or are they so out of style they've been discarded altogether? Who sleeps on the canopy bed that creaked on the left side but not the right? Were those book series ever finished? So many unknowns lie behind that closed door, and I'm not sure I want the answers. My one solace is that my name is still painted on the wall above the entrance, at least enough for me to make it out easily.

But the door is locked. My door never had a lock on it before.

You would think that it would've corroded enough over the years for that not to be an issue, but no amount of rattling can shake it loose. With everything else recognizable gone, I have my doubts that there's a key anywhere nearby, but I still double-check every drawer, nook, and cranny just to be certain. Even if I were alive, my scrawny arms couldn't muscle the door open alone, so that's out too. I'm not climbing the side of the house so I can freak out any clairvoyant neighbors. That's just rude. Funny, the longer I consider it, but still rude.

The only option left—the one I can't believe didn't occur to me immediately, wow—is to ghost through the wall, or try to anyway. I have no idea if this requires practice or not, but there's only one way to find out. Placing my hands up to brace myself in case I trip or run into something on the other side, I push against the door like I'm trying to hold it shut. At first it feels like nothing is happening; the door doesn't give and neither do I. Gradually, however, my fingers start to sink into it as if it's a curtain rather than a solid piece of wood. I blink and find myself inside when my eyes open again.

Down to the shoes kicked off by my nightstand and the pillows splayed across my bed, my room is entirely intact, just the way it was the morning we left for the cabin. Except now everything is mildewed and sun-bleached. What's left of the posters are hanging by single thumbtacks if they aren't curled up on the floor. The colors are faded off the bedsheets, the canopy torn down the middle. My starry cloud nightlight only has patches of paint left; it used to be purple and yellow. Once neatly posed, stuffed animals now lie face down in front of their shelves, along with moldy jewelry boxes and scattered paper. The curtains swing in the night breeze, tattered and colorless. It all lies in ruins like a forgotten cathedral.

"Well," I choke out through tears that have been building back up since I set foot in here. "I'm rotting in the bottom of the lake out there, so at least my room still matches me. He didn't take that away from me. This is still mine." Through sobs that echo through the whole house, I set to work trying to fix this mess. All the ripped paper and trash go in a pile by the door in the hall. All my toys and trinkets go back in their places, even if they're falling to pieces in my hands. My moldy shoes go back in the closet with my moldy clothes. Last but not least, I make my bed like I should have before we went on vacation, and then I crawl on top of the sheets and cry myself to the undead equivalent of sleep.

MUERTE

It's rare that we lesser reapers receive personal calls from our leader; he's terribly busy interfering with the Lines and keeping our ranks under his thumb, so we get little to no personal interaction with him, unless we've done something wrong. In which case he truly has no room to talk, especially not to me. Not knowing what I know now.

I've recently had a rather enlightening chat with several other reapers about his run-in with Merihem. The run-in that none but me were summoned to, as it turns out. He took her on alone, if they truly clashed at all, and then left her to take her vessel. Others have also noticed their coins being incorrect or not arriving at all as of late, so I took that chance to inform them of the imminent apocalypse to explain these oddities. Hopefully this didn't incite a full-blown panic among the others, but they need to be aware of the truth.

I briefly consider turning and fleeing from the cabin ahead until I remember my life alone is not at stake. Flit needs all the help she can get, and I will accept my fate for being that help, just as promised. None of us are quite sure what happens when a reaper dies; it doesn't happen often enough to be concerned about, given that we stay out of the thick of conflicts. We're just the cleanup crew, after all . . . carrion birds that walk and talk like Man.

The back door stands ajar, allowing the last of summer's breezes inside. Although the weather has cooled little in this part of the world, autumn will begin soon. The leaves in the forest will shift from rich emerald and jade to gold and ruby until the mountain ranges resemble walls of flame. The harvests will come in from the fields and will be prepared for winter. Humans will bundle up a bit more in the mornings and evenings, sip their warm drinks, and marvel at seeing their breath in the wind. I myself particularly enjoy the fall traditions surrounding Halloween; not to be cliché, but the reaper decorations are always amusing to me.

And I envy my brethren who are charged with supervising the Day of the Dead celebrations—such a festive occasion! It brings comfort to the rest of us that some humans choose to rejoice in a passed one's life rather than lament their loss. Eases our consciences a bit. Any thoughts of requesting a transfer to such duties leave promptly upon seeing Death's scythe dripping ichor and him gingerly bandaging himself up. He seems unperturbed by the gash that runs the length of his body but also dejected and exhausted. Like he hasn't a friend in the world, which I suppose he really doesn't. Flit is nowhere in sight, which is curious to say the least.

"Is everything alright?" I shuffle a bit closer to offer my assistance if necessary, hoping he doesn't hear the insincerity. "You requested to speak to me?"

He ties off the bandage, then nods silently, indicating a satchel in the window seat. "I would like you to deliver this for me, if possible. Do you recall my companion when we last met?" I nod in return, eager to know her whereabouts and why she left. "She no longer desires my company. She left some things behind that she may want, but I do not think she would accept them from me."

"O-oh, that's dreadful. Do you know where she is?" Of course he knows—he knows where every soul belongs and whether they're there or not, what kind of question is that? What I should've asked was, "Shouldn't you just hand me her coin so she can pass over, and I won't have to worry so much about her anymore?"

"I have an idea, yes. Her former place of residence in Lake Tahoe, California, is the first place you should look." He hands me a set of coordinates scrawled on a scrap of notebook paper. "If she is not there, report back here immediately."

"Of course. And if she doesn't take the bag?" I inquire as I turn to open a portal to my destination, the light sack strapped over my shoulder. At least she's probably safe for the time being and not kidnapped like I originally feared. She must've confronted him and escaped somehow.

"Leave that to Beatriz's discretion. I have done all I can for her."

So that was her true name. "Right. Be healed soon." I bid him farewell and step from the living room to a paved street. Dawn keeps pace not far behind me; the rising sun painting the white stucco homes and curved palm trees all shades of scarlet and indigo while the sky melts from black to blue. Sounds from the city begin to creep up the street, mixing with birdsong and the palm fronds rustling in the wind. Watching the world awaken nearly distracts me from my worry, which happens more often than I care to admit. We get so few days off to observe the places we flutter in and out of, so we must steal each second of quiet that we can.

It doesn't take long to find the house, decrepit and isolated at the end of the street, no signs of life within. Decay and patina sit well on some buildings, but this place was clearly abandoned with much sorrow and pain. It hangs over the entire block like a dust cloud in the desert, dark and suffocating. They clearly left unwillingly, whoever this family used to be, and took whatever happiness resided in this house with them. It's all gone now, with all of them dead or missing.

The front door opens with an awful squawk loud enough to rouse the most ancient dead, which is only amplified by the bare interior. Even if she were a hundred miles away, surely she could hear that and would come investigate. Of course, she could be one of those humans who avoids previously sentimental places to spare herself pain, and she could be anywhere else on Earth except nearby. Ghosts are funny like that, in that they don't always haunt somewhere familiar to them in life. Some are terribly lost souls in more sense than one, and that's what us smaller reapers are for. We are meant to be guides and little more.

"Beatriz? Are you here?" I call up the stairs, scanning each room for the wayward spirit I befriended. She doesn't appear to be on the lower level of the house, but I can sense her nearby at least. In theory, I could've just used my soul-sensing abilities to find her, but I didn't want to frighten her any more than she already is in this unusual situation. Poor thing doesn't deserve so much distress at once.

Another door creaks open above me, and a timid form emerges into the stairwell. "Muerte? Is that you?" The hope and fear in her voice are heartbreaking. Neither of us should be in these positions; she shouldn't be praying for a reaper's salvation, and I shouldn't be cleaning up after my superior.

"Now, I know you're tired of seeing me." I hold up the satchel as a peace offering, placing it on the bottommost stair. She finally recognizes me and practically flies down to embrace me. "But I was told to bring this to you."

As quiet as only the dead can be, she reaches into the bag and pulls out a leather-bound notebook with an ink pen attached to the side, a set of hardback novels, a piece of driftwood, some bones, several rocks, and a small angel figurine with one wing missing. This last object gives her great pause, as if it contains much more than ceramic and faded paint; she cradles it in her palm as though it is alive. Skeptical, she glances up at me briefly. "This is all you're here for? To give me this? He's not making you stalk me or try to talk me into coming back?"

"He could ask those things all he likes, but he will not get cooperation from me, or anyone else I've spoken to for that matter." I take a seat beside her so that we sit level with one another, "I-I would help you cross over, but you'd need your coin, and neither of us has it."

She pokes around in the smaller pockets of the bag in hopes that perhaps Death granted her his blessing for that last journey, but unfortunately a simple passing was withheld from her a second time. "Yeah, he couldn't let me have the one thing I actually wanted. He probably dropped it in the middle of the lake or something thinking he'd never need it again."

The poor girl looks so disappointed and frustrated; if she does linger on Earth long enough without being caught by the Court or the Host, all that despair will turn into power to manipulate the world of the living, and she could become a dangerous spirit. Those descended from the Lines are especially prone to becoming aggressive hauntings if not handled properly, which is why Death himself is the only one in charge of them. What made him shirk his duties with this girl, what made him allow her to linger this long knowing the possible consequences, greatly perplexes me.

"I am terribly sorry, my dear. I wish there were more I could do to help, but—"

"That won't be necessary."

We both jolt at the sound of a third voice joining our conversation; I know my scythe can protect us from anything that dares eavesdrop, but I don't appreciate being ambushed in the slightest! Under normal circumstances, I would play off the jump scare as a joke between colleagues, but with my companion's status, it hardly feels joyful to find out we are staring down a trio of angels. A Malakhim and one of the Authorities loom in the foyer below us while another stands watch outside.

"We can take her from here. Thank you, Reaper."

BEATRIZ

The phrase "rest in peace" must be an inside joke or code for something I'm unaware of because since I've died, I haven't had any peace at all. First, my soul gets kidnapped and my memories stolen by the Grim Reaper; now I'm hiding from somebody's goons behind a reaper that isn't much bigger than me. For all I know, these could be demons trying to disguise themselves, and we could both be as good as hellbound. Or they could be angels and we're about to get smote. Smitten? Either way, I'm not looking forward to it.

"Fear not, Beatriz," says the middle one as they lower their hand to me in greeting. The closer they get, the clearer the dim halos around their heads become. The two flanking angels wear armored helmets, so if they have halos too, they must be hidden underneath. "We are here to escort you home. Your long wait is finally over."

Muerte's eyes skip from me to the others and back, mirroring my confusion. "But—not that I think she doesn't deserve to pass over, of course—she doesn't have her coin, and nor do I. Unless one of you has it, she can't—"

"All in due time, dear friend," the angel reassures us. "Azrael's disruption of the balance will not go unpunished, and all will be righted by the proper parties."

Azrael.

Not Grim. Not Death. Not The Reaper.

Azrael.

In all our time together, he hadn't even bothered to tell me his real given name; he acted like he didn't have one at all. It makes sense to appeal to a girl who can't remember who she is by pretending you've lost part of yourself too. Make her think she gets to decide who you are because you think you've made the same decision for her. Then you both end up being wrong.

"Are my parents waiting for me?" I sit back on the stairs, rolling the small angel around in my hands. "Will I finally see them?"

The angel to the left finally speaks up. "As soon as our forces recover your coin, you will be escorted directly to your family's dwelling place. Until such time, you will remain in the Manor of the Host so that none of the Court may come into possession of your soul."

"We are also searching for your corporeal body so that it may be properly interred on consecrated ground," says the one on the right.

"I'll have to leave all of this behind to follow you, right?" The miniature peeks over my fingers; I hadn't decided whether or not to keep any of it before they showed up, but now that it has to stay here, I feel much more attached to what's left of my fake life. It's strange to compare the objects now to what they were before my death: The journal belonged to Mama even though she never wrote in it, but Papí had read the novels until their spines broke and pages frayed. The bones, rocks, and wood brought back memories of combing the shore as a child with my cousins and the neighbor kids. The broken angel belonged to a Nativity set Tia Jacquelyn gave us the year I was born. Once I turned about five or six, I decided it was meant to stand guard over Barbie tea parties and make sure I only put on the best clothes during dress up. It went with us on vacations, to show-and-tell at school, and hid in bags during sleepovers. It sat through my *quinceñera* on the table next to the cake.

My tiny angel lost its wing the night Azrael and Moloch took me. My hand swept it off the night table as I rose from bed and crept out of the house. It lay there until morning, when Mama found it fallen from its perch, one wing hidden beneath the bed skirt.

"I'm afraid so, dear. There may be facsimiles in your new home, but the actual physical objects must remain on Earth. They aren't made of the same material as souls or angels, so they can't pass through the gates." Muerte consoles me. "If you would like, I could leave them in your room upstairs while you go on ahead with them."

"What are you gonna tell him when you go back?"

A long, heavy silence hangs over the five of us. How would Azrael react to the angels finding me? Would he come after me, bang on the Pearly Gates, and demand I be returned to him? Or worse, come and try to apologize again? What if he has my coin and refuses to hand it over to the ones out looking for it? Would he run like he did from the prison or try to fight the angels sent to recover my key to the afterlife?

"Well, I'll tell him . . . I gave you the bag, as he asked, and that's all that I know." The angels are more surprised than me that the reaper is all but lying to their boss, but they're not as grateful as me to have a head-start on him. The little reaper bids us goodbye and collects my things from the floor, muttering as they climb the stairs as if they're embarrassed to even think about the situation. "What he did was utterly wrong and inexcusable, so if the wrath of Heaven awaits him, then who am I to interfere?"

"Come this way." The middle angel beckons me to a portal just outside the door, and soon the mortal world falls away for good. Finally.

CHAPTER EIGHT

BEATRIZ

I open my eyes to nothing for a second time. The angels have vanished; I am alone.

"No, no, this can't be happening. Not again." Panic swells, clawing at my ribs until it falls into the pit of my stomach like a lead brick. It was all a trap. It has to be. He'd never let me go that easy. I'll be stuck in Purgatory until he sees fit. If he ever does. No one will ever find me.

On the verge of screaming myself hoarse, hoping for rescue that will never come, my stilled heart leaps when a distant "Hello?" calls over my fearful cries. It sounds like a man's voice, but it isn't the one I'd been dreading. This one is much warmer, more human.

Spinning in the direction of the sound, desperate for a sign that this isn't square one all over again, I call back, "Who's there? Where are you?"

As before, the stark blankness of my surroundings is suddenly interrupted by a figure I can't quite make out at first. This one blends into the background, rather than standing out against it; the shape is cream-white and not much larger than me. Hard, angular pieces make up the bottom, while the top is more flowing and softer . . . and . . . moving?

The eyes I meet this time are set into a tan face, and they are dark, dark brown. They belong to a man sitting at a podium with a large book before him. His slender fingers are caked in black ink that hasn't had a chance to dry just yet, which makes the pages of the tome stick to his hands when he tries to turn them. He wears a simple, colorless tunic and sandals; it's a near replica of what I wear, minus the shoes. His hair and beard don't help him stand out either. It's all snowy white, and his hair curls against his head like a crown.

"Oh!" We exclaim simultaneously, one of us in surprise, the other in excited anticipation.

I almost ask him who he is, until the iridescent-silver gate looming over his shoulder and stretching into the distance comes into view. We've never met in person, but his name is immediately apparent.

"Miss Beatriz Torres, right on time!" Saint Peter declares, scratching my name down in the book with a black quill before descending from his seat. "Well, given the circumstances at least . . . Truthfully, you were meant to be here some time ago."

"So I've been told."

"Yes, well." He fans the air as if shooing a bug, adding a shrug at the end. "Azrael wasn't thinking clearly when he took you on that little detour of his. He's thrown everything off is what he's done." He stops short of elaborating as a trumpet blast thunders from behind the gates. It booms so loudly that for a moment I mistake it for a lighthouse foghorn. He gestures for me to stand beside him to get a better view of the source. "Not many earn the privilege to see this, dear girl, but this welcome is meant especially for you . . ."

"You mean that wasn't an alarm?" My head didn't quite turn all the way to face him before my eyes found something new to fixate on. Six beings stand on the other side of the fence, each one easily two or three feet taller than me and slender as a copse of willows. To call myself dumbstruck by their collective beauty was an understatement to say the least; it was a whole new speechlessness that not even Limbo could compete with.

They have to be the Heavenly Host.

However, given that no two sacred texts agree on more than three of their names, telling who is who is basically impossible. Azrael told me all their names and a little about each at one point, but given his proven unreliability, I doubt any of what he said was true.

Any onlookers could make an educated guess at identifying the Archangel Michael without much background. As the Warrior, Heaven's general, he dresses in a full suit of armor with a sword at his hip. His features are carved stern and stoic, but not in a menacing way . . . more like a fair but firm teacher. The chest-length, flaming red hair astounds me, though; I always pictured him with short, dark curls. I guessed the blue eyes right, just not the unearthly shade that glows with its own light.

Gabriel is another easy speculation, given that she holds the Horn that nearly blasted us off the clouds. Only she and Azrael bore physical wings on their bodies all the time, he claimed; being the Messenger, it made sense that she would use her wings for traveling and not just have them for show. The rest of them wear theirs in their clothing somewhere different. However, only one of them has pure white wings like a dove; the rest seem to be modeled after different birds.

Well, the birds would be modeled after them, since angels were created first.

The final angel in the line's feathers form long blue sleeves with white along the top of her arms and gray and black across her chest. Her dress is a shade of red I will never forget. The same shade that pursued us through the prison that day, the same hue that struck fear into the Reaper that his plan could unravel at any second. She almost saved me, but I was too afraid to seek her out. He made me afraid when I should've run into her arms the first chance I got.

But he isn't here to hold me back anymore.

"Don't be afraid, Beatriz." Saint Peter nudges me forward, as if he senses my lingering hesitation to approach them. "Jophiel and Auriel have been searching for you since your soul disappeared, so they're dying to finally meet you."

"Which ones are they?"

"The one with the sash around her eyes is Auriel, and the one with the black braid is Jophiel." He waves to get their attention, then introduces them as they head our way. "Then you have Raphael with the staff there and Cassiel in the purple. Gabriel is the bubbly little blond one next to the grouchy redhead. Michael might seem scary, but he doesn't bite." This assurance is loud enough that the angel overhears and finds amusement in the statement.

"Many demons would beg to differ," he replies to the gate guard with a voice as low as distant thunder, then lightens it a bit for me. "So this is the errant soul we've been after?"

Saint Peter shows him my name in his ledger; the ink is scarcely dry when he runs his finger across it. "Of course it's her, I wouldn't have gathered you all here if it were someone else!" he scolds Michael. "I would certainly hope your underlings are trained well enough to pick out the human they're sent to retrieve as opposed to grabbing the first one they see."

"Of course they are!" Gabriel jumps to defend the lesser angels. "It isn't their fault Azrael is so sneaky. He hid her in the most obvious place that we had already scoured countless times, and when we would get close again, he'd whisk her off somewhere else."

Not knowing what else to say or how else to join the conversation, I pipe up, "He hid me in Purgatory for a while. I don't know how long. We were in the cabin most of the time I was awake."

Raphael considers this added information carefully, rearranging his short locs with one hand and tapping the nails of the other against his staff. He reminds me more of a forest spirit than an angel with his deep green clothes and dark brown skin. "That must be how he kept her away from us for so long. Only certain spaces there are within our domain, and the other deities wouldn't think to interfere with Azrael's business." The rest of them came to the same consensus, so he continues, "He must've gotten too comfortable getting away with it and thought he was safe to let her out. That's when we finally made some headway in finding you."

I turn to Auriel with heavy regret. "If I had known to come to you in the prison, we would've been here a long time ago." Her sharp features and bronzed complexion remind me of the human women we met there, but her sash is in the way of her eyes. The way she turns to face me implies that she may not have any but doesn't seem to need them either.

"You were taught to fear us and seek shelter with him should one of us appear. You could not have known any different." Her voice is smooth and strong like a river; it has a natural hum.

The more lies that pile onto the lies I'm still trying to digest, the larger the pit in my gut grows; I feel like I swallowed all those rocks along the lakeshore, and they're trying to drag me down to the depths again. The tentative happiness we shared was fake, but I can't decide if knowing that is worse or if finding out the truth the way I did is. Maybe wondering is the worst of all.

"All the fault rests with Azrael. He chose to interfere with the plans laid in place millennia before you came along and kept you from learning your part in them as well." Cassiel's cheerful expression sours to match mine, and he kneels before me. He looks the most like me out of the group. He even looks to be the youngest, although none of them look old at all. His voice has the same effect of waking up with a warm, soft pillow on a cool autumn morning by the lake; all my worries are quieted for now. "He never told you what being part of a Line means, or anything about your Lines, did he?"

"No, not exactly. Or accurately. That would require him to be honest with me, and we see how well he did there."

"Things wouldn't be so off-course if she knew, little brother," Michael sighs. "Personally, I think all of them should be raised knowing their place in this world, but—"

"We tried telling them early. Remember the whole incident with Jonah?" Auriel scolds him, and though her eyes are covered, I can picture the exact expression they're making. So can the brother she's reprimanding and all the rest of her siblings too; their reactions range from stifled giggles to yes-yes-I-know-don't-remind-me moans.

"Well, I suppose now's as good a time as any to tell you. You may have to hear this speech a few more times, so I apologize if it gets long-winded," Cassiel continues where he was interrupted, and everything I thought I knew is turned on its head. "When the world was created, the plan for ending it was discussed among the creator deities, as is customary for every inhabited planet. A date was set, down to the nanosecond, at exactly midnight on the final day of the twentieth century. Then, these plans were passed along to us lesser beings so that we could help enforce them.

"Celestials were meant to guide the humans to their fate, not steer them in whatever direction pleased them at the moment. The gods' orders were not meant to be questioned nor disobeyed except under the direst of circumstances. Doing so on nothing more than a whim only leads to severe punishment. Few have fallen to these temptations, but those who have served as lessons to those left behind."

"Angels and other beings of light waged war against all the world's demons and their dark masters from the dawn of time for this exact reason; their plans contradicted our plans to the letter, and to preserve ours, we had to defeat whatever forces they raised against us." Michael says. Given Heaven's superior numbers—and ability to collaborate without tearing each other to pieces—forces of the divine typically win battles with less effort.

"How do the Lines play into all this?" I ask, glancing from angel to angel. I've met a few people from these families, and they all seemed pretty ordinary, myself included. Sure, I'm from two Lines, but that can't be all that unusual, can it?

Jophiel chimes in, "As per the set rules of our apocalypse, each of the fourteen members of the Court and Host must take human vessels and do battle on the earthly plane. These vessels will come from families that can be traced all the way back to those of biblical fame; while some Lines have faded from existence over the centuries, enough are left for each of us to have a vessel from a different family."

Cassiel informs me of a series of family trees that extend all the way back to the original humans and all the way to the branches on which they end, from the children that have yet to draw their first breath to the ancestors that have long since returned to dust. I can't help but wonder what it's like to have all those memories mixed in with your own personal thoughts. We may look the most alike, but his mind is on the polar opposite side of where mine was only hours ago. It's dumbfounding if I think about it too long.

"The demons are much more forceful about their decision than us." Raphael warns, "They possess the human of their choosing with or without their permission and will use the body recklessly until it can no longer hold itself together."

"There have also been whispers of them seeking out more vessels than they need in order to keep them from the angels," Jophiel says. However, she adds, until Armageddon is officially initiated, only reapers can distinguish between the Lines and other human souls. That being said, demons are not known for their discretion. There will be innocent casualties, as with any war.

"One of them already has a vessel," I inform the group, to their horror. "I don't remember her name—he called her Pestilence I think—but she took a girl right in front of us at a reaping." Of course, if not for Muerte partially witnessing the event, I would assume that was a lie too. Hell could've gotten a leg up on Heaven already, and it would be Grim's fault for smothering me in dishonesty.

"Wouldn't we have heard something if the Court already had a vessel?" Gabriel frets.

"Merihem has likely *chosen* a vessel, but according to our sources she has not taken possession of them yet," Michael tries to reassure everyone, but his tone misses the mark a bit. "Demons like to torment their vessels a bit, so she is probably stalking them until she grows bored of it."

"That's comforting . . ." All of them wince a bit. "So is everyone in a Line in danger of getting snatched up? I was drowned by a Knight or something, but he didn't possess me."

"A Knight? Were they working with Azrael or alone?" Raphael inquires. I honestly don't know. He'd never mentioned this guy before, and I'd never seen him before or since I died. They could've been working together, or just had a common goal and happened to run into each other. Until proven otherwise, I'm prepared to assume the worst: that he hired this demon to do the dirty work while he lurked in the shadows.

Turns out I'm not the only one either. "He knew exactly who Beatriz was before any of this started," Auriel agrees with my thoughts. "That's why he had her taken instead of any of the others. He knew what would happen if she went missing so close to time."

"Only certain members of the families can become vessels. You must come of age before a large battle, such as the one that has been delayed for so long, and either be a first-born son or daughter. That is how the Lines are tracked, by the first living descendant of each family," Saint Peter clarifies. If he was going for uplifting, he had less success than Michael.

"I'm an only child."

"And as per the tradition of the *quinceñera*, she came of age a year before the battle."

"And she's the end of two Lines."

"Ah. Well then," he sputters. "The good news is you can choose the angel you go into battle with. You have time to get to know them until we find the rest of the vessels, and you can all decide together." Was that really a choice at all? Yes, I could take any one of them as my guardian and companion, but I would still be fighting a war I knew nothing of until this very moment against creatures bent on killing everything in their path. Seems like a lose-lose situation all the way around.

The demons' goal, Michael explains, is to destroy the world of the living and rule over the ashes, not to rebuild humanity to its lost glory. If Heaven loses, Hell will take the mortal world apart and will then try to find its way up here to finish the job.

"Oh yeah, at least there's that." I definitely see the "possibly damned if you do, definitely damned if you don't" and despise it at both ends. The Reaper didn't give me a choice when he could have, and very much should have, and they don't have any other options to give me. I could always run, I guess, but I know the story of Jonah just as well as they do.

Michael bends so that we stand nearly equal and cradles his helmet under one arm so that he can reach out his other hand to me. "I know it seems like all of these decisions are being made without you being consulted . . ."

"Seems to be the theme lately." His palm and fingers are calloused and scarred, but his grip is gentle and open. He isn't trying to restrain me from pulling back.

"And I know how you may feel. None of us were asked if we wanted to be the harbingers of the Apocalypse either, but the alternative is letting the Court make the calls, and there will be no returning from that." I nod with a little less frustration and a bit more understanding, so he goes on. "So I will give you a choice in this at least. You can help us with our last mission before we start seeking the other vessels."

A muffled gasp ripples across the group, all except for Jophiel. She sneaks a glance into her mirror without pulling it from her shoulder and breathes a quiet sigh of relief. Gabriel isn't convinced by her brother's unusual decision-making, however. "Michael, are you sure? Isn't that too dangerous with her just being a soul? What if the Court finds out she's with us?"

He shakes his head to dissuade any further questions. "She will make that decision on her own. We are not here to imprison her as Azrael did." He turns back to me, closing his fingers around mine. "It's true what we are about to do is perilous, even for us, but I will let you decide if you want to join us after you hear our plan. Do you find this fair?"

"I mean . . ." I shrug. "At least you asked. What do we have to do?"

To which Auriel replies, "We are traveling to Hell. We must rescue our brother."

I don't think I heard her right, so I ask just to be sure I have my facts straight before agreeing to step one foot off this cloud. "So we're going to Hell? After we just talked about how dangerous it would be for me to be anywhere near a demon of any rank?"

"Yes. To the bottommost level, Judeccan."

"To rescue your brother . . . ?"

"Lucifer, yes." Michael keeps confirming what I thought—kind of hoped—I misheard. "He has served his punishment for what happened in the Garden, and it is time for him to retake his place among us."

The longer I think about what I know about that whole situation, the more I doubt he would want to come back. As most major religious authorities understand it, Michael is the one who cast him down in the first place. Why in the world is he going back to get Lucifer and expecting him to come running back to help them fight these demons they keep talking about? Sure, Heaven is a definite improvement from the bottom level of Hell, whatever that's like, but most people wouldn't be too gung-ho to help the ones that sent them there. It may not have been Michael's decision, but he still did it, and that's the most memorable circumstance in a situation like that.

Of course, this might just be how siblings work. I was an only child, like I said.

"He's more than served his time," Auriel huffs. "This rescue is twenty years overdue." She looks especially peeved about this disruption, as she explains it's her duty to maintain the balance of the world. Her underlings help monitor and control resources on Earth, while she collects repentant souls to keep Hell from gaining too big of a lead on Heaven's headcount. If I ever see Mrs. Allred again, I'll be sure to answer her question from before.

"So, after all is said and done, Lucifer gets to come back home to stay?" I can't explain why this suddenly worries me so much. Guess it's the undertones of being used, not unlike I was, as a means to an end. It wasn't fair then and it isn't any more so now, no matter who's involved.

"His banishment wasn't up to us. Father did what he thought was best at the time." Jophiel says, "He told us to wait until Lucifer had a chance to truly redeem himself, and now it's come." Saving the species you condemned to mortality and pain *does* sound like a good way to get back into people's good graces. Not everyone will be convinced he's changed of course, but it's at least a start.

"So how does one rescue an archangel from Hell?" It doesn't sound like any of them have undertaken such a mission before—they haven't mentioned any other missing siblings—and I know I haven't. The prison demon's portal was the closest I've ever been to Hell, and I'd rather hoped to keep it that way if possible.

"We have to slip through the levels above mostly undetected," Raphael continues, "but we may have to take out a few of the lesser demons to do so. Then we have to actually find him when we arrive in Judeccan."

"We don't really know much about what happened after he Fell." Cassiel picks at the flap of his messenger bag. "Some of the Malakhim claim they saw the Court capture him and . . ." He doesn't go into detail, but the way his eyes glaze over and his voice stops short tells me he knows every detail of what those creatures did to his brother.

Gabriel steps to his side and puts a comforting hand on his shoulder. "But we know where they're keeping him at least. They know we'll come to save him, and they don't want to make it easy."

Does anybody ever want to make necessary things easy?

"Now that you know what you would be facing if you travel with us, will you go, or would you rather wait here?" Michael squeezes my hand again to draw my wandering attention back to him. "You will be protected with or without us. The demons cannot enter here, and we will not let them touch you there, as long as you stay close and do as we ask."

How torn can I be about this? On the one hand, I don't want to leave this view; the clouds aren't the pure daytime white everybody thinks they would be—they're the saturated shades of violet, scarlet, and periwinkle after a sunset thunderstorm.

They roll and curl around themselves, forming shapes and shifting hues as light streams through them from different angles. Between the puffs, the sky is still visible so I can see what time it is down below on Earth. Here at the entrance would be a perfect spot to sit and wait and lose track of time talking to Saint Peter and the other souls that cross through here.

On the other hand, I've just about had my fill of sitting and waiting and doing nothing. Did it for twenty years without realizing it, and I can't get that time back. I can't shake the knowledge that I could've done so much in those years stolen from me, and, in a way, that gives me some empathy for Lucifer. He's been stuck in the same place, probably powerless, for centuries. He may not even know his family is coming back for him. Granted, he actually did something to get punished, but other than that, our stories are hardly that different. Of course, I could be totally wrong about him and the rest of his family, but there's only one way to find out which is the case.

I tighten the belt that still holds Azrael's dagger at my waist; he won't be getting that back any time soon. "Lead the way."

Michael allows himself the beginning of a smile, then stands to rejoin the others. "Very well. Gabriel or Raphael will have to carry you unless you can fly somehow."

"I wish." Some ghosts probably can, but I didn't get a chance to learn and had to walk everywhere.

Gabriel nods enthusiastically, volunteering for the task. "It's a wonderful feeling, unless you get motion sickness or have a fear of heights . . . or get cold easily . . . or—" She stops herself before she can list another downside. "I'm not making it sound like much fun, am I? I'll just let you decide for yourself, like my brother said." She lifts me into her arms like I weigh less than nothing. Holding Michael's hand felt like holding one of the stones from the lake after it had been sitting out in the sun. Being enveloped in Gabriel's arms feels like a blanket in front of a fireplace on a chilly autumn morning, but the brush of her feathers is more like a warm spring breeze finding me in the shade. She may have trouble putting me down when we're through with the rescue mission; this is the most at peace I've been since waking up dead.

The others take their time to adjust their armor—most of which is hidden under their robes until they shift them aside—and release their wings. Saint Peter vanishes briefly while we discuss our journey, but he returns around the side of the Gates pulling the reins of a golden chariot. "Just in case you can't carry him all the way back. He was a scrawny little fledgling, but he may not be much help getting out of there."

"Should we take it to begin with?" Raphael runs one dark hand along the side.

Jophiel shakes her head. "We would be too big a target if we took it from start to finish. We can get in quicker if we travel without it, but Peter is right, we may need it to bring him out if he's sick or injured."

Gabriel agrees. "I'll call it if we need it. Just leave it out here until then for me, won't you Peter?" I assume by "call it" she means using her horn, but I'm not quite sure how a horseless chariot works, especially not an angelic one.

"Will do. Safe travels to you all, and be swift about your return!" he calls to us just as Gabriel swan-dives off the cloud with me in her arms. I try to imagine the sudden dip as us coming over the first hill on a rollercoaster or jumping off the highest diving board at the pool instead of careening through the sky without a parachute. She wouldn't dream of dropping me of course, and I'm already dead, so it wouldn't hurt if she did, but the sudden burst of adrenaline catches me off guard. Only a short yelp escapes before the fall snatches the wind out of me.

We soar through the clouds much faster than expected; one blink and it's all blue sky. The layer of the world that holds Heaven goes by in little more than a kaleidoscopic blur, and it's not long before I can make out the shapes of the continents against the sea out of the tiny sliver of my eye that's open. Nerves have them wired shut, until a flash of white pries them open again.

"Don't worry!" Gabriel angles her wings to slow our descent and points to a ring of light behind us. "We just passed the Principalities guarding the path between Heaven and Earth. They keep demons from getting too close to home and stealing souls."

"Who guards us on Earth?" I finally get the courage to peek at the landscape we are descending toward. It's nothing but golden desert between two bodies of water; the one to our right is smaller, with some green patches and mountains around its edges. Roads wind around all of it like black spider silk. The heat from the sand rises to meet us the closer we come to the ground.

"Many of our kind roam the world to protect humanity, as it is our sworn duty above all else." Her perpetual smile wavers a bit when our eyes meet. Where was the angel meant to protect me? Whose slack cost me my life? I hope they've been dealt their punishment. I hope it's a long, arduous sentence somewhere unimaginably horrible. Should I hope that? I do anyway.

At last we land in the mouth of a cave, and all the angels file inside. Everyone, including Gabriel, folds their wings down so they disappear against their bodies and draw hoods over their heads. The Host almost look like reapers, except their robes are colors other than black and none of them have the bearing for wielding a scythe. They aren't cold and morose enough for the role to fit.

"Stay close, no matter where we are down there. If the Court finds out you're with us, they'll come straight for you." Gabriel lets me down but keeps one hand on my shoulder so I don't wander away by accident.

"They'll have to get through us to get to her, and the lesser ones aren't usually that stupid." Michael draws his sword, and the blade springs to life with flames that illuminate every inch of the cave. Surprisingly, it doesn't give off any heat even in such close quarters, but then again that's not regular fire. Holy fire, I suspect, only burns unholy things, and as far as I'm aware I don't fall under that category.

"It's not the little ones we need to be concerned about." Auriel whispers, "Beatriz could kill some of the little ones with one hand and both eyes shut."

Glad somebody has faith in me.

"Considering we aren't bursting through the front gates and announcing our presence to the entire realm, I doubt the Court will give us their full attention until we're on the way out again." Raphael predicts that, since we're taking one of the many unguarded side doors, we may make it to our destination mostly unscathed, but Jophiel advises us not to hold our breath on that. They could ambush us at any given moment from the time we cross from this world until the time we slam the Pearly Gates closed behind us. They're more than willing to play dirty.

"So how far down do we have to go?" I can't claim any familiarity with Hell's geography, so it can't hurt to ask. "I know you said the very bottom level, but how many are above it?"

Cassiel trots up from the back of the group, ever the walking encyclopedia. "There are nine levels in total. We'll be skipping Limbo coming this way; that's where other deities claim their virtuous followers. All of the wicked ones end up in one of the other eight realms, but each religion's afterlife is a bit different for its more honorable supporters." He describes the rest in the order we'll be going through—or skipping because we're taking a shortcut—and who goes to which layer.

Limbo, while mostly blank, usually appears to those within it in a way they associate with traveling between places. The most common fronts are crossroads, train or bus stations, or a hallway full of doors.

"Wait . . . that's not Purgatory?" Cassiel stops to ask what I mean. "The doors. When I woke up dead, I saw a line of doors, and Azrael told me that we were in Purgatory."

"Well, he wasn't technically lying that time. Purgatory is what lies outside that transitory area. Celestials use that space to travel rather than disturb the humans in Limbo with their presence." That's unfortunate for me then. If someone else had come along while we were wandering, maybe none of this would have happened . . . or he could've twisted that encounter even further to gain my trust faster.

Carnum, the second layer, is meant to punish those with too much lust in their hearts. Not just physical desire either, because lust for excessive power is on the same level as being a creep. In fact, the two usually coexist within the same person, which earns them a one-way ticket to this circle of the underworld regardless of which one is more prominent. I find the punishment—endless gusts of gale-force winds—a bit unusual, but Cassiel explains that it takes away their control of their movements and interactions with others, just as they would their victims. They have no way to influence their environment, so they get tossed around like ragdolls in a dryer, knocking into the other condemned and the cavernous room around them.

Prince Veraine, one of the Court members, is the only one immune to the wind, and he takes advantage of this by using the humans as target practice for his bow and arrow. We'll also be skipping that layer, however, given how difficult it is to travel through there without getting swept up ourselves or literally running into someone. Or impaled.

I wonder if a lust for revenge counts? Or would that fall under wrath instead? "So, even if you're innocent of that sin, the levels can affect you?" Talking in a whisper is made more difficult by the wind whipping on the other side of the cave wall, but no one in the group seems inclined to speak much louder.

Raphael leans in, his eyes full of regret. "No one is completely free of faults, Beatriz. This place is designed to find even the tiniest crack in your virtue and punish you for faltering."

"Everyone suffers here." Michael adds, "Even the Court are tormented by their sins."

The third level is Maxxhim, the level for gluttony. People who live lavishly with no thought for those less fortunate, who go out of their way to avoid charity and generosity and instead gorge themselves while others starve, are forced to live like neglected hogs. As in, they spend their days up to their waists in murky, sludgy water and being pelted by unending rain that stings straight through clothes, no matter how thick the fabric.

A small path winds through the middle of it, which is the way we trudge along for what seems like hours, lined with souls desperate for solid ground. But every time they get hold of a sturdy rock or root, it crumbles in their hands and they slip back into the muck.

They have to fight for every scrap of everything needed to survive, and not just with each other either; Michael warns me that this is the realm of the eldest of the Court, Prince Ezael, and that we must avoid coming into contact with him at all costs. His favorite pastime is personally hunting the damned in this level for sport, second only to sending his minions out to do it while he watches. He will think nothing of picking us off one by one like a wolf stealing sheep; I'm skeptical that one demon, no matter how powerful, could take out all six of my guardians alone, but they all assure me that he would try. My hand hovers closer to the dagger at my hip the longer we stay.

Little relief comes when we reach the fourth layer, Toman. The name of its sin rings a bell for some reason, though where I've heard it before eludes me. It shares some similarities with the one above it: greed and gluttony are not so different in their self-ishness, but here greed is more about material wealth than neces-sities. The people here were known for hoarding and spending wealth that didn't belong to them in the first place. Embezzlers in big companies, heads of nonprofits who lined their pockets instead of the fundraisers, even religious leaders who misused their churches' tithings have their place in line here.

Though wrapped closely in Gabriel's cloak, I can still see an arena to our left where a horde of demons stands. I can't hear anything except their wild screeching and the braying of some beast meant to resemble a horse. Calling it one would be a bit of a stretch. On the opposite end of the stadium stands another such creature, and both have a person strapped to their back with a jousting pole angling up from their hips. Gabriel didn't let me watch them collide in the middle, but the agonized screams and the demons' cheers assaulted my ears until we were well out of sight.

"Who runs that circle?" I ask her once the noise dies away. "I've heard of Toman before, sort of, but I can't remember where." It sounds stupid, but are my old memories pushing out my newer ones as they come back? Or did my memories being wiped have an unforeseen effect on making and keeping them? I don't know who to ask, or if anyone here could fix that if it were the case . . . or what to do if it's irreparable.

"Mammon is lord there, though I'd hardly call him a ruler the way the rest of the Court bullies him." she replies, though there is no sympathy for the demon in her voice. "He doesn't help his siblings when he has the choice, but he doesn't stop them either."

Could he be the demon that collected that horrid woman at the prison?

"I think I've seen him before with Gr—" I stop myself. "Azrael."

"Did he see you?"

I nod, and every angel tenses noticeably. "We have even less time than I thought." Michael's stride grows longer, and the rest of us have to jog to keep up, especially me. "If they know that one of the vessels was with Azrael, then they know we were scrambling around until now. We have to get—" He doesn't quite finish his sentence before an axe comes sailing through an opening in the wall, lodging itself barely an inch in front of his face. The whole group dives into the shadows to avoid being spotted, while he prepares to smite anyone that follows the weapon out.

We are passing by Aceteram, the punishment for the wrathful dead, when all six angels visibly tense and huddle even closer around me. Cassiel's description never rises above a whisper while we stand outside its borders. Aceteram is what most people imagine all of Hell to be—medieval torture devices interspersed across a battlefield, for lack of a better word. Demons personally torment everyone in whatever sick, twisted ways they can imagine for all of eternity, and if they're feeling particularly adventurous that day, they hold gladiator battles in the center. But, as with most of the other realms, the humans aren't only fighting among themselves: they have to fight the demons one on one. Occasionally it's a team effort, and all the humans get to take on all the demons in trench warfare, but it's usually an "everyone for themselves" situation. When the beasts are done for the time being, everyone's wounds will heal, and they will have precious seconds of peace . . . which only makes the rest of it worse.

Worst of all is when Princess Berith gets personally involved. She's a special kind of deranged, which is a feat when you're comparing the greater demons. She beats up her siblings, underlings, any human unfortunate enough to fall in her line of vision, even inanimate objects aren't safe from her frequent bouts of irritability. And she makes sure to sniff out her victim's most vulnerable pressure points and strike with all her wicked might, round after round, until there's nothing left to torture.

And I really hope she's not the one that threw the axe.

CHAPTER NINE

A PRISONER IN JUDECCAN

Knights and Imps are seldom a welcome sight. Imps are a nuisance of the highest order, and Knights are overpowered yes-men. However, judging by the devious look upon Moloch's face as he approaches, I deduce he has more than some petty errand to bring to Ezael. The eldest Prince leers past my cage at the henchmen approaching. "Come now, Knight, you mustn't hide your joyous news! Do tell the group what brings you to this lowly place in such good spirits."

They bow before the smaller creature steps closer, an equally hideous grin stretched across its features. "My lord, word has reached us from the Gorgons that guard the Black Gate . . . The girl Azrael stole has escaped from him."

"The vessel girl?" He twists his dagger into my side while he contemplates this revelation. They long to hear my cries of agony, so I remain silent.

Moloch nods in assent, confirming my tentative hope for the long-awaited Armageddon. If the Lines are back in play, as I suspected not so long ago with Mammon's appearance, that means things are back on track. The world is closer to its proper state. "Apparently, she discovered his treachery, and it quite enraged her."

"Well, naturally. Such a betrayal would be enough to infuriate the most patient of saints, I should think." Ezael steeples his bloody fingers thoughtfully. "She would be easy to convert to our cause, would she not?"

"That's the only trouble, sir." The Imp cowers away. "That's the last we know of her. There's no knowing if the Host has found her yet."

"I see." This is, unfortunately, true. She could be wandering the Earth to flee Azrael or in the clutches of any number of demons or other creatures. "Moloch, send the other Knights to inform my dear siblings of this news and bid them join me in the throne room. A meeting is in order, I suppose."

He withdraws his knife and leaves with a maniacal chuckle.

I am left to pray in deafening silence.

BEATRIZ

I can see a reflection in Michael's eyes as a demon approaches the hole in the wall; she's about his height with short-cropped black hair and jagged horns in place of a halo. Faint outlines of scars crisscross her face, and she looks ready to add more to her collection. Gabriel pulls me tighter against herself the closer the Princess gets. If she has to, she'll be ready to snatch me up and flee down the hall before Berith even realizes we're there, but Michael is clearly itching to decapitate this particular demon. She must be formidable for him to be so worried.

"On my signal, run and do not stop until you find Lucifer. Do not wait for me."

"But Michael—"

No one else objects when his eyes flash blue like the sea struck by lightning.

The shadow against the wall grows larger as the seconds creep by, flickering by the light of his sword. Her voice echoes down the hall around us with a demented snarl, "Oh, this poor wall . . . I meant to embed it in a good, sturdy ribcage. Guess I need some more target practice." Her gnarled hand reaches through the crevasse only inches from Michael's shoulder and almost connects with the hilt of her weapon until another demon calls to her out of sight.

"Madame! Lord Ezael has requested an audience with the rest of the Court." It bows to her briefly, then gestures toward the other side of the cave. I hear one of the angels whisper the name Abaddon.

She turns away from the axe, exposing her wasp-like wings to the corridor where we stand. "What does he want? I'm busy *not* being ordered around."

"It's about the vessels, milady. It's time to start searching fo—"

Berith reaches back at an unnatural angle, jerks the axe out of the wall, and coldly impales the demon next to Abaddon before he can continue its explanation. I can hear her shrug without watching her shadow, and I can hear the demon gurgling without seeing the blood soaking the floor. "Much better."

We don't dare breathe the sigh of relief we've been holding, not even when she's gone. We just run, or at least the angels do; Gabriel returns me to her arms and won't let go.

Verbin, the realm of Prince Asmodeis, sweeps by in a wall of fire that turns the inside of the cloak into a roasting pot.

If I were alive, I'd be dripping sweat and on the verge of a heat stroke; even now I'm lightheaded and queasy. His is the punishment for sacrilege: blaspheming against one's religion by violating its rules or by using your religion to persecute others for not following it of their own free will. Most, if not all, faiths have rules against that, whether all their followers acknowledge that or not, and the penalty for disregarding these rules is to burn at the stake as a heretic. The gods despise nothing more than humans befouling their names with their own hate.

Below that is Bellum, a world for the slothful and unmotivated. The ones who sit by and watch while evil occurs and do nothing, say nothing, are the ones who end up here. Here in this barren geyser field they don't have that option. There is no shelter from the constant onslaught of scalding lava and assault from demons sent by Princess Astaroth. Not that she actually does anything else to actively rule her domain, being the laziest thing to ever plague the Earth. If she could find a way to have a lackey breathe for her, she would do it in a rotten heartbeat. It sounds like we could walk right by her and she wouldn't even glance our way if we weren't already in her line of vision.

Next to last is Dulentan, the kingdom of another Princess, the demon of envy and waste. It reminds me of a hospital hallway, all sharp angles and being lost no matter which way you turn. There's no one here that I can see, but it feels like every wrong thing I've ever done is creeping up behind me. Merihem's realm is inhabited by the most corrupt of liars and the biggest backstabbers to ever live, up to and including the demoness herself. Her army of Imps torment the souls by poking and prodding at their minds until they find their worst betrayal, and then the demons repeat this lie until it drives the human mad.

Their ruler spends most of her time in the human world, however, spreading her own lies that sow the seeds of jealousy and carelessness; she convinces people that their friends all secretly hate them and that one little cigarette on the ground won't really hurt anything. She's laid waste to entire empires with a single rumor and has a pretty big hand in spreading epidemics all over the globe. Her goal is to spread the most discord and sabotage the deepest relationships, and she's damn good at it.

She's the one who drove me and Azrael apart, after all. If not for her attack at the hospital, he may have never uttered my real name and set me free.

No one specific rules over our final destination, given that it's apparently the worst of the nine circles, and none of them wanted to be stuck down there indefinitely . . . although with the family dynamic of the Court, they'd all fit right in in Judeccan. The final level of Hell is reserved for the treasonous type, that is, the ones who overthrow fair systems in favor of one that embodies their personal interests. Those who betray their loved ones, their homelands, their morals for material gain or political power find themselves here, encased in impenetrable ice. No one who has been sent here has ever escaped their own personal iceberg, much less the whole level.

And yet here we are with no ice pick and no idea where our angel icicle is.

The place doesn't seem all that big now that we're staggering across the slippery road right down the middle of it, but there's no way to gauge how deep the icy lake runs or how thick the glaciers along the walls are. Being the first one to ever get sent down here, Lucifer could be at the very bottom of the very bottom. They could've moved him to another level, and knowing the way the rest of this fiasco has gone, he'd be in one we skipped over. He may be dead by now, if the Court knew we were coming after him far enough in advance, or he could have escaped on his own and fled to Earth.

"Fan out so we can cover more ground, but don't lose sight of each other." Michael urges the others into a line so that they are only a wingspan apart. "It's easy to get disoriented in a place like this."

"Or eaten," I mutter as Gabriel sets me down. While there are no *visible* demons, that doesn't mean there are *no* demons at all. Come to think of it, the levels after Berith's were too empty for my liking, excluding the condemned. As fearsome and terrible as the Court has a reputation for being, I would've thought we'd run into at least some of them head-on, rather than narrowly missing just the one, especially if they were anticipating our arrival. None of their goons gave us any trouble either, which is equally convenient and troubling.

But maybe I'm just being paranoid. If none of the big demons want to be in Judeccan, the little ones probably don't either. And they could be more scared of fighting the angels than the angels are of being attacked by them, even with us being vastly outnumbered and on their home turf. That thought crosses my mind about the same time that a contradiction appears on the horizon. Several large contradictions, actually.

MUERTE

"I did as you asked." Every instinct within me screamed not to come back and warn him, but my anger compelled me to gloat. The High Reaper's comeuppance was nigh, and I had been right all along, though that fact did little to satisfy me given the details. One of our own had thrown a wrench into the universe's cogs and gears, betrayed us all. But most importantly, he betrayed the trust of an innocent girl, and for what? Though his actions were abundantly clear, his motives remain mysterious to me. More digging must be done before our master can be laid in his waiting grave. Few, I suspect, will mourn him.

He stands at the crossroads where Beatriz and I waited for him, unknowingly mere yards away from his deceit, burying a small pouch in the fork in the path. "And did she take it?"

"No. She left the bag and its contents in her bedroom and vanished soon after."

"Vanished?" Any alarm or concern in his tone rings false to my ears. He will garner no sympathy from anyone beyond himself after these revelations.

"She's where she belongs now, no thanks to you." Eons ago I never would've dreamed of raising my voice in this context, but that was before he discarded his sacred duty for selfish impulses. "As you will be in your due time. I know what you did to her."

"No." The High Reaper turns slowly as he rises to stand and returns his scythe to his grasp. He looms over me, thinking this will wither my resolve and send me cowering into the bushes like a frightened hare. He is wrong. Though terror races through every pore, I will not bow to him now or ever again. "You know what you have been told, just as Beatriz does. Neither of you know the full lengths to which I have gone in order to save us all."

"Save us? Are you mad?" If I didn't fear dying before revealing the full truth to my brethren, I'd strike him down where he stands. "What is it you think you saved us from by murdering that poor girl?"

In the distance, several angels materialize and march toward us from the depths of the forest. Like us lesser reapers, all the lesser angels of the same type tend to look alike, so there's no way to know if these are the same ones she and I spoke to earlier or if those sent for reinforcements. Not that it matters; I'm not the one they're hunting.

Disgraceful Death glances back at them and sighs, "The truth. It will bring more despair

than any lie ever could."

BEATRIZ

"Uh . . . I hope nobody had their hopes up just yet."

The entire line of angels halts in place, and at least half of them do double-takes toward the wall that now swarms with demons. Just below the din of insect hissing comes the clanking of armor, and through the same hole in the wall comes an endless stream of hobgoblins in mismatched armor. They trample unflinchingly through the field of ice, over frozen stalagmites and any body parts poking out of the snow. At least I think it's snow. Rather not ask and be proven wrong.

"The Court knows we're here." Michael's sword flares even brighter, sending the demons reeling back in fear. They aren't brave enough to attack us directly yet. There are caves and ledges all around us, but none of us are stupid enough to dive into one we can't see the back of.

"Follow me, we'll find a stronghold and fight them off as long as we can!"

"What about Lucifer?" My voice echoes a bit, but it's still difficult to hear over the ruckus heading our way. We've seen no sign of him since we arrived, and our time to search just got sliced down to mere minutes, if it's even that much now. The poor angels just finished one endless search for me, and now we're all trudging along on another.

"We'll have to split up to find him." Jophiel aims her mirror at the advancing line to distract them. Apparently, it shows prophecies to whoever looks at their reflection, and it's been known to drive some people insane with its knowledge. "Gabriel, take Cassiel and Raphael and sweep around behind us. The rest of us will fight them off."

"What about Beatriz? She won't be safe in either group."

Bit late for that sentiment, but there's a smarter option than standing behind Auriel's leg and throwing snowballs at demons. "You have healing powers, right Raphael?"

"Well, yes . . ."

"Then I'm coming with you." None of the search party objects, and soon we're slipping across the hellish tundra, desperately calling for Lucifer like shepherds seeking a missing lamb. If he's calling back, I can't hear him over the wailing souls we're weaving between and the clamor of battle to our backs. A few of the humans try to grab at the hem of my dress, but their arms are so cold that they snap like glass at the slightest movement and skitter away across the ice. Their voices are just as fragile, breaking off at random as they take harsh gasps of the burning-cold air around them; no one voice is distinguishable from the rest, but many of them are repeating the same things to people who aren't there.

"I did it for you!"

"It was the only way . . ."

"I would never betray you like that."

"You don't understand, it was for the best and—"

I kick that one's grasp away a bit harder than the others. I've heard this tune recently, and I don't care for the song and dance that goes with it. If their apologies and excuses were genuine, they wouldn't be here in the first place. Same goes for Azrael. If he had only been honest from the beginning, we wouldn't be tromping through this blizzard. I could still be lounging in my windowsill, journal filled to the last pages and shelf of treasures freshly dusted . . .

Well, actually no.

You don't share a home with the one who stole you away from yours over little more than a grudge. If he had told me the truth from the beginning, the whole truth of what happened to me and why, I would've come to the angels sooner. I would've fled at the sight of him, straight into the arms of whoever could keep him away from me. If it were all up to me, honestly, I'd trade him for Lucifer so that we could get out of here faster. It would serve him right to spend a few centuries wallowing in the consequences of tampering with my fate. If I were feeling especially spiteful about it, I would throw him into the horde that's chasing us to knock them off our trail.

A few stray demons find their way to us, and snowballs are just as ineffective as I feared. Raphael's staff works better to knock them around with, but not quite so well as Gabriel's trumpet. I thought it was loud from a few clouds away, but from only ten feet away I don't hear it so much as feel every cell—do ghosts have cells?—vibrate at the same frequency as the note she blasts over everything else around us. The demons directly in the path of the soundwave disintegrate to ash that tarnishes the snowy ground with red specks, but those to the sides sink to their knees in agony. I can't help but wonder if it's the frequency or her divinity that wounds them. I'll ask her later when we're not neck deep in living Halloween decorations.

My frantic search is abruptly derailed by one of the nasty Imps wheeling around the corner like a deranged racehorse; it collides with me at full speed, and we both slam into an ice shelf. The top crumbles above us, and I come to just in time to roll out of its way and watch the demon get flattened. The impact shoots me forward faster than my feet can move, and the floor embraces me once again. This time, however, my head connects with metal rather than ice, and the sound echoes like I'm standing inside a cathedral bell. "¡Ay! Right in the *cabeza . . .*"

My temple just missed the corner of this huge thing, which would've left me a cold lump on the ground ripe for the demons' picking. The strip of metal stretches out longer than I am tall in the opposite direction, and bars rise out of it every few inches; it's a cage, out here all by itself.

Wait.

I scramble to my feet, using the bars to steady myself on the slippery ground, and press my face eagerly into the cracks between them. But between the miles-thick ice and lack of natural light, my eyes can't make out any distinct shapes. This cage could be empty, and I could be getting excited for nothing. But I don't see any more cages nearby, so this must be somebody high profile who the Court doesn't want running around or buried where they can't reach.

"Lucifer?" Against my better judgment—I don't know how good demons' hearing is—I call into the shadows and hope to spy a loose feather or the hem of a robe the harder I stare. "You in there? Hello?"

Nothing, except the whisper of movement.

Fabric scrubbing across itself slowly.

Maybe a wheezing breath.

"Hey, I'm here with the angels." I lean as far as I can into the cage without getting stuck, "We're here to set you free . . . somehow." The door mocks me from the farthest corner with an iced-shut lock well above my head and no key in sight. There's no way for my scrawny arms to shake it from the hinges either, and the bars are too close together for either of us to slip through.

Scraping against the metal floor.

A soft thud, like a dropped apple.

The beginning of a pained sigh.

"Can you hear me? Say something back if you can . . . c'mon." Part of me wants to stick my arm into the cage to beckon him like a stray cat, but the rest of me acknowledges the lack of visibility and keeps my fingers firmly wrapped around the bars. "Please don't die on me, okay? Not after we came all the—"

An icicle sails past so close to my ear I can hear it sing like a missile, and it impales a demon trying to slink up behind me. It is followed by a voice as soft and low as autumn fog. When I turn to find its source, the eyes staring back are a more vibrant shade of scarlet than changing leaves could ever compare to, "Practice what you preach, little one."

CHAPTER TEN

BEATRIZ

"Lucifer?" The outline of his form is still barely visible within the cage, but now that he's sitting up, some details are easier to make out: a gaunt frame that puts Azrael's to shame, matted blond hair down to his shoulders, scars covering the left side of his face. Blood seeping down his ribs. But he's still so . . . pretty, like a marble statue come to life and swathed in stained-glass colors. He can hardly hold himself up from the looks of it, but he had enough strength to help me just then. "How bad are you hurt? Can you walk or fly or . . . ?"

"Not likely." He manages to crawl to the bars, but that takes most of any energy he may have stored up. His fingers fail to clasp around the bars, so they brush mine several times. None of the Heavenly warmth his siblings possess is left in his skin. He pulls a tattered cloak of slate-colored feathers around himself but continues to shiver nonetheless. "I hope my brethren didn't let you look for me alone . . . let's just say it was lucky I found that icicle a moment ago."

"I-I wasn't alone until just now. We got separated by these demons and—"

"Beatriz!"

"Where are you? Beatriz!"

"Oh!" I've been so absorbed in finding this angel that I didn't hear the others calling for me. Given the cold silence that's taken over, it seems the battle has died away, leaving only the Host's voices echoing off the ice and Lucifer's ragged breathing. His eyes track the sound of his siblings' voices as they approach, though he can barely keep them open for more than a few seconds. He's wasting away with every breath; if we'd gotten here a minute later than we did, it would be too late. It may still be. "Michael, we're over here, hurry! Over the ridge!"

Their armor rattles harder as the beat of their wings picks up speed and their voices grow louder and more desperate the closer they get to us. Gabriel is the first to crest the hill and the first to see our rattled expressions. She can't quite decide who to scoop up into her arms first, me or her long-lost brother, but the bars still stand in her way, so she settles for taking his hand.

"Oh, thank goodness, both of you are alright!"

I shake my head as best I can without snagging my hair in her plate armor while crushed against her. "He's not alright, look at him." She's so shocked that wriggling out of her grip is easier than I thought it would be. "We have to open the cage and get him home now, before somebody bigger than those ugly *pendejos* shows up."

"Somebody bigger won't be far behind. They usually send the Imps ahead of the stronger soldiers to wear down their enemies," Raphael says as he inspects the door for a way in. There has to be a weak point in the cage somewhere; even I know metal and cold don't mix well for long in Hell or elsewhere. He, Michael, and Cassiel set to work prying at the bars at random points with their hands—I hadn't even considered supernatural strength might be necessary—and Gabriel, Auriel, and Jophiel form a guard line facing the way we came in. I assign myself the job of making sure Lucifer doesn't keel over before we can free him.

He finds my willing proximity to him quite amusing. "Considering my reputation, I'm surprised at you, Beatriz." He wheezes my name; it sounds too much like the first time I spoke post-mortem. "Most humans wouldn't set foot over that hill if they knew who lay at the bottom."

"Yeah well . . . after spending the past twenty years with the Grim Reaper, I'm not easy to spook." I shrug, leaving out how fascinated I actually am with my current company. Cassiel filled me in on details of this horrible place and the members of the Court, but the Host still mystifies me. Sure, Azrael told me a bit about them, but only enough to make me more curious, and he wasn't the most reliable narrator. I understand some of their jobs, but I know only what I've seen in the past few hours about the majority of them. I didn't even know Jophiel, Cassiel, and Auriel existed until today. And everything I know about Lucifer is up in the air now that he's right in front of me, from the story of the Fall to his appearance. There's so much to ask, so much to observe, and no way to know how much time I have to do so or how to begin. Or where. Or with whom.

He tries to laugh, but there's too much pain to mask, and it becomes a cough instead. "Azrael is hardly . . . awe-inspiring company. All he does is tote souls about and grumble about overpopulation."

"You forgot about The Balance. We must uphold The Balance," Auriel grumbles under her breath. "As if he truly cares about maintaining equilibrium. He wouldn't know balance if it bit h—"

"Shh, if you say that too loudly . . . he'll show up." Lucifer grins drowsily, his eyes fluttering shut. "Speak of the Devil and all, you know." A groan sweeps through his siblings, accompanied by several eye rolls.

"If Azrael dares show his face in my presence," Michael grunts through the fruitless clang of his sword against the cage bars, "I will use his crooked, knobby head as a crowbar and then as a battering ram if necessary."

"Temper, temper, brother."

The eldest Archangel gestures to me, clearly in no mood to bicker with his captive brother. "Ask her then! We would've been here two decades ago if not for the Reaper's shenanigans."

Lucifer jolts with his last shreds of energy at the mention of the chosen families. "Oh, Michael, you didn't. You didn't bring a Line into enemy territory! Right under Ezael's nose!"

"If it helps, I'm already dead."

"It doesn't really," Raphael interjects, his staff bent so drastically I'm afraid it might snap in two. "Do you think the rest of these pitiful wretches are alive?"

He has a point to which I have no solid rebuttal. Fates worse than being stuck between life and death exist, if the circles we've passed through and the temperaments of the Court members are any indication. I'd prefer to avoid spending eternity locked in a frigid cage or being the bait dog in a demon fight. No matter what my, albeit missing, coin says about my afterlife, any one of the Princes or one of their cronies could swoop in and carry me away to whatever sick torture they're in the mood for today. The angels would have to choose between rescuing their wounded brother or hunting me down again, and I don't want them to have to make that decision.

Michael drives his sword into the snow in frustration, and its flames burn a circle around the hole. "This isn't working! At this rate we'll have to take the blasted cage out with us as well." Of course when he tries that approach, the cage won't budge from the ground either, no matter how many of them try to lift it. That would be too easy.

"Wait, let me try something . . ." There's no guarantee the same principles apply down here, but maybe if I can get through a locked door at home, I can find a way through this one. "Somebody lift me up to the lock. I can't reach it." Michael tosses his irritation aside to hoist me onto his shoulders and stands just beneath the lock.

"I suppose you can't do any worse than the rest of us," he huffs, "but what exactly do you have in mind?"

Rather than explaining, I press my hands against the metal until they sink into the mechanisms. It's the same as walking into the wall, except this time I'm feeling for the lock's pins instead of trying to pass through without disturbing anything. With the tips of my fingers, I move each one until it clicks into place and then turn a lever to release the lock. The door swings open and catches on the toes of Michael's boots.

"She did it!" Cassiel congratulates me from above, where he was trying to pry the top off the cage. Michael lets me down gently before nearly crushing me in a hug. He didn't strike me as a hugger, but I'm not complaining.

Raphael darts inside to assess Lucifer's condition more closely; the tip of his staff ignites, illuminating the hollows under his brother's eyes, the rib bones protruding from the tears in his clothes, and the clouds of his shaky breath. He can barely turn his head to look at the other angel, but when he does put his back to the bars, I notice something that should've clued me in to how horrible a state he's in.

His halo is gone.

All six of the others have luminous rings around the backs of their heads like Derby hats that fan out to frame their faces. They're not blindingly bright, but they give off enough light to see by, and Lucifer's is completely gone. Not even a stump or fragment emerges from the knots of his hair. No wonder I couldn't see him at first . . .

"How bad is it? Can you stand at all?" Cassiel peers in anxiously, no more than three steps inside the door. He barely meets Lucifer's eyes, not as if he's afraid of him, but more like a bashful child hiding behind a parent. He wants to reach out and comfort his brother, but maybe they weren't well acquainted before Lucifer was cast down.

"I think you're big enough to carry me now, Cass," he grunts as Raphael hoists him to his feet. Every bit of his weight leans on the other angel, and he staggers like a newborn fawn. Watching his stiff movements brings back memories of every pain and ache I've ever experienced and multiplies them infinitely. Angels are much harder to wound than humans, so the torment he's gone through had to be beyond mortal comprehension to leave him this way.

This is no joyous scene of reunion and triumph. We were only moments away from a funeral procession back to Heaven. And just when I thought my heart couldn't break any further for my new companions, Michael comes face to face with his forsaken brother for the first time in eons.

"Hello, Michael." The wind's howling almost drowns out the quiet greeting. "I wondered if you'd forgotten me down here. You didn't visit or write, you know."

"I know." Silent tears had been falling from his eyes for some time now, but Lucifer managed to hold his in until they were within arm's reach. The moment Michael speaks, both begin weeping openly. I'm afraid that Michael will crush Lucifer in the embrace they share, but it doesn't last long enough. The second wave of demons makes their presence known the second Lucifer's foot sinks into the snow.

Gabriel comes sprinting toward us, her sisters in tow, all of them frantic with the news of the approaching horde. "Knights! Four of the Knights and their underlings are approaching!"

"Which ones? Can you see their faces?" Michael shifts Lucifer back to the other two angels and mounts the hill just enough to peek over it.

"Does it matter?!" I squeak, in no hurry to deal with anything ranked above the last batch that attacked us. "We don't have time to stay and fight them, not with Lucifer hurt and me underfoot."

Michael snarls out of frustration and agreement, then motions for us to gather around him to strategize. "I see Belphegor, Samael, Abaddon, and Azazel at the end of the road, so the other four must be somewhere above. They mean to flank and overwhelm us."

"Gabriel, call down your chariot. Lucifer, Beatriz, and Raphael will ride inside and guard each other as we flee. Raphael can begin the healing process on the way home and provide them some defense should the rest of us fail." Michael's sword, of which the flame had petered out after being left in the ground, suddenly roars back to a handheld inferno. "We'll hold this position until it arrives. Take out however many come into range. We all need the practice."

"And they need a smaller army."

Everyone agrees wholeheartedly, but only a few of us have positions to take up to thin out their numbers. Gabriel mounts the highest point in our area and sounds a high trill on her horn that sounds like *Come here, come here, come here.*

Raphael remains at Lucifer's side with me while the others form a barrier around us; Cassiel stands the closest and is the only one without a weapon of his own. I expected him to act as an assistant healer or have something stashed in his bag to attack with, but he spends several minutes searching for a rock or chunk of ice he can hurl at an attacker should one break the line. When he finds nothing, Lucifer calls to him with a little more strength now. "My shield is at the back of the cage, on the ground outside. The whip should be under it." His brother scrambles for it before the demons get any closer.

"Give Beatriz the shield," Raphael suggests. "Hopefully they won't hit it hard enough to knock her backward."

"Hopefully, they won't hit it at all," I correct him. "Will I even be able to hold i—?" The question doesn't end before I find myself bearing a gold shield that stands nearly as tall as me. Thankfully, it isn't as heavy as I feared, but the unexpected weight catches me off guard and I stumble a few steps before regaining my footing.

The rest of the Host disappears from sight but not sound; their battle cries crash against the demon's howls, making for an ear-shattering din. Whole infantry lines fall before the angels, but more pour in by the minute to replace them. None have gotten past Cassiel and Auriel at the back yet. Still, I shiver as fight or flight wages a smaller battle inside my head. I don't know where I would run to escape this mess, but I do know I don't want to abandon those around me. I know they wouldn't forsake me. They care, even if it's not really their choice. They have to protect me. It's better than pretending to care when you do have a choice, right?

"Cuts quite the dashing figure, doesn't she?" Lucifer teases. "You didn't give her any fledgling armor at least? I hardly think a sundress will save her skin should a Knight find us."

"We left in a hurry. And this was Michael's bright idea, so take it up with him."

"Who knows . . ." I put my back to the two Archangels and peek over the shield, one hand on its grips and the other hovering by the hilt of my dagger. "Maybe they'll be so surprised I'm here that they'll keel over from shock and I won't have to fight anybody." Lucifer manages a real laugh this time, but he's still far too weak to get himself home. Gabriel's chariot sure is taking its sweet time to get here . . .

Of course, the demons it plows over probably beg to differ.

Just as one of the Knights—Raphael informs me it's Samael, judging by her fox-like features—meets with her reflection in Jophiel's mirror, the chariot comes careening up the road. Demons fall in its wake like tulips in the path of a runaway lawnmower. Those not directly in its way stop and watch in horror as their comrades get turned into infernal roadkill. As the chariot speeds closer, the angels fall back to follow it, leaving confused and flattened demons behind them. I don't even have the forethought to try and protect us from a hit-and-run with the shield, but luckily Gabriel gives one short whistle and our ride whips around us, stopping just close enough to load Lucifer in without jostling him too much. The chariot could fit all eight of us if necessary, but since we'll have six guards, there's enough room to lay him flat and give Raphael space to move around him.

There are not, however, any seatbelts or handles to latch on to, and I doubt the tailgate will hold all three of us if the chariot break-checks a demon or takes a curve too sharply.

"Y'know, on second thought, I think I'll walk back . . ."

"And be eaten by hellhounds? I think not." Raphael helps lift me over the high step into the bed of the chariot. "Sit with your back to the wall at the far end, I'm going to lay him down in the middle."

I scoot as far back as I can; Lucifer's head ends up resting against my knees, with the shadow of the shield covering his face. Like Michael's, his eyes glow an unearthly hue, but the one under the scars is duller than the other. Did the Court do that to him, or did those marks come from a battle before he Fell? Will Raphael heal those too, or is it too late to remove them?

He glances up at me, upside down, just as the cart lurches forward and upward. "For a human in such unusual circumstances, you certainly are quiet. I know better than most how curious you creatures are."

"I'm not used to having my questions answered." I prop the shield between me and the side wall and lean a little closer to him so we can hear each other over the rush of wind around us. "Azrael always lied or didn't tell me anything at all."

"And now you fear all others will do the same." He closes his eyes and sighs while Raphael busies himself healing the damage to his body. The green light from the staff swirls beneath his skin, highlighting his furrowed brows and thick lashes. It untangles the knots in his hair, turning them into gold waves that fall to his shoulders. Feathers missing along his cloak slowly regrow, and the dead ones fly out the back of the cart, leaving a gray trail in our wake. Lucifer watches them disappear and be replaced by swarms of demons pursuing us; he gives no sign that he is afraid. "Or are you fearful of what you might find out if you ask?"

"Both, I guess. The truth I found out didn't do me any favors."

"It seldom does." He gestures to the marred side of his face, which is starting to fill out a bit so he doesn't look so malnourished. "These scars and my banishment are what I got for giving the truth of good and evil to the first humans, and all their descendants inherited their suffering."

I follow his hand as it sweeps across the realm flashing by us. We're in Aceteram this time, rather than skirting around it. Lucifer flinches at every wail and crash of a weapon; he has the strength now to sit against the wall beside me, curled as far away from the hellscape as he can get. Raphael gives him a pained glance, but he shakes his head and urges him out to join the others guarding us. Demons arrive in dark waves with each passing minute, some groups so thick I can't see any light between them.

The sound of battle comes to me as if muffled by water; I am below the surface, listening but apart. The scene plays out around us in a Renaissance panorama whirling by in slow motion while we remain still. We're huddled so close that I can feel neither of us has a heartbeat; he instead gives off a hum, like the overhead lights in a hallway.

"Do you regret it?" I ask so quietly I'm not sure he hears me at first.

He doesn't turn, but he smirks as he finally answers, "Only if I think on it too long."

"I take it that's not a habit of yours?"

"Thinking? I've had nothing else to do for several millennia." He feigns offense, his smirk widening. He pulls the shield from behind me and places it in front of us facing the open back of the chariot. There isn't much fight in him yet, but there's enough "hold down the fort" that I let down my guard for a breath or two.

Then the chariot slams on the brakes just inside the next level, stopping so short it almost nosedives and flings us out. If he hadn't thrown his free arm out to catch me, I'd probably be skidding through the Pearly Gates right now.

"What in Father's name is—?!" Lucifer snarls and staggers to his feet, but he comes to a halt as quickly as the carriage did. So do the other angels hovering around us, each one wearing their own horrified expression. I dare to peek over the top and instantly regret it; between us and the only way out of Toman stand seven figures I can only assume are the Court. Mammon and Berith are fresh in my memory after our brief encounters, but the rest are only faces with no names to match. Each of them bears resemblance to a different bug, as the angels do birds, and in place of ringed halos, they sport uneven horns. Mammon and Berith look like an ant and a wasp, respectively, and down the line the others represent a fly, a mosquito, a cockroach, a termite, and a moth. The last one's wings would be beautiful if they weren't attached to such a hideously evil creature.

"We've been waiting a terribly long time to see you all again!" the termite Prince calls across the cratered wasteland, and I can feel the tension rolling off Michael. This one must be the leader, his counterpart and adversary.

"Move aside, Ezael," the eldest angel barks with a hundred times the volume of a megaphone. The walls around us drop pebbles and streams of tainted water as they tremble at his voice.

"If you interfere with our leaving, the world will be seven less of you beasts."

"Contrariwise, old friend," Ezael retorts, his tone sharp as a freshly forged knife. "If we interfere, you'll be one less human and a few less limbs." His dead-white eyes lock on to me before Lucifer can conceal me in his cloak, and he levels a twisted dagger in our direction. His family finds his threat entertaining and all raise their weapons in unison. Suddenly, the demons behind us look like a litter of kittens, Knights and all.

Lucifer's cape morphs into robin wings, and he's out of the chariot before the last feather rearranges itself. He swoops in front of the rest of our group and flares them out to their full span. Centuries of revenge have been stored away for a moment such as this, and they've all earned their own personal piece. "I will personally flay each putrid layer of your flesh from your rotted bones if you touch any of them."

If nothing else, his voice is back to full power.

"Lucifer . . . you look good for a dead dove." The roach girl coughs and sways as though she might faint, but she manages to stand upright, probably out of spite. Her voice sounds as cold and deadly as an ICU corridor, and she looks like a morgue escapee, so she must be Pestilence. She croons to me like a witch outside a gingerbread house, but the longer I look at her, the less of an appetite I have.

"So does your little friend. Pretty little birds don't last long down here."

"Cassiel, my whip."

His fingers barely close around the handle before the Court charges the Host, and I'm stuck just behind the front line.

LUCIFER

Both sides give a cry of "Take no prisoners!" and at last I have my chance to slaughter the ungrateful creatures who imprisoned me for all those years. I am the one who—inadvertently, of course—set them free with my greatest mistake, and they repaid me by dragging me through each realm and then discarding me in Judeccan when there was nothing left for them to torture. A scar for every level, a mark for every sin, and a burning hatred for each member of the Court. Yes, my brother may have cast me down, and the others may not have stopped him, but they had no hand in what came after I arrived here. They were only doling out fair punishment for what I did to humanity, not antagonizing me for sport.

My family did not break me, mend me, and then break me again.

They are all the hope I held on to for all these years, my only prayer for rescue.

And this girl of the Lines gives me hope for another chance to rule beside my siblings.

If we are this far ahead of the demons, with even just one human host, then I have faith that we will reign victorious in the end. This one is fearless, maybe foolishly so, but that fire can be tempered into skillfulness. Perhaps she is not the only one safe in Heaven's keep, but the only one brave enough to venture down into this pit. I have a good deal of catching up to do once these idiots are out of our way.

The four Knights who pursued us have caught up but choose to guard our way back rather than join the fight. Either they have indomitable faith in their masters' ability to win or they're smart enough to steer clear of us on the warpath. My bet is on the first option, as demons are far from bright regardless of rank.

"Lucifer, have you lost your mind? You're in no shape to fight!" Auriel scolds me with her foot on Mammon's throat. He does not appear pleased with their first meeting's outcome, judging by his bulging eyes and his fingers scratching frantically at her leg. He was never much of a fighter despite always being the first sent out into battle; all those years of the others whittling him down have done irreparable damage.

"The mind loss is debatable. As for the shape, you're right, but I have enough motivation to cover that, dear sister," I reply after dealing Veraine a blow to the temple, unfortunately missing both his diadem and his ridiculous horns, which would've added the desired insult to injury.

"I don't think that's how it works! In fact, I'm quite sure!"

"Oh? You don't think my beloved siblings and our new compatriot give me enough to fight for?" Beatriz's head pops up over the rim of the chariot for a second upon being mentioned, but she sees Berith turn in her direction and immediately seeks shelter once again.

"That is not my point, and you know it." Auriel kicks one demon to the side and exchanges him for his sister barreling toward the carriage. This is the most I've seen Astaroth move since the day we had the misfortune of meeting. "What good does healing you do if you run headlong into battle and get injured five minutes later?"

"It's been longer—" A wave of nausea hits me mid-sentence, one so powerful it causes my wings to stop beating, and I drop below the chariot's wheel before I can right myself. Merihem always fought dirty. She always did everything dirty, come to think of it. She is the embodiment of filth and waste, after all.

"Pity you made it all this way just to put your family in the same cage you crawled out of," she wheezes, dangling her reeking censer over my head. "We won't have enough room in Judeccan for all of you . . . perhaps we'll have to cut some of you up and feed you to the Gorgons."

"If your knives are as sharp as you all, that will take more time than you have left on this Earth, you rancid bitch." My whip coils around her throat, and with a fluid snap I send her crashing into the nearest wall. But true to her obnoxious nature, she doesn't stay down for long. "You'll be lucky if we leave anything of you behind when we're through."

A peal of her sickening laughter crosses the distance between us as she wipes the spittle from her mouth. "I am a Horseman, you winged rat. You couldn't dream of the power it would take to kill me."

"Oh, but I have dreamed of it, every night since I set foot in this accursed place." Each snap of the whip leaves a welt on her pale form, but she keeps coming toward me nonetheless. She is far too close to the chariot for my liking, given that Beatriz has only a dagger to defend herself with and no safe escape route. The Court has left her alone for the time being, but if they take enough of us down, they'll go straight for her and be gone before we can recover. Someone needs to take her to safety before the wrong side gets the upper hand.

Or before she draws too much attention to herself distracting the demons.

Berith misses a shot at Jophiel because our little cheerleader found a fragment of a javelin and threw it at her with surprising accuracy, then ducked back down before the demon saw her. It doesn't stick into her flesh or anything, but the impact is that much of a surprise. Ezael takes a rather nasty blow to the gut from Michael after a shout of "Hey, ugly!" catches his attention at the wrong time. Astaroth trips herself up trying to return insults and dodge Raphael's staff at the same time. While most of her victims are too occupied to truly retaliate, Merihem stands close enough to strike a dangerous blow if not intercepted.

Beatriz realizes this a moment too late, and she finds herself face to face with Pestilence herself. Her back is pressed against the wall of the chariot without even a breath between the two; not that she would want to breathe too deeply with that suffocating gas from the censer filling the space around her. No one, dead or alive, supernatural or mortal, is immune to the effects of whatever disease wafts from within that contraption.

But some of us have a higher tolerance for it.

As fast as my nearly withered wings will carry me, I fly to the chariot and knock the demon off her perch, which luckily sends the diffuser clattering to the ground below before the sickening mist can fully reach Beatriz. Unfortunately, it lands on the sharp edge of a discarded helmet and a crack forms in its side, thus coating the whole group in a dense fog of waste.

"Lucifer," the smallest member of our party coughs, sinking to her knees and covering her mouth with the hem of her gown. "What is that smell? I–I can't breathe."

"Stay close to the floor. It won't be as thick." As she huddles in the corner, I cover her with my cloak as well. The demons already down from their battle wounds cannot rise again to take their angel combatants with them, and the angels cannot stand another moment in order to deal the finishing blows against the demons. Now is our only chance to flee with a head start. "Michael, we have to go now, before we all perish from the gas."

"You'll never see the White Gates again!" Asmodeis shrieks between gasps of polluted air. "You won't even make it to the Black G—"

"Do shut up." Gabriel silences him with a trumpet blast as she guides the others into the chariot. Once we're clear of this fog we can retake our guard positions, but it would be far too easy to become separated with such low visibility. She warns us to hold on just as the chariot lurches forward again, flying blindly toward what we hope is the exit. There's no way to tell if the Court is pursuing us; until we reach Maxxhim, we have no way to know if we have escorts unless they attack again.

"Can we not fit down the side path in this thing?" Cassiel wobbles, the effects from the incense still lingering in his system. All his bookish wisdom and exact memories failed to protect him for the first time, and it clearly unsettled him to not have a solution.

"Too many demons block the shortcuts. The wheels would get tangled in their limbs and break." Jophiel watches our back anxiously. "We could send someone ahead to clear them out, but that would take time we may not have."

"We'll just have to take out the other four Knights and pass through the Black Gate. Most of them won't follow us past that point," Michael says.

"Moloch will try," I inform him. The Knights are bolder than my brother realizes; they may have followed rules about traversing realms many years ago, but all of Hell has grown restless in the last several years. They long for their leaders to reign over Heaven and turn Earth into an extension of their home. "Mahazael practically lives above ground, so he could be waiting on the surface rather than at the gates. As for Leviathan and Beelzebub, they will go for an ambush before the gate, without a doubt." One does not spend thousands of years around some-one else without learning their habits and personalities as well as their own.

"Be prepared for another fight, regardless of the partici-pants," Auriel grumbles, readjusting her blindfold where it ripped open. I'd forgotten the exact shade of obsidian her eyes were after all these years apart. She rarely takes the blindfold down, but that deep black is hard to forget; despite its darkness, there are still colors buried within. "Until we have passed Saint Peter's podium, we are not safe."

Tense silence falls, broken only by the perpetual storm that hovers in Maxxhim's sky. We are allowed a moment to regain our composures, to begin to feel our new aches setting in, and for me to take stock of my siblings more fully. They've all grown since I last saw them: Michael let his hair grow out, while Gabriel cut hers short; Auriel and Cassiel are no longer fledglings with down in their feathers; and Jophiel and Raphael have fully come into their unique powers.

And here I am, stuck only steps away from where I started.

I've been trapped down here for so long that I don't know who else I'm supposed to be but the rebellious prisoner. Most of my siblings won't remember me as anything but the defi-ant son who served as a lesson on disobedience. None of the humans know any different than the stories of me passed down by their ancestors, except perhaps the one with her hand ten-tatively wrapped in my cape. The demons only see me as a toy that they can torture and discard at will. I am all of the things they all think of me and yet none of them. I don't know what I should be, nor what I would rather be. I will have to decide this at some point, and it frightens me more than any other peril I have or will face in the coming days.

Beatriz notices what must be a terribly confused and pained expression on my face as we trade the rain for the gales of Carnum, and her own becomes concerned. She tugs softly at the cloak to draw my thousand-yard stare back into reality. "You okay?"

"Just ready to be home is all."

She nods, a bitter grimace forming from both the biting wind and the disappointment we both know. "Getting taken . . . or sent or whatever . . . away from all you've ever known against your will sucks. And nobody ever wants to make it easy to get back either."

"Going back after such drastic changes isn't easy, with or without help." I'm unsure of which of us I'm speaking to. "You possess knowledge no other human has ever gained, and I am Fallen. The person going back is not the one who left."

"Fallen?" she inquires. I expect she doesn't know the exact definition, although she's likely familiar with parts of the concept if she was religious at all in life.

"Stripped of my powers, basically. Much weaker than I should be."

"Will you get your power back once we're back up there?"

For that, I have no answer. Perhaps the others do, but the moment we enter the tranquil path through Limbo, they are robbed of the chance to explain. The Knights we missed in Judeccan are not the only ones standing at the Black Gates; the ones we've already fled found their way here before us.

And unless my ears deceive me, the Court is not far behind.

Beatriz quickly turns her attention to the obstacle ahead. "Uh, Gabriel? What are the odds of us jumping that line of demons in this?" There's no way around them on either side, and if we go through them at least one will find its way into the chariot with us, and it's already crowded as it is. With the aptly named Black Gates funneling us toward the Knights, we're going to have to get creative.

"Slim to none, only three of them can't fly. Cover your ears!" Already she has her horn leveled at the ones directly barring our exit, the poor bastards. They can run toward us with all their might or try to hide behind the pillars the Gorgons keep, but there is no escaping her deadly notes. Three of them are bowled over instantly, but the other four manage to hang on to the gate bars or roll themselves over faster than their kin. The louder she blasts, the faster the chariot speeds toward the door with little regard for what or whoever may be in its path. If we were to strike the wall at this pace or the gate should close, there'd be nothing left of any of us for the demons to pick apart.

Michael and Raphael lean out either side, sweeping the stragglers off their feet with staff and sword alike. Raphael nearly loses arm and all as we career through the Black Gate itself, and Michael takes a chunk of the pillar off. Jophiel shoves past our momentarily stunned brothers until she stands at the back of the carriage, her mirror aimed at our closest foes. One glance at its surface and the Court will be more concerned with its own fate than our demise for the moment. At least, the ones behind us will be.

In the heat of the moment, we all miscounted the Knights; they number one more than us, and the eighth one was missing from the assault we just barreled through. While we erroneously celebrate a clean getaway, Mahazael crawls from beneath a stone arch and snatches Beatriz into the air above us before anyone can grab her back.

"To underestimate the strength of Hell is to invite failure and death!" he jeers, dangling the poor girl by her hair in his filthy talons. He pulls her up closer, sliding his face and free hand along her skin as she squirms and shrieks. All her kicking and clawing only makes him hold tighter, lean in closer; fighting his grasp works as well as wresting yourself free from a boa constrictor. "But perhaps Lord Ezael will spare you after this pleasing offering . . ."

"Beatriz, no!" Gabriel teeters on the verge of desperate tears, her horn useless as long as she wishes no harm on the girl. Even dead, a direct blast from my sister's instrument would be incredibly painful.

"Someone strike him down!" Michael bellows, his eyes and sword aflame brighter than I've ever seen. "Rend him in two or leave nothing but ash, so long as—"

"But he'll drop her!" Raphael warns. "There has to be another way."

Panic sets in within seconds: the chariot makes an about-face to hover beneath them, but Mahazael won't stay still, and no one is bold enough to attack lest Beatriz get caught in the crossfire. If we cannot remove him from the equation, she is lost to us, but if we destroy him, she is still at risk. He may have accomplices down below as a backup should he fail to capture her.

"Michael!" Her pitiful screams of our names urge each of us to action we fear to take. "Gabriel, please! Somebody help me! Lucifer!"

Her tears catch rays of sunlight as they fall past, glittering like glass shards from a shattered church window. Her voice grows hoarse and tired, and her struggling gradually lessens until I can't tell if she's still fighting anymore. That is, until one slender hand slips free of his tail, grabs hold of her dagger, then plunges it into his writhing snake belly. He yelps but does not release her, though she twists the knife deeper into his lower gut. The blood seeping from the wound seems to spur her on, rather than repulse her to the point of relenting. Her cries for aid melt into vicious shrieks as she slashes away at her captor.

The idiot refuses to release the source of his pains, so I elect to send some encouragement of my own. "Get ready to catch" is the only notice I give my siblings before meeting the Knight midair with a flash of my whip. It snaps well above the girl's head, striking and wrapping around his serpentine face. Another swift jerk to the left loosens his grip enough that she slips through his claws and sails downward. In my haste and my siblings' scrambling, we all misjudge her trajectory, and the next thing we hear is a scream sailing by. Raphael is the first to collect himself enough to fly after her before another demon makes an appearance. She clings to him as ivy does the walls of a ruined castle, her sobs apparent even from this distance. He will bring her comfort as only he can and hopefully shield her from what's about to happen.

"Michael! Finish him while I still have a grip!" I call him to spend his mounting rage so that it doesn't consume his mind; he needs a clear head to plan our next moves upon returning home, and the thought of revenge will stand in his way. He needs to get it out of his system now.

I only hear one wingbeat before his flaming sword takes the head of the Knight from his shoulders, the wound cauterized by the holy fire. Mahazael drops into the sea without much fanfare, but that lull will not last long. For all their infighting and bickering, the demons will not tolerate strikes against their own, especially not now.

We have fired the first shot in the war.

BEATRIZ

If I never see another demon again, it'll be far too soon. And as far as I'm concerned, Raphael never has to put me down either; as long as he holds me, I don't have to worry whether what's under me is solid or about to drop away from my feet. These clouds to either side of the path look awfully transparent and sketchy, even though the dawn colors are as beautiful the second time as they were the first time I arrived at the gate. Our trek to and from Hell felt longer than only one day, but given my lack of time-sense, it could've been a whole week for all I know.

Not that it matters when it is—I'm glad to be as far away from the nine circles as I can possibly be, regardless of the date. Especially after stabbing the Knight and watching Michael and Lucifer cut him to pieces. If the other demons didn't already want our heads on spikes along their gate, they want the three of us for lawn ornaments without a doubt now. I know as angels it's part of their job to do away with creatures like that, but Michael decapitated him. Lucifer could have done it first if he'd yanked his whip a little harder. And I nearly cut his tail off.

It was so quick and without warning . . . so violent and intense. They've only just met me, and they are already willing to kill over me? For me? I'm not sure how to feel.

Am I bleeding? Is there blood on me? Or them?

My hands come away from my body clean, no matter how many times I check. Ghosts don't bleed unless they died bleeding. I guess. Raphael must've cleaned away whatever spilled on me from the knife fight.

Do demons bleed? Do angels?

There are black specks on Michael's face, but his sword burned all its evidence away. Lucifer has a black splash down his neck; his whip is already dark, so I can't tell if it's clean or not. Nothing comes off on his hands as he winds it around a loop on his belt. They all look so tired and bruised. Most are leaning on the fence to steady themselves.

"Is she hurt?" one of them asks Raphael. My mind is too loud to differentiate their voices. I think it's Lucifer, though, since he's standing closer to us.

"Doesn't look like it, but she's definitely shaken up," he says. "Mahazael dropped her from a good distance, and it wasn't a gentle descent."

Saint Peter drops his quill in shock. "One of the Knights had her?"

"Not for long," Michael assures him.

"As soon as the rest of them find the body, they'll be on the move, if they aren't already." Auriel's voice brings me back to the present as she speaks of the future. "We must begin preparations if we mean to stay ahead of the Court."

She goes on to explain, mostly to me, that while they know which Lines are eligible for this battle, they have to locate the individuals and convince them of their sacred duties before the demons find all of their humans and force them into it. The ideal outcome would be for the angels to find all seven of us and miraculously have enough time to find the other seven and hide them away to steal the Court's chance to do the same. None of them hold much hope for that to happen, nor do I. Our enemies are too crafty and underhanded to let us get away with that.

The others agree and file through the gates one by one; Lucifer is the last to cross over, and he hesitates beneath the archway. Saint Peter ushers him forward and welcomes him home, but he doesn't move until I tiptoe over behind him and peek around him as though I'm impatiently waiting in line. I almost trot in right behind him until I remember one tiny detail that might trip me up. "Hey, wait . . . did they find my coin? I can't go in without it, can I?"

"Well, you wouldn't be the first, but I'm not supposed to allow it." Saint Peter pulls something round and gold from a small satchel at his hip. "But we won't have to go that route today. One of the Malakhim found it in the strangest place . . . there was a dirt road leading to that cabin of yours and—"

"He put it at the fork, didn't he? The one that leads to the cabin or off into the woods?"

"At the exact center," he confirms, offering me the coin. "He watched them pick it up, then vanished."

I run my fingers over the letters and numbers etched into its surface, feeling the edges of my identity until I can see it in my mind, from the ornate crucifix carved into the middle to each word along the edge:

Beatriz Rose Torres

December 21, 1983

El Paraíso

And then a blank space where my death belongs.

CHAPTER ELEVEN

BEATRIZ

Um. That doesn't seem right.

"Something's wrong with it." I run my finger over the space where it should be, but there are no indications that it got scratched out or rubbed off. It's like nothing was ever there, despite the fact that I am very much dead. Did it fade off because of me not crossing over? Did my unusual death affect how my coin was made from the beginning?

"I noticed that myself when it first arrived." Saint Peter takes the coin back and examines it again. "I've never seen anything like this. Every coin is minted the moment a living being comes into existence, and both dates are present no matter how long or short the life is or how the being dies."

"Could Azrael have tampered with it somehow?" Raphael, perplexed, stands at the entrance and peers over Saint Peter's shoulder at the mystery. His siblings all shrug and shake their heads among themselves. "Is it even possible to change those coins?"

"No, reapers can't alter them." Everyone turns to me, surprised, as I explain Muerte demonstrating the indestructibility of the coins. "I've seen this before, with that girl in the hospital I was telling you about earlier. Part of her coin was blank like this too. The same part, actually."

"Perhaps it has something to do with them being vessels," Cassiel suggests. "They may have been left blank so Azrael would know to let them be, no matter what state he found them in."

"Oh yeah, he was totally gonna listen to a coin. If Merihem hadn't shown up, I probably would've gotten a new roommate that day," I retort. Azrael was fully prepared to take her until he was interrupted. And I'm quite confident that if we'd come across any other vessels, he would've spirited them away as well. His only qualm with the others would be having to kill them himself instead of calling Moloch or another Knight to do it for him.

"Does this mean the vessels cannot truly die until Armageddon is completed then?" Michael turns to Saint Peter, who can give him no answer. This is unprecedented. Unusual. Unforeseen.

Given this new development, an old concern of mine is renewed, "Will it let me in?"

No one responds except to exchange worried glances and to form a line behind the doorway. If I can't go inside, what will we do? How long will I be stuck outside like this? Jophiel tries to seek answers in her mirror—by holding it up to me despite the group's initial protests—but nothing helpful appears. Just a recap of what we already know, which she says is also suspicious.

"Only one way to find out." Lucifer offers his hand over the threshold, so I have to cross to reach him. "They let me back in, so the club isn't that exclusive."

I don't stop to wonder if he's right. One foot falls in front of the other, and in moments, the gate is at my back and I'm standing among the highest angels. We all wait for the reaction, for some unseen force to throw me backward out of his grasp and send me sailing through the clouds again, but I remain firmly planted on the edge of the golden street. A sigh of relief makes its way around the group, and then we move forward together.

"We'll give you an actual tour once we've got a plan sorted out," Cassiel says. "Right now, we need to go straight to our quarters and start discussing said strategy. I can tell you about it, though, if you like." His descriptions of Hell and explanation of the Lines filled in a lot of blanks for me, so I'm incredibly eager to hear what he has to say about his home. Ours now, I suppose, since I'm finally inside.

He begins with the White Gate—Pearly is a human-given nickname—that we just crossed through. Saint Peter has sat at his post for many centuries, verifying that each soul that passes his way is supposed to be there. Ordinary souls have one of the lesser angels escort them to their new home in the city beyond, while members of Lines get one of the Host to take them there. Demons cannot get past the gates, no matter how strong or determined they are; the gates form a barrier made of pure celestial energy that would kill them on contact. Even being close to it would be indescribably painful for a creature from Hell.

Enclosed within the heavenly wall is the City of Light, the place where the souls reside. Each family has their own little neighborhood made up of all their ancestors as far back as their name goes. Each home contains plentiful food and drink without the occupants ever having to leave; whatever they want, it will be there. Work is not required, but if one wants something to do, they are given the skills and means to do so for as long as they want. No petty discord exists here, nor sorrow nor sickness. All is well and wholesome, the epitome of peace.

"So, my parents are with the rest of my family somewhere around here?"

"Yes." Jophiel points to a fountain in the center of a town square. "A few streets down, I believe. Each square is marked by different plants, so no one gets lost while out visiting." She plucks a bright pink lily from a pot next to the road and hands it to me so I can commit the bloom to memory and find my way back.

"Some call those Surprise Lilies, others say Resurrection." Cassiel rubs the soft petals between his fingers as he walks by the terraces they're planted in. "I suppose either works. They pop up in droves in unusual places, and they come back every year."

"Surprises and resurrection. Sounds oddly familiar." I'm guessing that's why the lesser angels are hunting for my body, wherever it's been hidden. I doubt he was stupid enough to leave it at the bottom of the lake where just anybody could stumble across it. They said I needed to be buried in consecrated ground, but if I'm meant to be a vessel, it wouldn't make sense to leave me that way. Can't fight a war from six feet under.

"Father's always had a sense of humor . . ." Michael muses, chuckling a bit himself. Sounds like it's hereditary.

I wonder if it will feel different, being alive after being dead for so long. Will I feel the physical things around me the way I did before? Will my hearing or sense of smell be the same? My sight? I know I'll never think about anything or anybody the same ever again, that's for certain. Everything is so full of secrets I never would have considered, but now their possibilities are all too clear.

Beyond the edge of the City lies the home of the lower choirs of angels. There are so many of them that they do their respective jobs in shifts, taking turns resting and performing their duties. Seraphim, Dominions, and Authorities have a city of their own and live in apartments with a partner. While one recuperates, the other goes out for the day, and they trade off again that night. Malakhim all live together in a large complex like a YMCA center and go out as they are called upon. Thrones occupy an empty field and take turns relaying the prayers they receive to the Virtues, who are without a physical form. Principalities form the light barrier around Earth that we passed through, but if one is injured or worn down, it comes to Heaven to be replenished.

"What do angels do to relax? Do any of you sleep?" I ask.

"Not exactly." Lucifer speaks for the first time since we entered the gates; he's been busy silently soaking in everything around us, as a weary traveler returning home takes time to appreciate the familiar surroundings. "It's more like what humans call meditation, I would say. Not entirely awake, but not wholly unconscious either. We do get bags under our eyes if we don't rest, though," he adds, pointing at his own face. Behind the mischievous smile, the exhaustion from Hell is still apparent, and his siblings all wear a tired air to match.

"Hopefully, we'll have time to rest a bit before heading out again. We all need it," Gabriel sighs, her hand on his shoulder.

The Host also lives together in a mansion like the human souls do, though theirs is larger and does not change with their whims. They each have their own private room on one level, and above that is a conference room for making plans, a common room to simply mingle in, and access to the archives of all knowledge ever recorded. Cassiel admits he spends more time there than anywhere else and offers to bring me along any time I want. The human souls are allowed in there the same as the angels are, but their access point resembles an earthly library rather than showing its true form to them.

"Here we are, home at last." Raphael pulls open a wrought-iron gate at the end of a short walkway and ushers the rest of us in. Their home resembles a cathedral with its stained-glass windows and looming bell tower but also a palace with sprawling corridors and well-manicured gardens all along the front yard. Gabriel's chariot rests by the front staircase; it looks strange with no horses in front of it, now that I can take a better look. It doesn't even have the yoke thing to tie an animal to. Most of the outside is smooth and white, but the wheels and top and bottom edges are bright gold with wings carved into the lines.

There appears to be a guest house to the right of the manor, but so many huge, ancient trees stand guard out front that it's hard to make out many details of the structure. Or tell if anyone is inside. It's the decrepit cabin's twin, but instead of a lake view, this cottage would be in the mountains somewhere overlooking a beautiful valley. "Who lives there?" I try to peek through the branches with no luck.

"Oh, that's where Father stays when he isn't traveling on Earth or speaking with other deities on another plane."

According to Michael, the highest powers do not share a home. Each creator god or goddess has their own home realm, and any other gods in their pantheon also reside there. They will occasionally meet with one another here in the throne room atop the tower that overlooks everything; they plan the beginnings and endings of worlds, the reward and punishment for the actions of those below them. They form the gears that turn the universe and lead it down its path.

"Or poking around in Eden making sure the Twins aren't napping at the gates," Lucifer adds with a little bitterness. "I suppose I ought to tell them I'm back."

At the very edge of this world, behind a gate none may open except its two guardians, Urial and Eriel, is the fabled Garden of Eden. Since Adam and Eve were kicked out, only those two Cherubim and the animals that live there have been inside. It is the twin angels' duty to maintain the grounds and keep any wayward souls from finding their way inside before it's time. Lucifer, before he was cast down, acted as their leader and mentor, which is how he got into the Garden without raising alarms. They trusted him without question and were repaid with the worst kind of betrayal.

Maybe he isn't as misunderstood as I hoped.

"They've been asking about you," Auriel replies, hoping to offer comfort. "We aren't the only ones who missed having you here." He glances from his sister to the house next door forlornly but says nothing more and disappears into the main house. He isn't inside long before he staggers back out with a yelp of surprise. On each of his shoulders rest two angels about my size, both with their arms around him and wearing grins so big they must be painful to hold. It's a close contest of who's more astonished by this reunion, me or him.

"Captain, Captain, you're home!" the left one squeals, burying her face against his.

"We've been waiting all day for you!" Her mirror image rests his head on Lucifer's shoulder, and the shock finally disappears from his face.

"Awfully kind of Peter to save me the trip." He smiles softly and embraces them as best he can in the odd positions they're in. "I hope you two didn't give him too much trouble while I was gone." We all know he's teasing them, but their panicked glances at each other suggest they haven't caught on yet.

"They only asked where you were every third hour or so." Gabriel winks at the trio, but only the one being climbed seems to notice. "And they've been there much longer than a day."

"We took turns!" Eriel protests. "Eden always had at least one guard."

"Nobody got in or out. So there," Urial adds.

Lucifer shakes his head, though not hard enough to dislodge them from his shoulders where they cling, then addresses them in the tone of a parent giving a toddler a "very important" job to do. "I would expect nothing less from my favorite lieutenants. They haven't failed me yet, so this next mission should be simple enough." Now it was the older angels' turn to share concerned glances among themselves.

The Twins' eyes didn't literally light up at the prospect of new orders from their long-missing commander, but I'm sure they could have if they'd gotten any more excited. "Of course, anything you ask, we shall do our best!" They finally dismount from his arms, choosing instead to float at attention in the air in front of him. Their blue and white wings flutter excitedly, causing them to bob up and down in uneven bursts and their thick curls to flop around their faces.

"What should we do now?" Eriel tugs at a loose strand, twisting it into a braid. "It's not time to open the gates yet, is it?" Neither are sure what to make of me standing among their higher-ups, the lone vessel that isn't even whole yet. I wonder if they saw me leading the puppy into the Garden. Surely they would've gone running to the Host if they recognized me then.

"Not quite yet. We've only just gotten started," Gabriel answers, but she doesn't alleviate their curiosity or confusion.

Lucifer pauses, drawing the growing tension in the air as tight as a violin string. "I want you to patrol the outer gates as well as Eden. Start from either side of the Garden and work your way around the perimeter." When both little ones tilt their heads and blink their golden eyes, he goes on, "I know nothing can get in, I know. But we'll be expecting the other Creators soon, or Father will be at any rate, and we can't have broken fences when we have company over, now can we?"

"Of course not." Urial nods, pulling his sister along behind him. "We'll report any broken areas to you as soon as we find them." They both wave goodbye and disappear in two star-shaped bursts of light.

Auriel raises an eyebrow in his direction the moment they're out of sight. "Now you know as well as I do that our fence is impenetrable as the day it was built. What are you playing at?"

He returns her skepticism with his own. "I managed to slip in and out without getting caught more than you all would care to admit. I'd rather err on the side of caution than blind faith, if it's all the same to you, Auri."

Michael surpasses skepticism and leans straight into offense at the mere suggestion that Heaven could come under any sort of attack. "You think we aren't safe? That our enemies would be stupid enough to lay siege to us here?"

"I think too many of our enemies have decided to fight dirty this round and that nothing is above or beneath any of them." His gaze lands on me on its way across his siblings' faces, eons-old fear dancing in the fiery colors of his eyes. "The only ones we can trust to abide by the rules of engagement are standing here now. Am I wrong?"

No one speaks to the contrary, not even the eldest brother. With no argument to counter, the second-born archangel sweeps inside and strides down the hall without further comment. We follow suit.

LUCIFER

I don't remember these walls being so far apart or the hallways being so long or the rooms being so airy. Do we really need this much space just to exist? Being confined for so long made me appreciate the few inches I was given, but all this extra air is strange and disorienting. Not bumping into something with each movement or being surrounded by darkness with no reprieve of light makes me a little more than antsy. I'm not freezing to the point of numbness; each breath doesn't feel like inhaling razors.

This tentative peace does not suit me yet. I am too accustomed to fear and discomfort to revel in security; my restlessness has reawakened within these familiar halls, and it begs me to fly to unknown freedom. But, for the time being, I must remain grounded. I am needed here, even wanted if Auriel is to be believed. She's never been known to lie. If anything, she can be a bit too honest at times and often lacks the tact to temper her words.

"How much do we know about the other vessels already?" Beatriz turns round and round as she walks, her curiosity pulling her in circles. "I mean you know their names at least, right?"

"We've always known that," Michael says as he guides her into the council room. "Our trouble begins with getting to them before the demons can track down all of theirs, and all of us making it back in one piece. Ezael and his cohorts could be waiting around any bend."

Gabriel is a little gentler with her delivery. Of course, she doesn't have quite the vendetta our eldest brother has against the Court, so she isn't as impassioned about beating the stuffing out of their eldest brother. "We have to break into groups of two or three and locate them. One of us will speak to the human, explain the situation, and convince them to join us. The others stand guard and provide backup."

Beatriz nods along, absorbing what she's told. One can almost see the questions buzzing in her head like a frenzied swarm of bees; going from being told nothing and half-truths to having the universe's well of knowledge at your disposal must be overwhelming. "Can they say no? What would happen then?"

"Few would refuse once they learn the alternative. Demons are much worse company," Jophiel says.

"They can't refuse them either?"

"Try telling a Prince or Princess no and see how that works out," Auriel answers as she takes a seat at the end of the table to mend her blindfold while we have a moment of stillness. "They don't even ask the vessels; they give them the 'option' to join willingly or by force."

"They do try for willingness first, though," I add as I watch her flutter around the room, entranced by every view she encounters. "That way they can't be exorcized as an unwanted presence. Force is favored by the impatient ones." Demons that worm their way into a human without express permission can be removed with exorcism rites from the possessed person's religion of choice, so long as their soul can withstand the backlash. It's a lengthy, agonizing process that doesn't always leave survivors. We of the Host can also banish a demon from a human if we know who the demon is. Our mortality rate is slightly lower. Slightly. Angels can be cast out for the same reason with similar rites, but seldom have we been desperate enough to resort to force.

Beatriz pauses at a bookcase against the wall, tracing her finger along one of the lion-headed bookends thoughtfully. "Can reapers take vessels?"

Everyone stutters awkwardly around the question, which isn't surprising given her history with their leader. Personally, I don't know what she's worried about with Azrael now. If he's foolish enough to attempt to steal her back, he has seven terribly irate surprises awaiting him. Not only would the lot of us vehemently oppose the transaction, but our young ward has enough motivation to give him quite a struggle herself. And she has one of his own blades at her disposal. He and his underlings may profit from strife between others, but he never deliberately seeks out conflict.

"Azrael can, as he is one of the Horsemen, but he only has one Line he can draw from, and it isn't yours," Raphael says. "He must find a vessel from the Line of Methuselah, and you are of Lazarus and Elijah."

"Isn't he . . ." I can sense the gears whirring inside her mind until they click into place. She sighs heavily, "Of course we're related. He comes back from the dead, and I didn't go all the way."

"Funny how that works, isn't it?"

"Azrael is the only one limited to one Line," Michael butts in before any other bad jokes can be sprung on the poor girl. "The other fourteen beings in need of vessels can align with any of the eligible humans. Once they are joined with a vessel, they cannot choose another, and neither can the human, so consider your decision thoroughly when the time comes." He goes on to explain that the hosting isn't permanent, as once the battle is over, the victorious ones will return to their normal selves shortly. The losers will be given the opportunity to join the other side—we are giving that opportunity to the demon vessels, I should say—if they renounce their occupants and atone for their actions. Of course, they must genuinely regret their sins, so we may not save as many as we hope to.

"Do we have to find that person too?"

"No, that is Azrael's responsibility alone, but unlike us, he needn't worry about anyone else pursuing his vessel," Auriel responds. She considers her handiwork on her blindfold before returning it to its usual place. "He would be of no use to either party, and harming him would only draw the Reaper's ire for nothing."

"If you're Michael or Auriel's vessel, you'll get to meet him." Gabriel leans against one of the windows, the light from outside filtering through her halo and making it glow a little brighter. "They're Horseman too."

"As in the Four Horseman?" Beatriz tugs at her hair, which I assume was braided at some point but is now frayed and wild around her face; she resembles a doll lost in a meadow, innocent and tattered all at once. Gabriel beckons and offers to replait her hair while her questions are answered, so she sits in the nearest chair and lets my little sister go to work.

For the layperson, this revelation—biblical pun not intended, I promise—may come as a surprise, but the Four Horseman are not all demons or another entirely ill-intentioned race. Both sides have representatives, although it looks a bit biased with two angels and a reaper to one demon. Azrael's title is self-explanatory.

Michael offers her his title himself: "As the general of Heaven's army, I am the Horseman known as War." However, he did not earn this title through bloodthirst and warmongering but from his penchant for strategy and leadership.

Likewise, Auriel became the Horseman of Famine as the maintainer of Earth's resources. Her usual job is to ensure that famine does not befall the whole of the world and that souls are properly documented wherever they are destined to go. Her philosophy down to her core is "a place for everything and everything in its place." And she doesn't tolerate any infractions against it. I pity Azrael when they meet to discuss next steps; he claims to share her ideology, yet he trampled all over it for his own personal gain.

"Lastly, Merihem is Pestilence, which would be obvious to anyone who spends more than three seconds in her presence." That wench has never been mentally or physically well a day in her long, miserable existence and loves nothing more than to spread her misery to those around her. "I don't think she could do anything but cough and sneeze on everything in a ten-foot radius if she tried."

"She can't replace that smoking thing, can she? That was horrible." Our little compatriot shudders and is none too pleased to learn that Merihem's censer was one of a multitude. They even have different scents.

"The Horsemen come together and decide where our battle will take place and agree to the terms of victory and loss." Raphael steers the conversation away from plots to destroy Merihem's collection the first chance we get and back to the original discussion. "Then, they announce their decisions to the rest of the world so that the humans can make preparations for Judgment."

On the final day of Earth, if Heaven is declared the winner, all the little reapers will take their satchels full of coins and distribute them so that all the souls can be properly collected.

Urial and Eriel will work in tandem with Saint Peter to record all our new citizens and ensure they find their new homes. It's all one big party from there on out, with no obnoxious demons to interfere. Hell winning wouldn't be that organized. Those brutes would whip themselves into a frenzy until nothing was left, not the Court, not their lackeys, nothing. And Azrael would get to clean up their mess all alone.

"I hope Azrael's isn't the deciding vote." Beatriz grimaces at the mention of him. "He likes to make decisions for other people without their input."

"Azrael will be dealt with by the rest of the council after the other matters are settled, I assure you." Auriel matches Beatriz's scowl with one of her own. "He eluded us for far too long to allow him any reprieve."

"We will dole out a just punishment before he disappears forever, regardless of who wins," Michael adds.

"Disappears?" All the steel in Beatriz's gaze vanishes, replaced by an expression akin to regret. Until now, Azrael's fate post-Armageddon had gone unmentioned.

"After this battle, the living world will cease to exist, no matter who remains as victor," Cassiel explains. "Either Heaven or Hell will overtake the physical plane, and all the souls within it will be rendered deceased. Azrael, with no one left to reap, will fade away with the last souls to depart. Without life to end, there is no death."

"Oh." I can tell Beatriz doesn't want to sound concerned, but the forgiving nature of humans is hard to choke out of a soul. Perhaps she doesn't hate him as much as she wants to. She hates holding on to the rage that he left her with; it's like holding on to barbed wire and broken glass with your bare hands. "And the little reapers too?"

"Yes, they will go after him, I believe."

She nods, her face solemn and unreadable as she ponders their fate. Perhaps she hoped for one last chance at redemption for the death-bringers. Perhaps she sought vengeance with a little more sting at the end. Either way, she's greatly disappointed in the outcome we've laid before her.

"How long are we giving ourselves to find the rest of our humans?" Maybe we have enough time for her to decide and make peace with their fates, and her own, before they're gone.

"The eleventh month of their calendar, so three months' time from tomorrow. The council will be called the last day of November and the battle set from there," Auriel replies.

That seems an awfully short timeframe to find and train all fourteen with little to no experience in battle or the supernatural, much less supernatural battle. It doesn't feel wise to give ourselves such a slim window when we have no idea what the Court has gotten accomplished. "Will that be enough for all we have to do?"

"We are long overdue for this day, Lucifer. The human world is coming apart at the seams like an old flag because it wasn't meant to last this long," Raphael adds. Even he cannot heal all the damage that has been done, and it pains him beyond words.

"There isn't time to wait for anyone, not anymore." Auriel continues, "If we wait much longer, there will be nothing left to save."

Somehow, I doubt that. It's lasted this long past its expiration date, what would another month do? Another year? They fail to consider the time it will take to convince the selected humans—aside from the one currently watching my reaction—that they aren't hallucinating and that they are indeed capable of what we ask of them. Or the time we need to find them and to fend off any demons after the same people. Never in the history of planning has an event of this magnitude ever gone exactly the way it was supposed to, and three months isn't enough time to cover even the most basic of mistakes.

Nor is it enough time to appreciate what's being lost in mere days.

I have not seen the surface of the planet since Adam and Eve were cast out of Eden and I out of Heaven. Earth has seen many deaths and rebirths since that day; I imagine I would not recognize it, or what humanity has become, in the millennia since then. All the years I spent wondering wouldn't do justice to the truth, which is why I hoped to have time to commit their advancements to memory before Heaven replaced them. As an angel, I am all too familiar with perfection. It's all I knew for centuries, and then I knew its opposite in Hell. What I wanted—always wanted, since the first hour of this world—was to find a middle ground, something between ideal and torment. Earth, while it lasts, offers that medium, but the current plan doesn't offer the vacation time.

Arguing them all down from this plan would be as futile as baptizing a hellhound. There is no convincing Michael or Auriel to alter their course once they've made up their minds, and I have no intention of being cast down again for speaking up when I've only just escaped. However, that doesn't mean I'll sit idly by either; rebellion doesn't have to be brash actions and gaudy speeches. Sometimes it's quiet movements and unseen plans. Those in opposition don't have to know they are the opposition if it doesn't suit one's needs.

"Very well, I suppose." I give everyone the resignation they were hoping for and defer to Auriel for instructions. "Divide us up, then, so we can get a quick start tomorrow." The release of tension in the room after that is more palpable than the others want it to be, but not quite as attention-grabbing as the ill-concealed disappointment in Beatriz's face. She wanted someone to object to immediate Armageddon so that she could join with them, but she didn't want to cast the first stone herself. She probably thinks she has no say in it, no matter if any of us tell her otherwise. Humans tend to have such misgivings in the presence of beings like us. Most believe that they cannot possibly know enough to really converse with even lesser celestials because they see themselves as inferior and unworthy by their simple nature or some arbitrary sin.

The truth is that we are not so different from Father's last creations, and as such I may be able to secure myself an ally in our young guest.

BEATRIZ

After the meeting, Auriel splits the angels into groups to search for their vessels starting tomorrow morning: Gabriel will act as messenger between the trios; Michael, Cassiel, and Jophiel will take the east coast of the USA; and Lucifer, Auriel, and Raphael will take the west. Pinpointing the vessels' locations will become easier the closer the angels are to their known home state, but they have to check the surrounding areas too in case they've moved or are out of town. Once six more humans have been selected, they will be brought here—alive, like some prophets were—and given the same explanations I was.

The meeting of the Horsemen is the next logical step. One side of me wants to pick one of the angels on the council just to rub it in Azrael's face that his plan didn't work, that I escaped and he can't touch me anymore. I want to be the one to hand down his sentence personally. The other side never wants to see his face ever again and doesn't think delivering justice would be worth the pain that would linger long after. Thinking about his betrayal too long makes me ill and anxious; being in the same room as him would only amplify those symptoms and add more to the mix. Then again, the wounds he inflicted are still fresh . . . maybe with time I could face him again, but there's no guarantee I'll ever be ready.

And he'll never be ready to see me again.

He'll never have a good enough apology for what he's done. Nothing he could do would bring him back into my good graces, or anyone else's up here for that matter. Lucifer spent twenty years more than he should have locked away. Auriel and Jophiel spent those decades scouring the Earth for me when they could've been seeking the other vessels or trying to save their brother. Valuable time we'll never get back was wasted on his lies, and he fully expected to get away with it. He would have too if he had been more careful taking me around with him.

I don't know that finding myself embroiled in this impending war is much better, though. Sure, I've been involved in it all along, but jumping from one fire to another doesn't exactly cool the burns of the first one. Neither does knowing that no matter the outcome, the world I knew in life will be gone in a matter of weeks. It's already gone, given the amount of time that's passed since I died. Who knows if anything I'd recognize is even still there? If my house is any indication, I'd be a time traveler knocked out of my continuum, worse than a fish out of its tank.

I'm losing a world I didn't have a chance to know, and there's nothing I can do to stop it.

There might have been a chance if Lucifer stood a bit firmer in his disagreement, but he's seen the other side of disobeying these big plans and doesn't want to suffer the consequences again. Can't say I blame him, but I have a feeling he was hoping for the same inch of freedom I want. But all the angels have been resting since this morning, so I can't exactly conspire or commiserate with him about all the trips we could've taken before—

"You have a talent for finding me when I least expect it, Beatriz."

I don't want to use his joke from earlier, but it flashes through my head faster than I can swat it away. The thought is soon followed by me scrambling to reconcile the angel I see now with the one we hauled out of that cage the night before. His hair is above his shoulders now and much curlier than when we first got here. His clothes are all mended, down to a brand-new pair of brown leather boots and shinier chainmail. One of his eyes is still cloudy, but its iris stands out a little more now; his scarred left side brings to mind a harvest moon behind a sheet of fog.

"Oh, you know me, always looking for trouble." Judging by the fact he's sneaking out the front door of the mansion, that's exactly what I'm looking at. "Are you looking to cause some or . . . ?"

"Naturally. If I didn't, my siblings would begin to wonder if they brought back the real me." Lucifer chuckles with a wink. He's also wearing a knapsack not unlike Cassiel's, so he isn't going for an evening stroll down the street. He's skipping town entirely. "I hate to cut and run like this, but there isn't time to tiptoe around if the world is ending in a handful of weeks. And it's not like I won't be back before then . . ."

A glimmer of hope tugs me closer to him, but a stab of caution turns my head down each hall to check for eavesdroppers. "Are you serious? You're going to Earth alone?"

"Am I?" He tilts his head, and curls shift over his haunting eyes. "You wanted a grand tour before it disappears too, or did I imagine that look you shot me this morning?"

I didn't think he was paying that much attention to me, and I also think my subconscious is a little too bold for its own good. If he saw me watching for his reaction, then one of the less adventurous angels might have too, and they're all smart enough to put the pieces together once they notice him missing. They'll know that I know where he went and that I went right along with him, the same as Eve took that fruit at his bidding, knowing it was likely a bad idea but not concerning myself with that in the moment.

"You can't tell me there's not a rebellious streak in you somewhere, Beatriz." He opens the door just enough to let the sunset peek in over the top of the city below. "If there's only one thing I can still do in this world, it's find souls that share my defiant nature, and even some that outshine it." He opens it a bit more, wide enough for me to slip past him if my feet weren't rooted to the tile floor.

The halls are empty except for us, our silence, and the decision waiting for me.

Do I risk throwing our chances back to the Court by slipping off with only one archangel? Can he keep us both safe being Fallen? What will the others do if they catch us? Is living like this worth the chance of a fate worse than death all over again?

"This isn't forever, you know." The smug edge in his voice recedes for a moment. "We aren't abandoning our fight, just taking a detour. I plan to seek out a vessel on this little vacation, if you won't have me, of course."

"I can't take anybody yet. I'm still just a ghost," I remind him. Without my physical body, I'm just a tag-along for the time being. And I haven't known anyone here long enough to make that decision yet, but a road trip is a perfect opportunity to mull things over.

"You're much more than a simple spirit, dear girl." His eyes sparkle like twin candle flames, and he swings the door open the rest of the way. "Off we go then."

CHAPTER TWELVE

BEATRIZ

The door clicks shut behind us as the sun disappears below the horizon, leaving the hall dark and empty. Lucifer and I sweep down alleys between the neighborhoods to avoid being seen by anyone out enjoying the spring-like night. It never shifts into full nighttime that's too dark to travel in; the City of Light is covered in lampposts and lighted fountains that keep the streets visible no matter the time of day.

Immaculate flowerbeds keep the air sweet and humming with delicate butterflies and lazy bumblebees. Hummingbirds are harder to come by, but we spy a few sipping on a climbing vine a few streets from the mansion. I hadn't thought about wild animals being here, even though Eden is only a few blocks away and I've been to an animal's reaping myself. Those were both pets, though, and they must've belonged to a Line or Azrael wouldn't have been the one to collect them. Unless the same rules don't apply to animals, which would make sense if they can't be used as vessels. Nobody said they couldn't, but I feel like having an animal host would only be helpful if it were a massive, vicious predator. Puppies and barn cats wouldn't exactly strike fear into the hearts of Ezael and his crew.

"Is there a side door we can sneak through, or are we running through the front gate and hoping Saint Peter doesn't call your family?" I inquire, searching and sightseeing as we walk.

"A section of the fence came down when I was young, and it's well out of his sight. No one will see us, and the Twins will get credit for finding our escape route if they follow the fence like I told them to." We wait behind a garden wall for a couple to pass, then slink around the back of a cottage. I didn't get a good enough look, but it may have been Mr. Levitt and his wife we just dodged. Guess I need to add him to my visiting list when we come back. I did promise, and unlike some people, I keep my word.

"Getting past the Principalities won't be a problem either, but they'll be quick to find Auriel and report us. We may have to hide out for a few days, but the others will be preoccupied for most of our time."

"As long as we don't hole up in a lakeside cabin, we can stay anywhere you like." The streets are now clear of people as far as we can see, so we slip out onto the main road for a bit. His cloak skirts over the path like a sheet of oil on water, opalescent-black and smooth. The light from the lamps' flames weaves golden threads into his hair and eyes so that he glows as if his halo were restored. Now that I'm behind him, I can see where it broke off above the nape of his neck; there's a scar where no hair grows, and two raised spots where the ring would start and stop.

"I prefer the mountains, personally. The smaller ones, not the ones that nearly reach up to here and spend most of their time covered in snow," he replies. "Never was fond of water, or meddling reapers."

"You don't think he would try and come after me again, do you?"

"Something interesting I doubt anyone has told you yet . . . If an angel of any rank is grievously injured or killed, members of their choir receive a signal that draws them to their exact location so aid can be rendered or vengeance exacted. If Azrael is stupid enough to pursue you while you are in my care, he's stupid enough to call the whole Host down on himself," he says resolutely while admiring the flowers along the path. "Do you think he's that much of an idiot?"

A beat of unamused silence passes, but he doesn't shrink back from my glare. "I'd use a stronger word than 'idiot' if you're asking what I think he is."

"Fair point." Lucifer readjusts the strap of his bag over his shoulder. "He will be dealt with one way or another, never you fret. Your body and peace will be restored to you if I have to tie him up and antagonize him myself."

"I don't know about the peace part. That seems like it's going to be scarce for a while."

"It's the least I can do." Lucifer reaches back to playfully brush my bangs out of my eyes. Some warmth has returned to his touch, but the chill isn't gone yet, like the first breath of spring after a long, harsh winter. "You helped my siblings set me free, and you're accompanying me on this last hurrah. In fact, I feel as though I'm one favor short of us breaking even."

I don't want him to only help me out of some imagined obligation, but there's a sincerity to his promises that makes me believe that won't be the case at all. Of course, it wouldn't hurt to cash in that second favor early.

The next corner we round brings us back to a familiar square full of lilies, and I'm suddenly reminded of the deepest ache I've been carrying. Somewhere on this street, my parents are surrounded by even more of my family that has passed on, some that I know and some that lived and died generations ago. I have all my memories back now, and the need to seek their comfort has come back with them. "Can we stop for a minute? I need to . . . it's my parents, I—"

Lucifer's smirk falls into a bitter shadow of a smile. "You gave me my family back, so I'll not begrudge you seeing yours." He finds himself a seat by the fountain and shoots me a cheeky grin. "Have fun explaining who's outside waiting for you, though."

"It's not like I'm bringing a boy home." I shrug as I approach the door of one of the houses, searching for Mama and Papí's names on the wall. "They'll probably just look at you funny." He laughs skeptically, and I find a shiny gold placard that reads:

Joseph & Liliana Torres

Est. August 2000

I get in one knock before the door creaks open.

LUCIFER

Members of the Torres family are staunch believers in door-sized windows on every wall, it appears. The large group gathered in the front living room is visible from every angle, as is their reaction to the newest member crossing the threshold. Children cease their running and giggling to ogle a girl scarcely older than they are, and adults halt previous conversations to wonder whose direct descendant she could be. Beatriz follows the gaze around the room, searching for familiar faces. She didn't recognize the older gentleman who let her inside until he explained he was her grandfather on her mother's side. He must've died before she was born or when she was too young to remember him clearly. Human minds are unlike ours in that way; we remember everything from the first breath onward in perfect detail, as if we experienced it only moments ago. Every gleaming triumph and every agonizing failure gets filed away so neatly, no matter how you try to scrub it clean from your mind.

I can see my own memories overlaying the scene before me: each child that clamors into her arms is Gabriel begging me to throw her off a cloud so she could learn to fly, or Cassiel climbing onto my shoulders to reach a book in the library. Every adult embracing her is Raphael offering comfort or Michael giving advice. The love and amazement in her eyes are mine before I sacrificed all that joy to foolish pride, and the subtly dwindling hope to find her parents in time mirrors my thoughts before she appeared outside my cage.

She briefly meets my gaze through the window between us, and that first meeting replays the moment she looks away. I could compare it to a human on the brink of death seeing a silhouette of their savior and mistaking them for one of us, but that would be too overdone.

Everyone thinks angels come to the rescue just as the last breath is inhaled, but no one ever considers the alternative of demons torturing you until you crave it. For more years than I can even begin to relay in mortal terms, demons filled my every waking hour with their torment. Some days it was physical agony: plucking my wings down to the bone, throwing me to the starving hellhounds, leaving me at Berith's nonexistent mercy. Other times they left me completely isolated and half-drowned in Maxxhim or burned me at the stakes of Verbin for years on end. But worse even than freezing to death alone in Judeccan were the hours spent in Dulentan in Merihem's personal chambers.

Ordinarily, souls left in her care are subjected to their own lies until they are driven to madness, but the Court sought to drag me even lower. Instead, I listened to the lies each hellspawn spread throughout the human population on my behalf . . . all the tales of me luring the pious to sin, the obscene rituals done in my name, proclaiming my hatred for mankind. Any truth in their words belonged to the Court and the Court alone. I had no genuine part in any misdeeds after The Fall, no matter what those monsters portrayed me as.

However, after centuries of hearing their deceit and seeing its consequences, the falsities found their way deep under my skin. I started believing them myself; I believed everyone had forsaken me for the image that remained and that the rescue party was little more than a mirage born of my desperation to deny that fate. Until the moment Beatriz called to me with warmth no demon could mimic, and the light of her soul broke the dark backdrop of my prison, my mind braced itself for another round of misery. She is my tether to hope, to restoration.

And it brings me great pain to spirit her away from her own peace.

She only just recovered her family—far more of it than she bargained for—after Azrael stole her away, and here I am luring her back out of the White Gate like some winged siren. Yes, she agreed to come even before there was a suggestion, but without said suggestion, she wouldn't be so rushed in reuniting with her parents. She could come and go from our manor as she pleased, reconnecting with them and sowing new bonds among the Host. No fear of capture by the Court or stumbling across Azrael would disturb her mind if I'd only kept this plan to myself. But it's too late to convince her of that now; even if I were to slip away and explore alone, she would hunt me down and demand an explanation for my abandonment. Beatriz is not the kind to let such actions slide by without retaliation.

A door clicks closed, breaking the quiet spring-night ambience and putting me on high alert. Now would be an awful time to be caught unawares and escorted back home to my undoubtedly incensed siblings. Fleeing almost immediately after they took the time to free me and absconding with the only human in our possession will have a strong feather-ruffling effect that will linger until our return. Luckily for our fledgling journey, the sound's source is only my companion exiting the house, not a battalion of Authorities searching the villas for missing persons who fit our descriptions.

"Find who you were looking for?" I must admit I wasn't truly watching her interact with her family after a while. Getting lost in my own head tends to blur out my vision of the present, so I didn't see her parents come forward from the crowd.

To my surprise, Beatriz shakes her head. "They're visiting Papí's family a few streets down. Don't know when they'll be back home, so I told them I'd come see them when we're done on Earth." Tear tracks glisten on her cheeks, but no heavy air of sorrow surrounds her. Pure joy can be their only cause, and the proof is in the soft smile that hardly lifts her mouth.

"You told them what we were doing?"

"Not exactly. I told them I was helping a friend look for something important, which isn't really a lie . . ."

"No, I suppose it isn't." I lift myself from the bench and resume our trek to the broken fence, Beatriz trotting alongside me as if we're only taking a casual stroll through the town. I don't think she quite grasps the drastic nature of our actions or the severity of the consequences should we get recaptured by either side, or she doesn't care as long as she isn't dancing on the end of someone else's strings. Perhaps she craves the danger Azrael sheltered her from, and perhaps I am a fool for bringing her into the thick of it. "You may not have another chance to back out of this later, Beatriz. Once we leave Heaven, I don't intend to turn around for some time. I understand if you want to return to your family and wait—"

"Lucifer, whatever happens, whoever wins, I will be with them again in the end." Caution hides in her confidence, but it isn't slowing her down by a step. "But I don't even know the world we'll be fighting for. I'll never rest knowing that, and neither will you. We've been restless too long. We have to go. Together." The finality in her words leaves no room for doubt.

We arrive at our exit as night paints the sky below all the darkest shades of blue and violet. White-hot stars burn in the distance, framing the curves of her face with a silver aura. If it were a bit brighter, she could have a halo of her own, but although she stands on her tiptoes at the edge of the clouds, nothing behind her can give her wings. If I were to back out now, she would carry on regardless; she is no Eve in need of leading astray. This rebellion belongs to us both equally.

"Very well, let us jump rather than fall."

Being carried about by angels is quickly becoming second nature for her; I only had to open my arms a little and Beatriz soon rested against my side. She's no heavier than the Twins, but she's much easier to hold on to, given that she holds still. Her laugh echoes off the clouds like chapel bells on the way down, one arm across my shoulder and the other outspread in the shadow of my wing.

As we pass the shield of light around the planet, a trumpet blast shakes the air, signaling to those below that the end is approaching.

AZRAEL

Living as a fugitive until the end of time appears to be my fate now.

The Host thinks me meddlesome at the very least and an insidious traitor at worst, and they only have one side of what occurred. Not that I believe Beatriz embellished the truth or anything of that sort, but she still lacks the full story. And if she were still as upset as when she fled the cabin, I can only imagine how humanity's foremost protectors took offense at the actions that led to those tears.

Gabriel, the least violent of them all, may come for my head herself. She, as a guardian of children's souls, takes it as a personal affront if someone so young is traumatized so deeply. However, her assault may be waylaid by her sisters seeking their own vengeance against me. Jophiel's carefully laid plans and their subsequent backups scattering to the winds undoubtedly perturbed her beyond measure. Auriel, meant to be my partner in keeping the world on-kilter, likely bears the most rage against me if Beatriz is not considered. None of the Archeia are to be trifled with, but even I fear her retribution. As a fellow Horseman, we would be on more even footing than her siblings would, which gives her ample opportunity to open my position for a new hire.

The Court got little more than amusement from my game of keep-away, but I suspect at least a few of them got their hopes up that, should my grip falter, the girl would find her way into their hands first. How disappointed they must have been knowing the angels carried her through their realms like a trophy and escaped intact with Lucifer in tow as well. Ezael was beside himself in his rage when I came to collect Mahazael from the Dead Sea after his failed kidnapping attempt.

"I hope you've had your fun, Reaper. You've cost me one of my men and two of my prizes," he snarled. "This will not be forgotten nor forgiven." He tends to simmer and boil over like an unwatched teapot, so if he fails to keep himself in check, that temper will cost him and his brethren even more dearly before all is said and done.

And he will not be the one to feel it; he did not even glance in the direction of the portal used to send the serpent Knight to his fiery grave. The seven remaining warriors, however, bow their heads in their fashion of reverence. While the Court cannot stand the sight of one another for more than a few hours at most, the Knights at least consider themselves comrades in arms. This will be a hard blow for them in the coming war, especially if any of their strategies relied on Mahazael's skills.

"You will have to wait like the rest of them for your vengeance upon me." The smoke wafted across the water until no evidence of his death remained but the solemn faces around me. "There will be an awfully long line, you see."

"That's if he makes it through the Horsemen's meeting with Auriel and Michael," Merihem gloated. "There may not be anything left for the rest of us once he pays them for his mistakes."

Whether they all acknowledge it or not, we are all only one wrong choice away from certain destruction, be it of ourselves or a truth we hold sacred or those we wish to protect. All it ever takes is one misstep, and all could be gained or lost in an instant. I have already made that mistake and multiplied it tenfold in no time at all, thus condemning myself to the role I hoped to avoid. But moping over my earth-shattering failure will get me nowhere quickly. There was no permanent escape in the cards, of course, but an extended delay would have suited me, as well as much of the living population.

Take the fellow on the other side of the window of this funeral home, for example. Not the dead one in the visitation room. Any concerns he harbored are long gone by now. The one at the antique rolltop desk, meticulously signing paperwork and collecting files, could use a vacation from his dour work. He is only days away from realizing this after his long and storied career in this business, yet I wait just outside the door. Not to reap his soul but to bring him the truth of his lineage. I am his fate, and he is mine. He does not know he is the last of my vessel's Line, and I expect he will not take the news well. Most before him did not. Others often spoke of retrieving their vessels for apocalypses past, describing their mostly invulnerable forms being shot, stabbed, whipped, and burned, to name a few of the futile assaults.

The humans have no idea of their part in this until the last moment. Never have in the long history of god-engineered catastrophes. Of course, that leaves them with little real choice in the matter. Rarely do they realize this, even if they are plainly told as much, and some of them could not care less. We shall see which of the two this last one will prove to be.

I dip under the roof of the porch and approach the front door to knock. I could simply appear inside the same room he stands in, but history has proven that an unwise decision. Entering the funeral parlor as a mourner would is much more appropriate and less likely to end in fisticuffs.

"It's open," he calls, likely expecting someone coming to make funeral arrangements for a loved one. The foyer glows with the dim pink light morticians use to disguise the pallor of death, and warmth spills through the room to ward off the chill of a reaper's aftermath. Even I look almost human-toned, I notice in a nearby mirror. What a peculiar occurrence. To be one of the furthest things from them and yet to look this simi- lar, even only for a moment.

No one else occupies the building but us two. All the other offices are dark and silent as the tombs they work to fill. The scratch of his pen fills the otherwise empty air; if a floorboard under my feet had not creaked, he likely would not have looked up until I entered his room.

He does not shout or leap backward. He blinks slowly three times and holds his breath until I momentarily worry that he has forgotten how to. Given that breathing is mostly an involuntary reflex for humans, however, he could forget but his body would not. Self-preservation usually roots itself in the nerves, muscles, and bones rather than the mind.

"You, uh . . . must not be too busy tonight, if you're com- ing to me personally." A tiny exhale escapes as he sets his pen off to the side; his paperwork has suddenly taken a backseat. He quips to hide his nerves. "Or do you do this for everybody?"

"No, Mr. Ginn, only a select few are granted my company, and you are one of them." I sit—as best I can in the limited space afforded to this room—across from him on the fainting couch against the wall. In my travels across the ages, it came to my attention that lowering myself to their approximate level rather than looming in doorways like some horror film antagonist tends to calm humans down. To them, this posture indicates peace-seeking rather than menace.

He hums a note of understanding, folding his hands on the desk before him and fixing a businessman's smirk on his face. "That's J.T. to you, just like the rest of 'em. You're not coming to fire me as a mortician, are you?"

"Hardly," I humor him. "This is a business visit, not a personal one."

He hums again, the sound mixing with hints of relief. He knows he will not die this night, but I am unsure whether he knows the rest of our history together. Some families pass down such encounters with the supernatural as folktales to their descendants, while others lock them away as disgraceful secrets never to be revealed. Some of his past relations were warned of my coming, but that tradition may have died before reaching him.

"You see, I need your help with a matter of celestial consequence. Only you can help me, as you are the last of your Line." J.T. has no siblings, no children, no blood kin to speak of really. Those few who are left would not fall within the strictures either way.

"And what is my 'celestially important' job? Are we swapping places or something?" J.T.'s cool expression does little to mask the brewing skepticism underneath. He is a salesman of sorts after all, and he recognizes a bad pitch when he hears it. "I believe I'm a little short for them robes you got on."

"Not so much swapping as joining. There are those who seek to destroy the mortal world, and I ask you, John Thomas Ginn of Methuselah's Line, to stand with me against them." Thunder rumbles softly outside, not quite a storm yet but not the cloudy calm that greeted me when I arrived. "You may truly be my last hope, so how do you feel about sabotage?"

GLOSSARY

ANGELS

Michael (MY-cull): Firstborn archangel of The Host and leader of Heaven's army of Dominions & Authorities. Also known as the Horseman of War.

Lucifer (LOO-ci-fur): Second-born archangel of The Host and former captain of Eden's Cherubim (CHAIR-ub-im) guardians. Captive of the Court of Hell.

Raphael (rah-feye-EL): Third-born archangel of The Host and divine healer. Leader of the miracle workers known as the Virtues.

Gabriel (GAY-bree-ull): Fourth-born archeia (are-KEY-uh) of The Host and Messenger of Heaven. Leader of the Malakhim (MAL-uh-kim).

Jophiel (JOH-fee-ull): Fifth-born archeia of The Host and Prophetess of Heaven. Leader of the prayer receivers known as Thrones.

Auriel (ARE-ee-ull): Sixth-born archeia of The Host and leader of Earth's guardians known as the Principalities. Also known as the Horseman of Famine.

Cassiel (cass-ee-EL): Seventh-born archangel of The Host and leader of Heaven's caretakers known as the Seraphim (SAIR-uh-fim).

Eriel and Uriel (AIR-ee-ull and YUR-ee-ull): Guardians and caretakers of the Garden of Eden.

DEMONS

Ezael (EH-zay-ull): Firstborn prince of The Court and ruler of Maxxhim (MAX-him), the realm of gluttony.

Asmodeis (as-moh-DAY-is): Second-born prince of The Court and ruler of Verbin, the realm of dishonor.

Merihem (MAIR-eh-hem): Third-born princess of The Court and ruler of Dulentan (doo-LEN-tin), the realm of envy. Also known as the Horseman of Pestilence.

Ashtaroth (ASH-tuh-roth): Fourth-born princess of The Court and ruler of Bellum, the realm of sloth.

Veraine (ver-AYN): Fifth-born prince of The Court and ruler of Carnum, the realm of lust and pride.

Mammon (MAM-uhn): Sixth-born prince of The Court and ruler of Toman, the realm of greed.

Berith (BAIR-ith): Seventh-born princess of The Court and ruler of Aceteram (ACE-ter-am), the realm of wrath.

KNIGHTS

Abbadon (uh-BAD-in): Knight of Wrath

Azazel (uh-ZAH-zull): Knight of Greed

Beelzebub (bee-EL-zeh-bub): Knight of Gluttony

Belphegor (BEL-feh-gore): Knight of Sloth

Leviathan (leh-VEYE-uh-thin): Knight of Envy

Mahazael (muh-HA-zeye-el): Knight of Lust

Moloch (MOH-lock): Knight of Sacrifice

Samael (sam-eye-EL): Knight of Pride

REAPERS

Azrael (az-reye-EL): The High Reaper, also known as the Horseman of Death.

Muerte (MWAIR-tay): The only named lesser reaper, whose name translates to "death" in Spanish.

www.ingramcontent.com/pod-product-compliance
Lightning Source LLC
Chambersburg PA
CBHW032243310726

48973CB00008B/2267